Praise for these bestselling authors

Carole Mortimer

"Carole Mortimer dishes up outstanding reading!"
—*Romantic Times*

Catherine Spencer

"Catherine Spencer pens a truly wonderful read."
—*Romantic Times*

Diana Hamilton

"Diana Hamilton [creates a story] that is spellbinding
from beginning to end."
—*Affaire de Coeur*

Carole Mortimer is one of Harlequin's most popular and prolific authors. Since the publication of her first novel in 1979, this British writer has shown no signs of slowing her pace—she has published over 125 books. Carole was born in a village in England that she claims was so small that "if you blinked as you drove through it you could miss seeing it completely!" She adds that her parents still live in the house where she first came into the world, and her two brothers live very close by. Carole lives in a beautiful part of Britain with her husband, children and menagerie of pets, including a dog acquired several years ago in Canada, which is actually half coyote!

Catherine Spencer fell into writing by happy accident. Ready for a change of career, she eavesdropped on a conversation about writing for Harlequin and decided this was too good a challenge to pass up. With the blithe ignorance of a nonswimmer leaping into a shark-infested pool, she resigned from her job as a high school English teacher and fired off her first submission to Harlequin Mills & Boon's editorial staff. Although her first two submissions were rejected, the third effort made the grade. Since then, she's sold over twenty-five books. Catherine is married and lives with her husband in White Rock, a small seaside community south of Vancouver, British Columbia. She has four grown children, five grandchildren, two dogs and a cat, all of whom are perfect!

Diana Hamilton is a true romantic and fell in love with her husband at first sight. They still live in the fairy-tale Tudor house where they raised their three children. Now the idyll is shared with eight rescued cats and a puppy. But despite an often chaotic lifestyle, Diana has had her nose in a book—either reading or writing one—ever since she learned to read and write, and plans to go on doing just that for a very long time to come. Diana has published over forty books for Harlequin and is a *USA TODAY* bestselling author.

CHRISTMAS
Secrets

Carole Mortimer
Catherine Spencer ~ Diana Hamilton

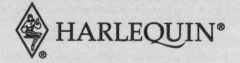

HARLEQUIN®

TORONTO • NEW YORK • LONDON
AMSTERDAM • PARIS • SYDNEY • HAMBURG
STOCKHOLM • ATHENS • TOKYO • MILAN • MADRID
PRAGUE • WARSAW • BUDAPEST • AUCKLAND

ISBN 0-373-83618-X

CHRISTMAS SECRETS

Copyright © 2004 by Harlequin Books S.A.

The publisher acknowledges the copyright holders of the individual works as follows:

A HEAVENLY CHRISTMAS
Copyright © 2004 by Carole Mortimer

CHRISTMAS PASSIONS
Copyright © 2004 by Kathy Garner

A SEASONAL SECRET
Copyright © 2004 by Diana Hamilton

This edition published by arrangement with Harlequin Books S.A.

® and TM are trademarks of the publisher. Trademarks indicated with ® are registered in the United States Patent and Trademark Office, the Canadian Trade Marks Office and in other countries.

www.eHarlequin.com

Printed in U.S.A.

CONTENTS

A HEAVENLY CHRISTMAS

Carole Mortimer

CHAPTER ONE

'YOU wanted me?'

Mrs Heavenly was aware of the soft, fluttering sensation behind her that told her she was no longer alone. But her attention was so intent upon the vision that she didn't want to leave it, even for a second!

At last! She had waited a long time for this particular plea for help to come. Almost too long, she acknowledged ruefully. But at last it *had* come.

She looked up to smile warmly at the young angel who stood before her. Faith. Yes, she would be perfect for this particular assignment. Warm, compassionate, and with a mischievous sense of humour that had almost been her undoing a couple of times in the past. But in this particular case Faith's qualities were more suited to the problem than the equally admirable ones of Hope or Charity.

'Come and look at this, my dear.' Mrs Heavenly encouraged the angel to step forward and share the vision with her. 'It will help you to understand the problem that has—thankfully!—been presented to us.'

Faith stepped into Mrs Heavenly's vision, eager to learn what her assignment was to be. Christmas was only two days away—always a fraught time of year for humans, when the inadequacies in their normally busy lives often became glaringly obvious. It was also a time when they often cried out for help to cope with those difficulties.

'This incident happened a short time ago,' Mrs Heavenly told her softly, a smile on her cherubic face.

Faith gazed down interestedly at the scene being enacted below them.

A tiny woman of about thirty—startlingly beautiful, her fine-boned body clothed in a black trouser suit and cream blouse, and with golden-blonde hair cropped close to her head—was stepping lithely out of a lift, her expression one of determination as she marched down the carpeted corridor to rap sharply on an oak door at the end of the hallway.

'She looks rather angry,' Faith murmured.

Mrs Heavenly nodded unconcernedly. 'She invariably is,' she informed Faith lightly.

'Why—? Goodness, who is *that*?' Faith gasped as the oak door swung open to reveal a man almost as handsome as Gabriel himself.

Or Lucifer, she decided as an afterthought. His hair was so dark it was almost black, his eyes so dark a brown it was difficult to see where the iris stopped and the pupil began. As for his looks—they could only be described as devilishly attractive.

'Is he her husband?' Faith prompted breathlessly.

'Hardly.' Mrs Heavenly smiled. 'Listen,' she encouraged softly.

'Ms Hardy,' the man greeted dryly. 'To what do I owe this unexpected pleasure?'

Olivia, despite the obvious derision in his tone, stared back at him unmovingly. Ethan Sherbourne had occupied the apartment directly above hers for over a year now. But apart from an occasional greeting to him—on the rare occasion they happened to get into the lift together—or to one of the constant stream of women that seemed to flow in and out of his apartment, Olivia had remained firmly detached from the man.

The only other exception being when his mail became confused with her own. Which it had already several times this Christmas.

'Yours, I believe.' She held up the pink envelope she carried with her.

He raised dark brows as he reached out a lean hand and took the envelope, checking the writing on the front before holding it up in front of his nose and sniffing appreciatively.

'Gwendoline,' he announced knowingly.

Olivia repressed a delicate shudder. 'I didn't realise women still did that sort of thing,' she commented scathingly.

Neither did Olivia understand why Mr Pulman, the caretaker of this exclusive apartment building, should think she might be the recipient of a scented Christmas card!

Ethan Sherbourne gave a roguish smile. 'Only certain women,' he drawled huskily.

Utterly stupid ones, in Olivia's opinion. But she was sure Ethan Sherbourne wasn't in the least interested in her opinion. She wasn't tall, willowy— or young!—as the majority of women trooping in and out of his apartment seemed to be.

She gave a cool inclination of her head. 'I'll leave you to open your card—' She broke off with a frown as the lift doors opened down the corridor, immediately releasing the ear-splitting wail of a baby. A very young baby, by the sound of it, Olivia realised, wincingly.

She turned slowly in the direction of the cry, just in time to move out of the way of the young woman striding purposefully towards Ethan Sherbourne's apartment.

The roguish smile had been wiped off Ethan Sherbourne's face the moment he looked at the approaching virago. 'Shelley...?' He betrayed his uncertainty with a frown.

The tall, youthfully leggy blonde, looking not much more than a child herself, gave him a humourless smile, the screaming baby held firmly in her arms. 'I'm surprised you remember me,' she snapped. 'We met so briefly.'

'Of course I remember you,' Ethan Sherbourne

returned smoothly, sparing a reluctant glance for the shawl-wrapped bundle in the girl's arms. 'And this is…?'

Olivia stood to one side of the hallway now, an unwilling but at the same time fascinated eavesdropper on this conversation.

The girl—for, on closer inspection, she most certainly was a girl, probably no older than twenty or so—was gazing down at the screaming baby with a look that somehow managed to combine motherly love and sheer terror at the same time.

'Here.' She thrust the child into Ethan Sherbourne's unsuspecting arms.

The screaming—to its mother's obvious frustration—instantly ceased, although emotional hiccups quickly followed.

'She obviously prefers you to me, anyway,' the young woman choked tearfully—as if this was the final straw as far as she was concerned. 'Her name is Andrea. Everything she needs is in here.' She took a holdall off her shoulder and dropped it onto the floor. 'She will want feeding in about an hour. I just can't cope any more.'

With a last heart-wrenching glance at the baby she turned on her heel and ran back into the lift, desperately pressing the button to close the doors.

'Shelley—!' Ethan Sherbourne's cry of protest died in his throat as the lift doors closed on the distraught mother, followed by the sound of its descent.

At the same time his raised voice startled the baby in his arms, and it began crying again.

Its obviously distressed cry shot through Olivia's nerve-endings with the sharpness of a knife, and her face was pale as she grimaced painfully.

'Where do you think you're going?' Ethan Sherbourne demanded grimly, his voice raised above the baby's wail.

Olivia had turned, intending to follow the young mother's example and escape from the situation!

She turned back to Ethan Sherbourne, her brows raised. 'I've delivered your card—which I received by mistake.' She shrugged. 'I thought I would leave you to deal with this...second delivery of the day alone,' she explained dryly.

Dark brown eyes narrowed icily at her obvious sarcasm. 'Don't be so damned stupid,' he snapped, striding out of the apartment to move forward to the lift and press the button for its return, the pink-wrapped bundle—still crying—held awkwardly in his arms.

Olivia gave him a considering look. 'Where are *you* going?' Not too far, she didn't think; she doubted this baby was going to wait for another hour to be fed.

'After Shelley, of course.' He rasped his impatience, looking more harassed by the second. The baby's initial response to being held in his arms rather than its mother's was definitely gone for good. 'What the hell is wrong with her?' he demanded exasperatedly of Olivia.

Olivia looked stunned by the question. 'What on earth makes you think I would know?'

'You're a woman, aren't you?' Ethan's agitation was fast reaching danger level. 'At least...' his gaze moved over her trouser suit '...I presume you are. Where the hell is the damned lift?' he grated between clenched teeth.

'Maybe if you stopped swearing—'

'You think that might stop the baby screaming?' He conveyed his doubt with another frown.

'No,' Olivia answered reasonably. 'I would just prefer it if you did.'

If looks alone could kill, Olivia knew she would have been struck down in that moment. She only just stopped herself from taking a step backwards as Ethan Sherbourne took a threatening step towards her.

'Er—your lift seems finally to have arrived.' She pointed past him with some relief to the waiting elevator, its doors open invitingly.

He glanced from the open lift to Olivia, and back again. 'So it has,' he acknowledged. 'Here,' he offered.

And promptly deposited the baby into Olivia's arms!

Not welcoming arms. Not waiting. Not even willing. In fact, her initial feelings of satisfaction at one of this man's past relationships having caught up with him—with a vengeance—disappeared totally as she found *she* was the one left holding the baby!

'Mr Sherbourne—'

'I have to try and catch up with Shelley,' he told her firmly before stepping into the lift. 'Take care of the baby until I get back with her mother.'

Take care of—!

The lift doors closed, leaving Olivia alone in the hallway.

No, not alone…

A now silent baby lay in her arms, staring up at her with unblinking trust, Olivia realised as she reluctantly looked down at Andrea.

Olivia's legs began to shake, quickly followed by the rest of her body, until she knew she was actually in danger of collapsing completely. But with a very young baby in her arms that was not a good idea.

The door to Ethan Sherbourne's apartment still stood wide open. Not particularly inviting, but this baby was, after all, Ethan's responsibility.

Olivia managed to reach one of the armchairs in the ultra-modern lounge before her legs collapsed beneath her. But only just. She was shaking all over, her breath coming in short, hyperventilating gasps.

How dared Ethan Sherbourne do this to her?

How *dared* he?

*   *   *

'Mr Sherbourne is certainly in need of a little divine intervention,' Faith murmured sympathetically as the vision in the apartment stilled.

Mrs Heavenly straightened, shaking her head. 'Mr Sherbourne isn't the one requesting our help, my dear.'

Faith blinked. 'Well, of course Shelley is very troubled—obviously overwhelmed by mother-hood— No?' She frowned as Mrs Heavenly shook her head again. 'Surely not baby Andrea...? No, of course not,' she answered herself. 'But that only leaves...'

'Olivia,' Mrs Heavenly confirmed with satisfaction. 'Yes, my dear, it's Olivia Hardy who needs our help this Christmas.'

Faith glanced back to the woman stilled in the frame. Beautiful, and obviously successful, as she lived in such a luxurious apartment building; in what way, Faith wondered, did such a woman need the help of one of Mrs Heavenly's angels?

CHAPTER TWO

FAITH continued to look at the frozen vision of Olivia. 'I don't understand,' she said after some time had elapsed. 'Olivia appears to have everything going for her.'

Mrs Heavenly gave a sad shake of her head. 'Appearances can sometimes be deceptive, my dear.'

'But she is successful in her career?'

'Very. Junior partner in a very prestigious law firm.'

'And beautiful, by earthly standards, too.' Faith studied the image before her; to her Olivia looked very beautiful indeed. 'Is she married?'

'No,' Mrs Heavenly answered slowly. 'Nor does she have any children.' She pre-empted what she thought might be Faith's next question.

'Ah,' the young angel murmured with satisfaction.

'Nor does she *want* a husband or children,' Mrs Heavenly added pointedly.

Faith felt more puzzled than ever. 'But she has asked for our help?'

'Oh, yes.' Mrs Heavenly sighed her satisfaction. 'For the first time in ten years Olivia has sent up a prayer. And I don't intend letting this opportunity pass us by.'

Faith felt no nearer to knowing in exactly what way Olivia Hardy needed their help, but she trusted Mrs Heavenly's instincts implicitly. If she said Olivia Hardy had not only asked for help but was also deserving of it, that was good enough for Faith. If only she knew in what way she *could* help…!

'Watch what happens next,' Mrs Heavenly invited as she saw Faith's continued confusion.

The frame in the vision instantly shifted, and the sound came back too—the tiny baby was hiccupping again in between drawing in shuddering breaths.

Olivia looked down at the tiny being in her arms. The baby, although still very young, looked well cared for; her cheeks were round, her skin a healthy pink, and her blue eyes gazed back unfocused at Olivia.

The pink blanket Andrea was wrapped in was clean, and she wore a pretty pink woollen suit beneath, plus a matching hat that hid the colour of her hair. If she had any!

'You're going to get too hot in all this wool, aren't you, poppet?' Olivia spoke gently to the baby even as she eased herself up out of the chair to lie Andrea down on the thickly carpeted floor and began slowly unwrapping her.

Almost like a Christmas present—except a baby

was the very last thing Olivia wanted, for Christmas or at any other time!

The hair beneath the woollen hat, Olivia discovered a few seconds later, was a startling black. Exactly like her father's, she realised with a disapproving tightening of her mouth.

She wasn't a prude, by any means—in her career it was best not to be! But Shelley had looked no older than twenty at most—possibly even younger than that—and Ethan Sherbourne, although very attractive in a devilish sort of way, and obviously physically fit, was a man in his early forties. And, from the little Shelley had said before her abrupt departure, the relationship between the two of them had been so fleeting the young girl had been doubtful that Ethan Sherbourne would even remember her!

To Olivia this whole situation seemed just so irresponsible. It was also one that could easily have been avoided. In her opinion, Ethan Sherbourne, with his obvious maturity, should have been the one to avoid it!

Selfish, Olivia instantly decided. Totally lacking in thought for anyone but himself and his own pleasure. He lived here, in sumptuous luxury, with a harem of women at his beck and call, while a young girl like Shelley, obviously not in the same financial bracket at all, by the look of her worn clothing, was left to bring up her child—and Ethan Sherbourne's!—completely on her own. It was men like him who—

'She had already disappeared by the time I got downstairs.' A disgruntled Ethan Sherbourne strode forcefully into the apartment, slamming the door behind him.

'Why didn't you just follow her back to her home?' Olivia reasoned—it was what she had expected him to do, after all.

'For the simple reason that I have no idea where she lives!' He scowled darkly at Olivia as she stood up with the baby held in her arms, now minus her blanket, hat and woollen outer suit. The pink Babygro that she wore beneath was slightly too large for her. 'How old do you think she is?' Ethan frowned.

Olivia raised blonde brows, already disgusted enough by the fact that he had no idea where Shelley lived without this too! 'Don't you know?' After all, if the relationship had been as fleeting as Shelley had implied it was, then it shouldn't be too difficult for Ethan Sherbourne to take a guess at his daughter's age!

'I would hardly have asked if I already knew, now, would I?' he snapped, moving to the array of drinks that stood on the side dresser, pouring out a large measure of whisky into one of the glasses and taking a large swallow before holding the decanter up in invitation to Olivia.

'No, thank you,' she refused coldly; she didn't think his getting drunk was going to help the situation at all!

'Suit yourself.' He shrugged before downing the rest of the whisky in the glass. 'At a guess, I would say she's somewhere between two and four months old,' he decided.

Perhaps not so fleeting a relationship, after all. Certainly not the one-night-stand that Olivia had been imagining. 'Her name is Andrea,' she bit out caustically. 'And I would agree—she's about three months old.'

Ethan's mouth twisted scornfully. 'In your expert opinion?'

Olivia drew in a sharp breath at his insulting tone. 'Now, look, Mr Sherbourne—'

'Oh, for goodness' sake, call me Ethan,' he retorted impatiently. 'After all, with Shelley's abrupt departure, we seem to have been left joint custodians of a very young baby!'

'*We* most certainly have not!' Olivia walked determinedly across the room, putting the baby firmly into Ethan's arms. 'In her mother's absence, Andrea is one hundred per cent *your* responsibility.' She stepped back pointedly. 'And, as such, I think you should be aware of the fact that Andrea needs her nappy changed,' she added with satisfaction. 'It's probably the reason she's so upset,' she guessed shrewdly.

Ethan raised the tiny baby slightly, his nose wrinkling with distaste at the obvious aroma that came up to greet him.

'I presume her nappies are in the bag—along with her food.' Olivia moved to pick up the shoulder-bag Shelley had dropped earlier, unzipping it to find everything in there that baby Andrea would need for an indefinite stay: several changes of clothes, uncountable nappies, and enough formula and bottles to feed her for a week. 'Here.' She handed Ethan one of the tiny disposable nappies, wipes, and barrier cream, and was completely unsympathetic as he tried to balance those as well as hold the baby.

Dark brown eyes opened wide. 'You expect me to change Andrea's nappy?' he said with obvious disbelief.

'*I* don't expect you to do anything,' Olivia assured him lightly. 'But I think Shelley does!'

Ethan gave up all pretence of holding on to the things she had just handed him, dropping them—but fortunately not the baby!—onto the carpeted floor. 'Well, let me inform you—and Shelley too, if she were here—'

'I think that's probably the appropriate word—*if* Shelley were here,' Olivia said sweetly. 'Which she isn't. Which only leaves you—'

'And you,' he pounced quickly.

'No way.' Olivia shook her head decisively. 'Shelley obviously believes you are more than capable of caring for Andrea.' Although in the same circumstances Olivia didn't believe she would have been so positive! 'I suggest you start fulfilling that belief by changing the baby's nappy.'

Those dark brown eyes looked at her suspiciously. 'You're enjoying this, aren't you?' he finally said slowly.

When it came to the distressing circumstances of Shelley being put in a position where she didn't know where else to turn to for help—no. But the fact that this arrogant Casanova had finally been given his comeuppance—yes, she was enjoying that!

Ethan Sherbourne was everything Olivia disliked in a man: arrogant, self-satisfied, too good-looking for his own and everyone else's good. And on today's evidence—totally amoral.

'What I happen to think about this situation isn't important,' she dismissed. 'Making the baby comfortable is, however. I'll just get a towel from the bathroom for you to lie her down on.' Which she did with no trouble whatsoever—the lay-out to this apartment was exactly the same as her own on the floor below. 'There.' She doubled the dark blue towel, placing it on the floor before looking expectantly at Ethan Sherbourne.

His cheeks were flushed as he scowled back at her darkly. 'I am not—' The baby began to cry once again. 'Maybe I am,' he muttered between clenched teeth, before moving down onto his knees and lying the baby gently down on the towel. 'How do I get into this thing?' He pulled ineffectually at the Babygro, turning the baby from side to side in his effort to find an opening.

'There are usually poppers on the insides of the legs— Oh, for goodness' sake...!' Olivia showed her impatience as he lifted the baby's legs to the left and then the right, almost turning the poor little thing over onto her face in the process. 'She's a baby, not a sack of potatoes!' Olivia bit out as she dropped down onto her knees beside him.

'Sacks of potatoes only need opening and the contents peeling—not having their nappies changed,' Ethan muttered with distaste as Olivia easily released the hidden poppers and freed the baby from the lower half of the all-in-one garment before moving out of the way. The pungent aroma was much stronger now. 'I can't believe I'm doing this,' he said a few minutes later, the soiled nappy discarded, one of the wipes held gingerly in his hand.

Olivia felt it diplomatic to take the nappy to the kitchen and dispose of it at that moment. Mainly because she didn't think Ethan Sherbourne would appreciate seeing her bent over in hysterical laughter—at his expense!

He had looked so ridiculous kneeling there on the carpet, wearing what looked to be—and probably was!—a black silk shirt and tailored black trousers, as a happy Andrea blew bubbles up at him, her joyfully kicking legs making it difficult for him to finish what he had started.

If one of his harem could only see him now—if *all* of them could see him now—they might not be quite so available to him!

That thought had the effect of sobering Olivia, if nothing else. She washed her hands before returning to the sitting room, and came to an abrupt halt as she saw Andrea was still minus her nappy while Ethan Sherbourne lay on the carpet beside her, copying her bubble-blowing antics.

Olivia felt a sudden tightness in her chest. Ethan didn't look so ridiculous any more. In fact he looked as if he was definitely enjoying himself.

He glanced across at Olivia as he sensed her standing there, his expression softened from playing with the baby. 'She's beautiful, isn't she?' he said huskily.

Olivia didn't even glance at the contented baby. 'All babies are beautiful, Mr Sherbourne,' she told him hardily.

'I thought I asked you to call me Ethan,' he reminded her softly. 'And you are…?'

'Olivia,' she provided stiffly, knowing it would be completely churlish to refuse to give him her first name—as well as non-productive; he only had to ask Mr Pulman for it if he really wanted to know.

'Olivia Hardy,' Ethan repeated mockingly as he

sat up to look at her with laughing brown eyes. 'It sounds like one half of a comedy duo!'

Angry colour darkened her cheeks. 'In the circumstances, what does that make you?' she returned scathingly. 'If you'll excuse me,' she added abruptly, before he could come out with some clever reply, 'I have some case notes I need to go over this evening.' She moved towards the door, anxious to escape now.

'Of course,' he agreed, standing up. 'You're a lawyer, aren't you? Exactly what sort of lawyer?' He followed her over to the door, standing in the doorway as she stood waiting for the lift to arrive.

'A good one,' Olivia came back derisively, glancing back at him in surprise as she heard him chuckle.

'I'll just bet you are too,' he replied appreciatively. 'Olivia—' He broke off as the sound of the baby whimpering could be heard behind him.

Olivia's mouth thinned humourlessly. 'I believe that is your cue to feed her,' she told him as she stepped inside the lift. 'Good luck!'

Ethan grimaced. 'I think Andrea is going to need that more than I am!'

He was probably right, Olivia decided as the lift began its descent. Sorry as she felt for Shelley in her obvious desperation, she couldn't help thinking that the other woman should have chosen someone with more competence at the task than Ethan Sherbourne obviously had. Even though, as

Andrea's father, a more appropriate minder couldn't be found!

As she let herself into her own silent apartment she could still hear the baby's cries, whether real or imagined, so she moved to switch on the television and drown out the noise—instantly turning the volume down as she realised she was probably the one responsible for disturbing the neighbours now! Besides, no matter how loud the television, it didn't stop Olivia from worrying about the baby.

Would Ethan Sherbourne know how to feed Andrea properly? Did he know how to make up the formula? To use sterilised water and not some straight from the tap? To tell if the milk was the right temperature for Andrea to drink? That he had to wind the baby after every ounce or so to prevent her getting tummy ache?

Olivia switched off the television impatiently, striding through to her bathroom to turn on the shower before going into the adjoining bedroom to undress. A shower might help to relax her. Anything to take her mind off what might be going wrong in the apartment above her.

Except that it didn't.

She stood under the punishing jet of the power shower for over ten minutes, desperately trying to channel her thoughts into the case she was working on at the moment. And failing miserably. How could she possibly think of work after the disturbing sequence of events earlier this evening?

Finally she came back through to her bedroom, wearing a peach-coloured silk robe, and looked around her appreciatively at the lovely things she had bought to surround and calm her. It was all the best that money could buy: a Mediterranean-style kitchen, antique furniture in every room, brocade drapes at the windows, luxuriously sumptuous carpets on the floors, several original paintings hanging on the cream-coloured walls.

And yet as Olivia looked around her she knew that it wasn't enough. That it never had been...

She sat down on the side of the bed, knowing exactly what she was going to do now and powerless to stop herself.

The photograph lay in the bottom drawer of her bedside cabinet—the only thing in that particular drawer. Her hand shook slightly as she picked it up, the tears streaming hotly down her cheeks even before she looked down at the picture.

Oh, God, Olivia pleaded emotionally, please, please help me to get through this!

CHAPTER THREE

'WHAT...?' Faith moved slightly in an effort to see the subject in the photograph Olivia held, only to be disappointed as Olivia suddenly clasped it against her chest, those tears still falling down the paleness of her cheeks.

Mrs Heavenly straightened, moving a hand gently over the vision and instantly dispersing the images into a wispy cloud. 'As you can see, Olivia's prayer is for help to get through Christmas.' She smiled at Faith. 'Not too difficult an assignment, I would have thought.'

Faith looked searchingly at her mentor. That wasn't exactly what Olivia had prayed for...

'So there you have it, my dear,' Mrs Heavenly told her brightly, shuffling some papers on her desk. 'The scene is already set for you to be able to do that quite easily. It's just a question of continuing to bring Olivia and Ethan together—'

'Ethan Sherbourne?' Faith couldn't hide her surprise. 'But isn't he—?'

'Ethan isn't exactly what he seems,' Mrs Heavenly assured her kindly. 'In fact, he could do with a little divine intervention himself! But I think on this occasion it might be better if... Don't be too visible, my dear,' she encouraged Faith. 'Neither Olivia nor Ethan are…well, shall we say that neither of them is particularly…a believer?'

Was it her imagination, Faith wondered, or did Mrs Heavenly's gaze no longer quite meet her own…?

Ridiculous, she instantly answered herself. Mrs Heavenly was the most open-hearted of all the—

'Poor Ethan.' Mrs Heavenly had opened the vision once again, was shaking her head regretfully as she looked down. 'Although he does seem to be coping well, in the circumstances,' she commented admiringly. 'Perhaps now would be a good time, Faith…?'

'Of course.' Faith drew herself out of the speculative trance she had lapsed into. 'Time I was going,' she agreed.

'But remember, Faith!' Mrs Heavenly called out to her before she disappeared. 'No matter what other distractions might occur, Olivia is the subject of your assignment.'

'I'll remember,' Faith assured her softly as she floated down to Earth.

And she *would* remember. But that didn't mean she couldn't try and be of some help to Shelley and Andrea while she was about it. Possibly even to Ethan Sherbourne too…

The photograph was back in its drawer and Olivia was wearing grey silk pyjamas. Her dinner of smoked salmon and salad was on the glass-topped dining table with a glass of white wine at exactly the right temperature for drinking, when a loud knocking on the door interrupted the calm enjoyment of her meal.

Who on earth—?

The wailing of a distressed baby penetrated the thickness of the door to her apartment, the tranquillity she had so determinedly made for herself instantly shattered.

Ethan Sherbourne and his—and baby Andrea, Olivia instantly realised. What could possible have gone wrong now?

Whatever it was, she knew she couldn't just ignore that cry; Ethan Sherbourne could stew in his own juice, as far as she was concerned, but the baby was another matter entirely.

'What have you done to her now?' Olivia demanded as she wrenched the door open—only to find herself staring into an empty hallway!

But how—? What—? She had been so sure...

She had to have been mistaken; there was no way Ethan could have knocked at her apartment and then disappeared back into the lift before she opened the door. Besides, what would be the point of him doing such a thing?

Olivia shook her head dazedly, closing the door to walk slowly back into her dining room.

She barely had time to sit back down and take a sip of her wine before that knock sounded on the door a second time. The crying of the baby was slightly fainter this time, but still audible to Olivia's acute hearing nonetheless.

She stood, striding angrily over to the door this time. This evening had already been traumatic enough; she was decidedly not in the mood to play childish games with Ethan Sherbourne!

'What on earth do you think you're playing at...?' Olivia's angry tirade trailed off abruptly as she opened the door and found the corridor empty again, a glance up and down the hallway showing her that there really was no one there.

Well, she wasn't going to give Ethan Sherbourne the chance to play this childish prank on her a third time. It wasn't in the least funny, and she intended telling Ethan Sherbourne so!

It took her exactly two minutes to throw off her silk pyjamas, pull on designer denims and a loose black shirt and slip her bare feet into a pair of loafers, before marching determinedly out of her apartment. She got into the lift, pressing the button for the next floor and stepping out to stride forcefully down the corridor and put her finger on Ethan Sherbourne's doorbell. And kept it on. Two could play at this game!

Ethan opened the door and barely had time to

raise surprised brows before Olivia pushed him firmly to one side and strode into his apartment.

She looked anxiously around the sitting room, finally turning a blazing grey gaze on Ethan Sherbourne as he stood just inside the room, curiously returning her gaze. 'What have you done to her?' Olivia demanded coldly. 'And don't tell me nothing,' she added impatiently, before he had time to answer, 'because I could hear her crying all the way downstairs!'

'I doubt that very much,' Ethan drawled as he walked further into the room. 'The only reason I bought this apartment was because I was assured by the agent that the building is completely soundproof.'

Olivia snorted softly to herself. No doubt he had been thinking of his harem at the time!

'I don't care what you were assured,' she returned. 'I definitely heard her crying.'

'I presume by "her" that you mean Andrea?' He derisively turned the tables on her after her earlier comment to him. 'And exactly what do you *think* I've done to her?' He folded his arms across his chest as he faced Olivia, his expression deceptively calm as he looked at her with mild curiosity.

Grey eyes flashed warningly as Olivia glared back at him. 'How should I know?' she replied shortly. 'Judging from previous evidence of your ability to know the needs of a young baby, you've probably tried to feed her steak or something equally unsuitable!' She looked around the room for a second time. 'Where is she?'

'Changed. Fed. Played with. Fast asleep.' He continued to look at Olivia, now with amusement.

'But I heard her,' Olivia said restlessly. 'I definitely heard her crying.' Although she equally definitely couldn't hear the baby crying now...

Ethan slowly shook his head. 'I don't think so.'

'Then where is she?' Olivia was low on patience at the best of times—at the moment it was non-existent!

He sighed, dropping his arms down to his sides. 'If you promise to be quiet, I'll show you.' He raised dark, questioning brows.

Her cheeks flushed fiery-red. 'Of course I'll be quiet,' she clipped. 'What—?'

'If you'll excuse my saying so, you haven't shown much sign of it in the last few minutes,' Ethan observed.

Olivia had been about to question him sharply again, but at these words her lips clamped together. Although she couldn't resist another glare in Ethan's direction.

'Better.' Ethan gave a mocking inclination of his head. 'Follow me through to my bedroom.'

Under other circumstances Olivia would have told him exactly what he could do with such an invitation. But in her concern for Andrea she resisted any such response, instead following Ethan into the bedroom situated directly above her own, lit by a low-voltage lamp on the bedside table.

What looked suspiciously like a drawer lay in the middle of the sumptuous king-size bed, and nestled securely inside that drawer, covered with a many-times-folded satin sheet, lay baby Andrea, looking absolutely adorable as she slept contentedly.

Also looking as if she had been like that for some time...

'Satisfied?' Ethan asked softly at Olivia's side.

She swallowed hard, nodding wordlessly. Whoever she had heard crying a few minutes ago, it obviously hadn't been Andrea.

In the circumstances, Olivia felt very reluctant to mention those two knocks on her apartment door which had accompanied the sound of crying...

'That was—the idea of a drawer for a bed—it was very inventive,' she told Ethan awkwardly once they had returned to the sitting-room.

Ethan eyed her wryly, 'Didn't you think I could be inventive?'

Her cheeks coloured heatedly at his obvious double meaning. 'To be honest, I've never given the matter any thought!' she assured him quickly.

'Stay for a drink now you're here?' he asked, moving to the array of drinks on the dresser.

Olivia thought longingly of her uneaten dinner, her rapidly warming glass of white wine. But her continuing concern for Andrea—despite the fact that Ethan seemed to be proving better at baby-minding than she would ever have imagined!—was of much greater importance at this particular moment.

She deliberately ignored the offer of a drink. Socialising with a man like Ethan Sherbourne was definitely not on her Christmas list of things still to do! 'What are you going to do about Andrea?' she asked.

'"Do" about her?' Ethan repeated softly.

Olivia frowned. 'Well, you can't just keep her here!'

'Why can't I?'

'Because—well, because—' Olivia's exasperation was such that she could hardly speak.

'What else do you suggest I do with her, Olivia? Call the authorities? Have her taken into care, over Christmas of all times? Cause all sorts of unnecessary complications for Shelley once she realises what she's done and comes back to reclaim her baby?' He shook his head, pouring red wine into two glasses, his expression grim as he held one of those glasses out to Olivia. 'Or perhaps you intend informing the authorities yourself?' he added harshly. 'Part of your duties as a responsible lawyer—?'

'Don't be ridiculous!' Olivia cut in instantly, drawing in a long, controlling breath. 'I have no wish to make this situation any worse for Shelley. I just don't think—'

'That I'm capable of looking after Andrea?' Ethan interrupted challengingly.

How could she possibly claim that when he had already more than proved that he was?

'No, it isn't that.' She sighed irritably. 'I just— I don't drink red wine!' She put her glass down untouched as she realised she had taken it from him without realising what she was doing.

'Pity. Apart from the odd emergency—like earlier,' he drawled, 'I drink very little else but red wine.' He straightened. 'So, you agree with me that until Shelley returns to claim Andrea she stays here with me?'

She hadn't said that at all! His lifestyle—days spent in his apartment being visited by a string of beautiful women, evenings and weekends spent with whoever—was not compatible with caring for the young baby that Andrea was.

But what was the alternative…?

Besides, there was one other important factor in this scenario—he was the baby's father.

'Unless you have any other ideas about what I should do?' Ethan prompted smoothly.

Olivia frowned at the question. 'Me?'

'Yes—you,' Ethan echoed mockingly. 'You could offer to care for Andrea yourself. Although I suppose a baby would mess up your sterile lifestyle.'

Olivia bristled angrily at this last remark. 'And what about *your* lifestyle?' she flew back. 'Exactly how do you intend explaining away baby Andrea's presence to your other—*friends*? Friends like Gwendoline of the perfumed Christmas card,' she reminded him as he would have spoken. 'Not with the truth, I'm sure,' she added.

'You think that wouldn't go down too well…?' Ethan asked thoughtfully.

Not unless those other women were completely stupid—no! But then, Olivia had no evidence to prove that they weren't exactly that! A couple of them had even been chatting and laughing together beside Olivia in the lift one day as they went up to his apartment.

'This is ridiculous!' she exclaimed. 'I only came up here—'

'Yes—why did you come up here?' Ethan put in huskily.

Her gaze faltered at that throaty tone in his voice. 'I told you. I heard Andrea crying—'

'And I have since proved to you that you couldn't have done,' he drawled. 'After I had changed her I warmed a bottle and fed her. Then I tickled her toes and played with her for a while before she fell into an exhausted sleep in my arms. She's stayed asleep for at least the last hour,' he ended firmly.

Olivia didn't dwell on thoughts of his playing

with Andrea; it didn't quite fit in with the mental image she had of him...

But his claim did make a total nonsense of those two knocks on her apartment door earlier and the sound of a baby crying!

And if it hadn't been Ethan knocking on the door, or Andrea crying, then who—or what?—had she heard...?

Maybe she hadn't really heard anything? Maybe it had just been her imagination, after all? If that were the case, then this Christmas promised to be even harder to get through than all the others had been!

And it was obvious from Ethan Sherbourne's sceptical expression that he believed she had used the claim as an excuse to come back up here to his apartment!

Arrogant, conceited pig!

'Obviously, as you say, I was mistaken,' she answered him frostily. 'I'm sorry to have disturbed you.'

'Oh, don't apologise, Olivia,' he replied softly. 'I've rather enjoyed being disturbed by you!'

He probably had too, Olivia realised impotently.

'Goodnight!' she said suddenly, turning sharply on her heel and leaving before he had the chance to say anything else facetious.

The man was nothing but a womaniser. Even with his own illegitimate daughter in his apartment he hadn't been able to resist the impulse to flirt with her!

Olivia hoped the baby kept him awake all night!

It had been too soon, Faith decided as she looked at Olivia's face when she re-entered her apartment, easily able to gauge Olivia's mood as one of complete antagonism towards Ethan Sherbourne.

Oh, well, there was Christmas Eve to go yet— Christmas Day, too. And miracles had been worked before in much less time than that.

Besides, Olivia's brief absence from her apartment had given Faith the opportunity to take a look at that photograph Olivia kept hidden away in the bottom drawer of her bedside cabinet.

Faith only hoped Mrs Heavenly hadn't been watching—her mentor might see her behaviour as cheating!

CHAPTER FOUR

OLIVIA felt absolutely exhausted as she made her way home on Christmas Eve.

Her client had decided, after Olivia had worked on her case for weeks, to reconcile with her husband, and as such had no further need to sort out the custody of their child. The fact that the reconciliation would probably only last as long as Christmas—maybe as long as New Year if the couple were lucky—meant that Olivia would have to restart the exhausting business of pinning down the husband as soon as her office reopened in January. Not exactly a good way to end a year's work!

The office party had also taken place this afternoon and early evening. It was an event Olivia usually tried her best to avoid, but she had been prevented from doing so this year by a personal request from one of the senior partners.

'Not good for company morale not to have the management in evidence,' was how Dennis had put it—when all he had really wanted was the legitimate excuse of Christmas mistletoe to try and kiss her. If one of them—she wasn't sure who—hadn't inadvertently knocked some files off the top of a cabinet, thus diverting attention from the fraught situation,

Olivia was very much afraid she would have had to slap him on the face!

Yet another situation she would have to sort out when she returned to work in the New Year, she acknowledged with a sigh. Not that there was anything wrong with Dennis; he was only about ten years older than she was, single, attractive, and had made it more than obvious to her over the last few months that he was very available. She just wasn't interested.

Rushing to the local supermarket when she had finally managed to escape—conscious of the fact that the larger shops would be closed for the following three days—and having to fight her way through frantic last-minute shoppers for the few fresh provisions she would need to see her through that time had been the final straw for Olivia in what had already been a disastrous day.

She just wanted to close her apartment door on the rest of the world, pour herself a glass of chilled white wine, put her feet up on the sofa as she drank it—and hope that she could somehow avoid even knowing it was Christmas!

The first, second, and even the third of those needs was soon satisfied. But the knock on her door, even as she sat back on the sofa with a contented sigh, seemed to imply that the fourth one wasn't going to be quite so easy...

Especially when she opened the door to find

Ethan Sherbourne standing outside, with baby Andrea reclining in a baby buggy, deep blue eyes wide open as she looked about her curiously.

Olivia's gaze rose slowly from the baby to centre questioningly on Ethan Sherbourne.

He smiled. 'I went shopping for a few things today that I thought I might need,' he explained.

Olivia was curious as to how he had done that with baby Andrea in tow, but determinedly didn't ask the question. She did not want to know any more about this situation than she needed to. Did not want to become involved!

'You look tired.' Ethan looked down at her concernedly. 'Had a tough day?'

Olivia gave a startled blink, feeling the sudden rush of unwanted tears as they stung her eyes. It had just been so long since anyone had asked her how her day had been, let alone noticed how tired she looked…!

She swallowed hard, pushing the momentary weakness to the back of her mind. 'Probably not as tough as yours,' she allowed dryly, standing firmly in the doorway. She did not intend inviting him— or Andrea!—inside.

In the time she had lived in this apartment building Olivia could probably count on one hand the amount of times she had actually seen or spoken to Ethan Sherbourne. Even then it had only usually been as the two of them had passed, either going in or out of the lift. In the last twenty-four hours she had seen him almost as many times as in the whole of the previous year—and spoken to him far too much for her liking!

Ethan shrugged now. 'It really wasn't that bad. Andrea is still at that stage where she sleeps more than she's awake.'

He didn't exactly look frazzled, Olivia had to admit—in fact, he looked in better condition than she did!

Once again she wondered what the man actually did for a living. He obviously hadn't been at work today if he had been shopping and looking after Andrea all day.

'What can I do for you?' Olivia prompted sharply.

Ethan was wearing a jacket over his silk shirt and tailored trousers—looked, in fact, as if he was on his way out...

'It isn't for me,' he answered smoothly. 'It's for Andrea. You see—'

'The answer is no,' Olivia cut in, before he could even finish what he wanted to say. He *was* dressed to go out, damn him! 'Most definitely no,' she repeated firmly. 'I've only just got in, and I haven't even had a chance to eat dinner yet. I was going to take a long, leisurely bath before—'

'Settling down for the evening,' Ethan pounced with a triumphant grin, pushing the buggy inside her apartment and running one of the wheels over

Olivia's toes in the process. 'There's absolutely no reason why you can't still take that long, leisurely bath—Andrea is far too young to look and tell!' he pronounced suggestively. 'She's just been bathed, fed and changed too, so—'

'Is it me?' Olivia followed him through to her sitting room, completely exasperated with his railroading behaviour. 'Or have I just told you that I'm busy?'

'I have to go out, Olivia,' Ethan interrupted, his teasing tone of a few seconds ago completely gone. 'And I can't take Andrea with me.' He answered what he had guessed—correctly—was going to be her next question.

'Why can't you?' She glared at him. But from the way he was dressed she already knew the answer to that; the particular member of the harem he was meeting this evening wouldn't understand about baby Andrea!

His gaze shifted slightly, no longer quite meeting hers. 'I would really rather not say.'

Olivia's eyes widened incredulously. 'You would really rather not—? Now, you just listen here, Ethan Sherbourne—'

'I would love to, Olivia—but I'm already late for my appointment.' He handed her the bag he had slung over his shoulder before bending to kiss her lightly on the cheek. 'I promise not to be late,' he told her on a teasing note.

'Ethan—' Olivia gasped—only to discover she was already talking to herself. Ethan had closed the apartment door softly behind him as he left.

Leaving her alone with baby Andrea for goodness knew how long. Olivia gave absolutely no credence to Ethan's claim that he wouldn't be late.

She just couldn't believe he had done this to her! Or that he had kissed her...!

She raised a hand to touch her cheek, surprised to see that her hand was shaking slightly. And her cheek felt as if it were burning.

Dennis Carter had tried to kiss her fully on the lips earlier, tried to grab hold of her behind a filing cabinet, and all she had felt was revulsion. Ethan Sherbourne merely kissed her on the cheek and she was quivering like a schoolgirl.

Which just went to prove she was more in need of that leisurely bath and quiet dinner than she had realised. Ethan Sherbourne had gone out to spend the evening with one of his legion of women-friends, literally leaving Olivia holding the baby, and she was standing here in a daze because the damn man had had the nerve to kiss her on the cheek.

Too much cheap wine at the office party. That had to be the answer.

A slight whimper from Andrea brought Olivia back to a complete awareness of her predicament. Whether either of them liked it or not, it seemed they were stuck with each other—at least for several hours.

Olivia went down on her haunches beside the buggy. 'I'm not at all happy about being abandoned by Ethan in this way myself,' she assured the baby wryly. 'But learn from this experience, poppet.'

She reached out and gently touched one of Andrea's tiny hands. Her baby fingers immediately clenched about one of Olivia's own. 'We're both left sitting at home while your daddy goes out.' She tried to get up, suddenly finding herself unable to move as Andrea continued to hang on to her finger. 'That's it, poppet.' She smiled. 'We women have to stick together, don't we? How about we go into the kitchen now, to prepare me some dinner?'

She gently released her finger before straightening to wheel the buggy through to the adjoining room.

She found herself chattering away to the baby as she moved about the kitchen, sitting at the breakfast bar to eat her food rather than going through to the dining room as she usually did because Andrea seemed absolutely fascinated by the array of shining pots and pans suspended from the rack in the middle of the kitchen ceiling.

She really was the most adorable baby, Olivia decided as she watched Andrea yawn tiredly before falling back into a contented sleep.

Whatever trauma had occurred in Andrea's life in the last twenty-four hours—her mother's desperate flight, then being cared for by the inexperienced Ethan Sherbourne, and now being left with yet another complete stranger—Andrea remained impervious to it all, completely unaware anything was wrong in her young life. Or that she wasn't completely loved and cared for.

Not so Olivia, whose heart ached for this helpless little being as she wondered what on earth the future would hold for her.

Andrea, like all babies, deserved to be loved by her mother *and* her father—to be brought up and loved in as stable a homelife as possible. Even if—as in this case—her parents chose not to live together. Somehow Olivia couldn't see this being so for Andrea.

Once again Olivia felt the tears falling hotly down her cheeks. Tears that she hadn't cried for so long. Tears she hadn't allowed herself to cry.

Damn Ethan Sherbourne for involving her in the mess he had made of his life! And double damn him for just leaving the baby here with her like this!

When he returned—from the arms of whatever woman he was spending the evening with!—she was going to tell him exactly what she thought of him.

Exactly!

'How's it going?' Mrs Heavenly enquired interestedly as Faith stood before her.

Faith sighed. 'Slowly.'

'Tomorrow is Christmas Day,' the elderly angel reminded her gently.

Faith was well aware what day tomorrow was. And she had been doing everything she could to try and bring about a miracle for Olivia. But it was rather difficult when Olivia herself—despite having asked for help—was so adamantly against finding happiness.

Look at the way she had behaved with that lovely Dennis Carter at the office party earlier. The poor man was completely besotted with her, had apparently been inviting her out to dinner with him for months, and today he had finally plucked up the courage to kiss her—and look what had happened.

From the angry gleam in Olivia's eyes following that attempted kiss, what would have happened if Faith hadn't chosen to knock some files onto the floor and thus divert Olivia's attention was that Olivia would actually have slapped the poor man. And goodness knew, as Dennis was effectively one of Olivia's bosses, what the repercussions of that might have been!

Faith gave another sigh. 'Olivia is—a little difficult,' she said, with understatement.

Mrs Heavenly gave a sympathetic smile. 'No one said this job was easy!'

'No,' Faith agreed slowly.

'What are they all doing now?' The cherubic face looked up at her enquiringly.

'Ethan has gone out. I have no idea where,' Faith reported. 'Olivia has fed Andrea, and the two of them are now fast asleep.'

'I see.' Mrs Heavenly looked serious. 'How do Olivia and Ethan seem together now?'

Faith pulled a face. 'It's a little difficult to tell— Olivia is either furiously angry with him or else she's in tears.' She shook her head. 'I don't—'

'In tears?' Mrs Heavenly echoed softly. 'Olivia has cried again since we saw her yesterday?'

'Buckets,' Faith confirmed reluctantly, totally astounded when Mrs Heavenly gave her one of her beaming smiles. 'What—?'

'Whatever you're doing, Faith, it seems to be working.' The elderly angel nodded her satisfaction. 'But I would get back down there now, if I were you,' she advised quickly. 'Ethan is standing outside Olivia's apartment about to knock on her door.'

'The mood she was in before she fell asleep in the chair, she's likely to have an axe in her hands when she answers that knock!' Faith opined, before quickly making her descent.

Hopefully she would be in time to prevent Olivia from actually using that axe!

CHAPTER FIVE

'AND just where do you think you have been till almost midnight?' Olivia demanded to know as she opened the door to face Ethan Sherbourne, having glanced at the clock to check the time before answering his knock.

Ethan raised dark brows before glancing down at the gold watch on his wrist. 'Eleven-thirty-one is hardly midnight,' he returned calmly.

'It's hardly early, either—' She broke off her tirade as Ethan grinned at her unconcernedly, darkly frowning her irritation at his reaction. 'And just what is so funny?' she snapped, not in the best of moods anyway, after being woken from her dreamless sleep.

'It's just that I haven't had someone tell me off for being late home for more years than I care to think about.' His grin turned to a throaty chuckle. 'It's rather nice,' he added wistfully.

'Nice!' Olivia echoed incredulously. 'What on earth could possible by "nice" about being shouted at because you're late home?' Really, the man was even more exasperating than she had previously realised.

Ethan smiled ruefully. 'That someone cares enough to mention the fact, I suppose.'

Olivia drew in a sharp breath. 'It isn't a question of caring, Ethan,' she assured him. 'I am merely bringing it to your attention because it's well past time you took Andrea home for the night!'

'Where is she, by the way?' Ethan glanced past Olivia into her quiet and seemingly deserted apartment.

'After the speed with which you left earlier, I'm surprised you care,' she scorned.

His smile instantly faded, dark eyes suddenly intense as he looked at her. 'Believe me, Olivia, I care.'

The softness of his tone, the conviction behind his words, was enough to make her blush uncomfortably; after all, the situation behind Andrea's birth was still all guesswork on her part. 'Andrea is fast asleep in my bedroom,' she assured him quietly, holding the door open wider for him to enter. 'I'll take you through—'

'Leave it for a moment,' Ethan rasped before dropping down into one of her armchairs, suddenly looking very tired. 'This has been a very fraught evening,' he said heavily.

The word *good* instantly sprang into Olivia's mind. If he chose to go out with one of his women instead of facing up to his responsibility towards Andrea, then he deserved—

'I've seen Shelley this evening, Olivia,' Ethan

continued wearily. 'If you wouldn't mind, I would like to tell you about it.'

Olivia was absolutely stunned to learn she had completely misunderstood the reason for his disappearance this evening. Not only that, she was also taken aback that he actually wanted to talk to *her* about it.

But did she want to know? Did she want to become any more embroiled in this situation than she already was? The answer to both those questions was a resounding no! And yet...

'Would it be too much to ask if I could have a cup of coffee while we talk?' Ethan looked up at her gratefully.

The last thing Olivia wanted to do was make him a cup of coffee, and thus delay his departure from her apartment any further. But one glance at the strain so evident beside his eyes and mouth and she relented enough to go out into the kitchen and make them both coffee.

Whatever Ethan and Shelley had had to say to each other this evening, it obviously hadn't resulted in Shelley coming back with him to collect Andrea. Which was a little ominous, to say the least.

'Thanks.' Ethan took the mug of coffee from her as she held it out to him a few minutes later. 'I am sorry about my hurried departure earlier,' he apologised. 'But I had learnt from a mutual friend where I could find Shelley, and I wanted to get there before she realised I was on my way and had a chance to disappear.'

Olivia sat down in the armchair facing his, quietly sipping her own coffee as she waited for him to continue; after all, he was the one who wanted to talk.

Ethan breathed deeply after sipping the reviving coffee. 'This is good coffee,' he said approvingly.

Which made Olivia realise it had been some time since she had made coffee for anyone but herself... Strange, but in the time she had lived in this apartment she couldn't remember ever inviting anyone back here—not even a female friend. She hadn't known until this moment just how reclusive she had become...

'I'm just delaying things, aren't I?' Ethan acknowledged, completely misunderstanding the reason for Olivia's sudden silence.

'You really don't have to tell me anything,' she assured him softly.

'Oh, but I do,' he asserted firmly. 'I've inadvertently involved you in this tangle; the least I owe you is an explanation. You see—' He broke off as the sound of Andrea's crying from the bedroom suddenly filled the air. 'I think I need to have a word with that young lady about her sense of timing,' he said affectionately, putting his empty coffee mug down on the table before standing up. 'I'll go,' he assured Olivia as she would have stood up too. 'After all, you've stood the evening shift!'

Olivia sank back down into her armchair, watching him as he strode over to her bedroom door and quietly let himself in, speaking soothingly to Andrea as he did so. In truth, after Ethan's innocently spoken words, she couldn't have stood up now if she had wanted to!

She was glad of the respite of his absence; he could have no idea of how his casual comment had evoked painful memories—memories that had been forcing themselves back into her conscious thoughts more and more the last couple of days. No, Ethan could have no idea—and Olivia intended making sure it stayed that way!

Although she couldn't say she was altogether sure she was happy with his presence in the intimacy of her bedroom—no matter how innocent his reason for being there. It was so obviously a completely feminine room, with its lace and satin décor in creams and golds, and only the presence of a double bed gave evidence that she hadn't always slept alone…

'Is she hungry again, do you think?' Ethan asked concernedly as he returned with the still crying Andrea in his arms.

'She could be,' Olivia agreed, standing up. 'I'll go and warm one of the bottles you left earlier.'

In fact, Olivia had been amazed by his organisation when she'd opened Andrea's bag earlier. There was everything in there, including several made-up bottles of formula, that she could possibly need to look after the baby for several hours.

Curiously, Ethan Sherbourne was proving more and more just how inexperienced he *wasn't* when it came to caring for a young baby...

'This is cosy, isn't it?' Ethan remarked several minutes later, with the baby lying in his arms sucking contentedly on her bottle as he once again sat in the armchair opposite Olivia's.

It wasn't quite the description Olivia would have used; overly familiar was what sprang to *her* mind. In fact, explanation or not, she couldn't wait for Ethan to leave now—and take the baby Andrea with him!

'It's rather late,' she replied tersely, deliberately not answering his own comment. After all, there was no reason why he couldn't go back to his own apartment and feed Andrea there. And leave her in peace.

'You're right; it is.' Ethan grimaced in agreement after glancing at the clock on her fireplace, which now read fifteen minutes after midnight. 'Young babies have no appreciation of the difference between day and night, do they?' he added with a fond glance at the obviously alert Andrea.

'How should I know?' Olivia returned stiffly.

'You shouldn't,' he accepted lightly. 'By the way,' he added softly, 'Happy Christmas.'

Olivia opened startled grey eyes, before frowning heavily. Of course, they were now fifteen minutes into Christmas Day. She swallowed hard. 'Happy

Christmas, Ethan.' Her voice choked on its unfamiliarity with those two words.

He gave her that spontaneous grin once again. 'I bet I'm the last person you thought you'd be saying that to this year!' he said, explaining his humour.

Or any other year! Ethan Sherbourne just wasn't the type of man she wanted to spend any time with—let alone the early hours of Christmas morning.

'I'm sure you could say the same thing about me.'

Ethan gave her a considering look, head tilted on one side, those brown eyes darkly probing. 'Why should you think that?' he finally asked—just when Olivia had almost got to the stage where she thought she couldn't stand that piercing gaze on her a moment longer!

Now it was Olivia's turn to smile. 'I'm hardly the type of woman you would usually choose to spend time with,' she stated derisively.

He frowned his puzzlement. 'And how would you know what type of woman that is?'

Her smiled widened. 'I've seen several of them in passing, on their way up to your apartment,' she told him candidly.

He looked at her quizzically for several long minutes. 'But don't you know what I do—?' He broke off as Andrea, having let the bottle slip from her mouth, now let out a sound of protest at being deprived her food. 'Silly pumpkin,' Ethan murmured indulgently as he repositioned the bottle.

Olivia stood up abruptly, unable to stand the intimacy of this situation a moment longer. They might almost have been a family. A father and mother talking softly together as the baby was fed. It was an image that was totally unacceptable to her.

'Would you like some more coffee?' she offered abruptly.

'That's very kind of you,' Ethan said warmly. 'But I really think Andrea and I have taken up enough of your time for one evening,' he added with obvious regret.

From the look of the milk still left in the bottle, and the speed with which Olivia knew the baby drank, he was going to be here for some time yet. 'It will only take me a second or so to pour it; it's already made in the percolator,' she assured him, and she picked up his empty mug. Once again she needed a few minutes to herself, and getting fresh coffee provided her excuse to leave the room.

'In that case...thanks.' He made himself more comfortable by sliding down the chair. 'If it's any consolation, Olivia,' he called after her as she went through to the kitchen, 'this isn't quite how I envisaged spending my Christmas, either!'

Which was exactly what Olivia needed to hear to put her equilibrium back on its usual even keel!

Of course this wasn't how Ethan had expected to spend his Christmas! No doubt he had one—or possibly several—of his harem lined up with whom to spend the hours of Christmas. But baby Andrea's appearance had ensured that just wouldn't happen.

And, Olivia told herself firmly before returning to the sitting room, she mustn't ever think Ethan was doing more than playing with her, in the absence of one of those women, with his occasional flirtatious remarks to her. The poor man probably couldn't help himself! To imagine anything else would be pure stupidity on her part.

'Are you doing anything tomorrow—I mean today?' Ethan asked conversationally, after glancing at the clock once again.

Olivia slowly put his coffee mug down on the table in front of him before moving decisively back to her own chair. What business was it of his how she intended spending her Christmas?

She thought longingly of the two new classical CDs she had bought to listen to during the next two days. She had no intention of even switching the television on for any of that period; the superficial, over-jolly seasonal programmes were total anathema to her. She had bought a delicious Dover sole to grill for her lunch today, knowing it would be very enjoyable with a glass of light white wine.

Yes, her Christmas—such as it was—was all taken care of.

'It's Christmas Day,' she answered dismissively.

'Exactly.' Ethan grinned.

'I meant there will be nowhere open,' she said coolly.

'I meant, are you going away to see family? Or anything?' he pursued lightly.

Olivia wasn't fooled for a moment. By 'anything' he was obviously referring obliquely to the possibility that she might have a male friend she was seeing.

She thought briefly of Dennis Carter, who had casually suggested that he might call her on Boxing Day, to wish her a Merry Christmas. Somehow Olivia had the feeling his telephone call might include an invitation to spend the day with him.

'I am spending the holiday period at home. Alone,' she added bravely.

'Come upstairs and spend the day with Andrea and me,' Ethan suggested instantly, sitting forward to look at her intently. 'Don't refuse until you've thought about it, Olivia,' he said as she would have done exactly that.

She didn't need to think about it; the idea of spending Christmas day—any day!—in the company of Ethan Sherbourne, with or without the presence of baby Andrea, was totally unacceptable to her. Although without Andrea the invitation would probably never have been made at all...

'I've been out and bought a tree, and decorations,' Ethan added persuasively. 'In fact, the tree still needs to be trimmed,' he admitted. 'I'm not sure where the time went today—yesterday—but I simply didn't have time to do anything but put the tree in a pot.' He looked around Olivia's apartment, which was totally lacking in any sign that it was indeed Christmas, least of all a decorated tree surrounded by presents! 'We could do it together later this morning, before opening our presents,' he suggested cajolingly.

Olivia had listened with growing horror as he outlined his plans for today—for all of them! 'I—'

'I've bought you a Christmas present, Olivia,' Ethan put in softly. 'At least, Andrea and I have,' he added huskily.

Olivia's stare was now one of shocked amazement, her cheeks fiery red. What did Ethan think he was doing, buying her a Christmas present? He had no right—

She didn't have anything to give him in return! Or Andrea either, for that matter...

'Do come, Olivia,' Ethan persuaded, putting the now replete Andrea into her pushchair before gathering up her things in preparation for leaving. 'It will be much more fun. For Andrea, I mean. And you did say you don't have any other plans...'

It was time to stop this. And stop this now! 'Andrea is hardly old enough to care one way or the other,' Olivia replied sharply.

Ethan looked sad as he straightened. 'But *I* would know, Olivia,' he said. 'This is her first ever Christmas, don't forget. I want it to be special for her.'

Olivia could hardly see how her own presence would make it that! 'I said I was spending Christmas alone,' she bit out harshly. 'And that's because that's the way I prefer to spend it,' she concluded rudely.

Ethan unconcernedly wheeled Andrea's laden pushchair towards the door. 'No one should spend Christmas Day alone,' he said lightly. 'We'll expect you about nine-thirty, okay?'

No, it was not okay! Of all the arrogant—

'Ethan—' Olivia broke off as he stopped suddenly in front of her, bending to pick something up off the floor. 'What on earth is that?' She peered at the piece of green foliage Ethan now held in his hand.

Dark brows rose over quizzical brown eyes. 'Don't you know?' Ethan teased, suddenly standing much too close to her.

Olivia resisted the impulse to step back; she was a mature woman of thirty-two, not a gauche teenager!

She frowned down at the sprig of greenery, the white berries that decorated its branches making it unmistakable. Mistletoe! Now how on earth had that got here? She certainly hadn't brought it. Maybe it had got caught up in her shopping at the supermarket earlier, and dropped to the floor as she'd carried the bags inside? However it had got here, she did not like the determined glint in Ethan's eyes as he held the mistletoe up over the two of them!

'It's bad luck not to kiss under the mistletoe,' Ethan told her gruffly.

Olivia found herself held mesmerised by the

warmth in those compelling brown eyes. 'I've never heard that before,' she replied breathlessly.

'That's because I just made it up,' Ethan admitted, before his head lowered and his lips claimed hers.

Olivia felt as if an electric shock had coursed through her body at the first touch of those softly sensual lips against hers, which parted slightly as she gasped in reaction. Then the kiss deepened as Ethan's mouth took firm control of hers.

His arms moved about the slenderness of her waist and he pulled her against the hard length of his body, his hands trailing down the length of her spine.

Olivia wanted to scream, and shout, to push him away—but more than any of those things she wanted the kiss to go on and on for ever!

Her body felt on fire, her limbs fluid, her only reality Ethan and the erotic exploration of his lips against hers.

He was finally the one to break the kiss, his breathing shallow as he rested his forehead against hers. 'Wow!' he murmured throatily.

Wow, indeed. Olivia could never remember being so aroused by just a kiss. And from Ethan Sherbourne of all people…!

'Nine-thirty in the morning?' he prompted, his arms still firmly about her waist.

She moistened dry lips, hardly daring to breathe. 'Yes.'

'Good.' He nodded his satisfaction as he stepped

away from her. 'You don't need to bring anything—just yourself,' he said warmly.

Olivia was still standing where he had left her as he quietly closed the door behind him and Andrea as they left. She didn't dare move yet, in case her legs didn't hold her when she did!

Worst of all, despite her earlier protestations, she now seemed to have agreed to spending Christmas Day with Ethan and his young charge!

'The mistletoe was a nice touch,' Mrs Heavenly praised Faith warmly.

Faith made no response. Arranging for that piece of mistletoe to be there in front of the door, where Ethan would easily find it as he left, had been a brainwave on her part. But she didn't want to sound as if she were feeling too self-satisfied; there was still a long way to go on this assignment.

Although that kiss under the mistletoe *had* resulted in Olivia agreeing to spend Christmas Day with Ethan and the baby...

'This evening alone with Andrea was very hard on Olivia,' Faith said instead. 'Are you sure she's up to spending Christmas Day *en famille*?'

Mrs Heavenly smiled sadly. 'I have a feeling it will either be the making or the breaking of her.'

That was what Faith felt too. 'I'm not sure—'

'Olivia lacks faith in herself, as well as in other people, my dear,' Mrs Heavenly pointed out gently. 'One day, in order to start living again, rather than just existing, she has to make a leap of faith. I be-lieve Ethan Sherbourne has been chosen for her to leap to.'

'Which is where I come in,' Faith put in. 'But I do wish Ethan had had the chance to finish explain-ing to Olivia about those other women in his life.'

Was it her imagination, or did Mrs Heavenly's cherubic gaze suddenly not quite meet her own? Surely she hadn't—?

No, of course not. She was being silly. This was Faith's assignment. Mrs Heavenly wouldn't have given it to her if she hadn't thought she could handle it.

'All in good time, my dear. All in good time,' Mrs Heavenly dismissed brightly. 'Now, if I were you, while Olivia is sleeping I would take a few earthly hours' rest myself.' She beamed up at Faith. 'This promises to be a very busy day for you.'

It certainly did. Faith only hoped Olivia wouldn't change her mind later that morning, and cancel spending the rest of the day with Ethan and Andrea…

CHAPTER SIX

SHE must have changed her mind about the sensibility of spending the day with Ethan and Andrea at least a hundred times since early that morning! After Ethan had left, during the long sleepless early hours, and again after she'd got up and showered. But, despite all that indecision, it was now nine-thirty and she was standing outside Ethan's apartment, preparing to ring the doorbell in order to announce her presence.

It was all the fault of that piece of mistletoe, of course; Olivia still had no idea where it could possibly have appeared from. But without that Ethan would never have kissed her—and she wouldn't have responded!

She still felt a fluttering sensation in her chest every time she thought of that kiss they had shared. Her only consolation was that it probably hadn't meant a thing to Ethan; he probably viewed kissing her as having done his good deed for the day!

'Merry Christmas!' Ethan greeted as he opened the apartment door and kissed her lightly on the cheek. 'Come in.' He clasped her arm to pull her inside. 'You're just in time to watch Andrea open her presents.'

Olivia stared in astonishment at the tiny baby as she lay on the thickly carpeted floor, surrounded by more Christmas presents than Olivia had ever seen before!

'Do you think I went a bit overboard?' Ethan said uncertainly as he saw her expression. 'This is such a completely novel experience for me,' he explained. 'I almost bought the toy store out!'

She wouldn't be at all surprised. And some of the things he had purchased were obviously way beyond Andrea's age range—the tricycle, for example. But no doubt Andrea would grow into it.

As for the novelty factor; no doubt finding out he was a father *was* a novel experience for him!

'They must have loved you,' she teased, before going down onto the carpet next to Andrea. She was dressed smartly but comfortably today, in black trousers and a red jumper, as Christmas was being foisted on her anyway, she had decided she might as well enter into the Christmas spirit! 'Happy Christmas, poppet.' She kissed Andrea on one creamy brow. 'I brought you a present too.' She held up the gift wrapped in pink tissue paper.

'That's really kind of you,' Ethan said admiringly as he watched her unwrap the present for the baby.

Having Ethan tell her earlier that he had a Christmas present for her had initially put her in rather an awkward position—because she didn't have one for him. Or Andrea. But then she'd thought hard... Ethan hadn't been too difficult to sort out; she had simply wrapped up the two CDs she had originally bought herself for Christmas. Andrea had been a different matter altogether...

'Christmas is for children,' she answered Ethan distractedly, holding up the brightly coloured rattle that she had just unwrapped. As with all young babies, Andrea was transfixed.

'You know something,' Ethan said slowly as he watched Andrea excitedly waving her arms as Olivia gently shook the rattle. 'I think I should have saved myself the trouble of buying all this—' he waved his arm over the pile of unwrapped presents '—and just bought her one of those!'

'It's a little like when we were children and found the boxes more interesting than the contents!' Olivia laughed in agreement. 'But don't worry; she'll grow into all of these,' she assured him lightly.

But her mood wasn't in the least light as she waited for his next question, which was sure to be where, exactly, had the rattle come from? Because it obviously wasn't the sort of thing one had just lying around in case a baby came to visit. If Ethan asked, she had decided she was going to tell him that she had been out yesterday and bought the small gift for Andrea...

'This is for you.' She held out the other slender parcel she had brought with her.

He frowned at the present. 'Olivia, you really didn't have to—'

'*I* was always taught to say, ''Thank you very much. It's very kind of you'',' she rebuked gently.

He looked decidedly uncomfortable. 'Thank you very much. And it *is* very kind of you. I just—'

'You don't know what it is yet,' she interjected, relieved when he at last took the present, and turning away to play with Andrea while he unwrapped it, suddenly feeling embarrassed. What if he didn't like classical music? What if—?

'I can't believe this!' Ethan burst out incredulously seconds later. 'It's amazing. I actually went out yesterday intending to buy myself this particular CD.' He held up the Mozart. 'I just didn't have time after going to the toy shop.'

'You probably wouldn't have been able to carry it, either.' Olivia looked at the pile of presents under the tree still to be opened, slightly incredulous herself that Ethan should have the same taste in music as herself. Incredulous that they should have anything in common at all!

'Probably not.' He chuckled. 'Is it okay with you if I put this on now?'

'It's your gift,' she replied.

'In that case…' He suited his actions to his words, then came back to sit with Olivia and Andrea under the enormous tree, the beautiful sound of Mozart's music filling the apartment. 'This is for you.' He picked up a parcel, the red shiny paper adorned with gold ribbon and a bow. 'I'm useless at wrapping gifts, so I had the woman in the shop wrap it for me,' he admitted.

Olivia's hand shook slightly as she accepted the present. It was light, and soft to the touch, making her wonder what could possibly be inside. She was almost afraid to open it and find out!

'It won't bite.' Ethan grinned at her obvious hesitation, brown eyes warm with humour. 'I told the saleslady that you were probably a 32D, but you can always take it back and change it if I got the size wrong—'

'Ethan!' Olivia gasped her protest—and not just at his implication that the parcel contained a bra. He had also guessed her bust size exactly!

He laughed. 'Just trying to stay in character for you,' he explained. 'I had the distinct impression last night that you believe me to be something of a womaniser...'

Olivia avoided meeting that humorous brown gaze, deliberately ignoring his last remark as she spoke. 'I don't believe for a moment that there's a bra in here!' she exclaimed.

'A bikini?' he taunted.

'Wrong time of year!'

'A slinky camisole?'

Her cheeks were the bright red of her jumper by this time. 'Not that, cither,' she retorted firmly, putting herself out of her agony—and depriving Ethan of his source of teasing!—by ripping open the glossy red paper.

Inside, wrapped in tissue paper, was a delicate cashmere wrap the colour of milky coffee.

Olivia eyes filled with tears as she looked at it and touched its beauty. It was years since anyone had bought her a completely personal gift like this; her usual Christmas presents consisted of products for the bath or chocolates from the far-flung members of her family. Her parents always sent her a cheque, with the excuse that they had 'no idea what to buy her'.

This wrap, exactly the right colour to complement her fair colouring, was so—so absolutely right...

'Do you like it?' Ethan said uncertainly at her continued silence.

'Do I *like* it!' Olivia looked up at him, her eyes still swimming with those unshed tears. 'I love it!' She held the wrap close against her chest.

He looked at her quizzically for several long seconds. 'You know,' he said slowly, 'and please don't take this wrongly!—but I always thought you were rather a cold lady. Distant. Happy keeping yourself to yourself.' He shook his head. 'In the space of the last fifteen minutes I've seen you laugh and I've seen you almost cry. What—or who—have you been hiding from, Olivia?' he prompted.

She swallowed hard, wondering what Ethan would say if she were to answer *herself*…?

The last ten years she had deliberately presented herself with a gruelling schedule. After having worked to put herself through university, and struggled for several years at the bottom of the ladder, very rarely taking time off, she now found herself as junior partner in a prestigious law firm. But it had all been done at a price: no self-questioning…

And she wasn't sure she was up to Ethan questioning her now, either!

'You're being silly,' she dismissed, turning away abruptly, folding the red paper back over the wrap before putting the present to one side and turning back to Andrea. The baby, at least, was still gurgling happily.

There was a continued silence behind her for several minutes, as if Ethan were weighing up the pros and cons of persisting with his questioning…

Olivia held her breath as she waited for his decision.

'We can't just sit here doing nothing, woman,' he finally said briskly. 'There's still a tree to dress, and then vegetables to prepare for Christmas lunch!'

Olivia stood up, moving Andrea to a safer place away from the base of the tree they were going to decorate. 'Are we having turkey for lunch?' She couldn't keep the surprise out of her voice.

'Of course,' Ethan confirmed in a tone that questioned if there was anything else they could possibly have for lunch on Christmas Day. 'I'll have you know I got up at six o'clock this morning to put it in the oven!'

'I'm impressed,' Olivia teased.

'So you should be,' he responded. 'Here, have some tinsel.' He handed her a bright green string of it from the box of decorations.

'The lights should go on first; that way you don't knock the other things off,' she told him knowledgeably.

'I stand corrected,' he returned with a mocking bow, bending down to pick up a box of coloured lights and then handing the plug to her. 'Better?'

'Much,' Olivia answered dryly, turning to watch as he draped the lights over the branches.

It was rather a large tree, reaching almost to the ceiling, and it took them well over an hour to hang all the decorations. But the end result, they both agreed, was well worth the effort.

In fact, as the two of them stood back to admire their handiwork, Olivia thought she had never seen such a beautiful tree. It made her feel like crying all over again!

Strange—in the last forty-eight hours she had cried more than she had allowed herself to do over the last ten years. Oh, she was well aware that Andrea was the prime reason for this breach in her defences, but Ethan had his own way of breaking them down too...

She gave an involuntary start now as she felt his arm drop lightly onto her shoulders, turning to look at him questioningly.

'Now it really is Christmas,' he said.

The room sparkled and danced as the tree decorations reflected the illumination from the coloured lights, the whole thing giving the room a magical air.

'I don't think your youngest guest is too impressed,' Olivia said wryly, giving a pointed look in Andrea's direction, relieved to have something to break the spell of enchantment she had felt stealing over her.

Christmas was like that, she told herself firmly, a time to be over-emotional. It had nothing to do with Ethan. Or with her.

The baby, obviously tired out from her unusual morning, had fallen asleep on the carpeted floor.

Olivia felt an emotional lump in her throat as she watched Ethan gently pick the baby up in his arms before carrying her through to his bedroom.

Over-emotional or not, she realised she couldn't stand much more of this. She felt constantly on the edge of tears. The memories that were crowding in on her becoming almost unbearable.

'What is it, Olivia?'

She turned sharply at the sound of Ethan's voice,

realising that her emotions must have been reflected on her face as she saw the way he was looking at her so concernedly.

'Don't!' she choked, giving a desperate shake of her head. His kindness was something she couldn't take at this moment—not when she was already feeling so vulnerable and exposed.

He strode forcefully across the room, grasping the tops of her arms to look down at her searchingly. 'Talk to me, Olivia,' he encouraged huskily. 'Tell me what it is that's tearing you apart in front of my eyes?'

She couldn't! If she once started talking she knew she wouldn't be able to stop. It was something she just didn't dare do.

'Olivia?' He shook her slightly in his frustration at her silence.

She swallowed hard, fighting back her feelings of panic; she didn't have to do anything she didn't want to do! 'I thought you said we had some vegetables to prepare,' she reminded him stiltedly.

'Damn the vegetables!' he barked impatiently. 'I don't know what this is, what happened to you in the past, but you need to talk to someone, Olivia—'

'Aren't you being rather arrogant in assuming that someone should be you?' she cut in, blonde brows raised as she met his gaze unflinchingly, her defences firmly back in place after his attempt to step over a line she allowed no one to cross. Absolutely no one!

Ethan's mouth tightened at her deliberate challenge. 'I don't see any other men lining up for the privilege!' he responded harshly.

Olivia flinched at his own deliberate retaliation. Obviously they were both people who came out fighting if thcy felt they were being backed up against a wall!

'Your arrogance is in assuming I wish to confide in anyone, let alone you!' she returned hardily, grey eyes glittering with anger now.

Ethan stared down at her wordlessly for several long seconds before releasing a hissing breath. 'I realise it's what you're angling for, but I refuse to fight with you.' He shook his head. 'Today of all days!'

'Peace on earth, goodwill to all men and all that,' Olivia replied derisively.

'And all women,' Ethan drawled, releasing her to step back.

Olivia felt suddenly cold with the removal of his hands from her arms. 'I thought the last applied to you the rest of the year, too,' she said tersely.

His eyes narrowed at the barb. 'Back to the womaniser accusation, are we?' he countered. 'Things are very rarely what they seem to someone on the outside, Olivia.'

'I don't believe Andrea is a figment of my imagination!' Olivia returned staunchly.

'Andrea?' he repeated. 'What does she have to do with it?'

What—!

'Well, if you don't know, I'm not about to tell you!' Olivia snapped disgustedly.

Was the man totally beyond conscience? Beyond shame? Oh, not for the fact that he wasn't married to Andrea's mother; it seemed that was many men's personal choice nowadays. But nothing could alter the fact that Shelley hadn't trusted him enough to confide her problems to him. Or that he had continued with his own rakish lifestyle long after their affair was over…!

Ethan drew in a harshly controlling breath. 'I realise my efforts as a grandfather may not meet your exacting standards, but I can assure you that I am doing my very best to make this as good a Christmas for Andrea as I possibly can…'

Olivia didn't hear another word he said after 'grandfather'. *Grandfather!* He was Andrea's grandfather—not her father, as Olivia had assumed?

Assumed…

Yes, she had assumed, given all the circumstances, that he had to be the baby's father. But no one—not Shelley, nor Ethan himself—had actually said that he was.

Maybe, in the circumstances, it hadn't been such

an unusual assumption to make. But, as it now turned out, it had been an erroneous one.

She couldn't believe it; Ethan was Andrea's *grandfather*!

'I had no idea Ethan was Andrea's grandfather!' Faith exclaimed concernedly, knowing that she had been guilty of making an assumption too.

Mrs Heavenly looked up in surprise. 'Back again already, my dear?' she said kindly.

Faith drew in a deep breath. 'I said—'

'I heard you, my dear,' the elderly angel replied soothingly. 'Would it have made any difference if I had told you all the circumstances behind Andrea's birth? After all, it's Olivia who asked for our help, not Ethan,' she reminded her gently.

Faith shifted uncomfortably, reluctant to admit that until a few moments ago, when Ethan had revealed that he was Andrea's grandfather, and not her father, she had been feeling the same prejudice towards him that Olivia obviously had. Angels weren't supposed to feel prejudice...

'Probably not,' she answered evasively. 'I was just a little—surprised to learn the truth, that's all.'

Mrs Heavenly smiled. 'Not as much as Olivia was, I'm sure!'

'No,' Faith acknowledged ruefully, clearly remembering that stunned look on Olivia's beautiful face. 'Maybe there is hope for those two finding each other, after all...' she added thoughtfully, as she remembered that other emotion on Olivia's face as she'd looked at Ethan with new eyes.

'I told you. It's faith that's needed in this case, my dear,' Mrs Heavenly reiterated.

'Of course,' Faith accepted, knowing herself to be mildly, if kindly, rebuked and straightening determinedly. 'I'll get back and see what I can do to help.'

'You do that, dear,' Mrs Heavenly agreed, blue eyes warm. 'I must say I think it's all going extremely well so far,' she said happily.

'You do?' Faith said hopefully.

'Of course.' Mrs Heavenly smiled. 'Don't you think so?'

'Ethan is really rather a nice man, isn't he?' she realised slowly.

'Nothing less would do for someone as special as Olivia,' Mrs Heavenly assured her.

That was what Faith had thought. Had realised. Now all she had to do was return to Earth and avert the argument that had been brewing when she left.

She only hoped she hadn't left it too late!

CHAPTER SEVEN

Now that she knew the truth, Olivia could view Ethan's behaviour over the last couple of days from a new perspective, and there was respect for him in her eyes now as she looked across the room at him.

Whatever plans of his own he might have had for Christmas, they had obviously been shelved in favour of Andrea's needs. In fact, not only had he put his own life on hold, he had gone out of his way to make this Christmas as wonderful for Andrea as it was possible for him to do so. Olivia very much doubted he usually bothered with a tree—or lunch with all the trimmings, for that matter!

Which begged the question: What sort of man was he really...?

Olivia now found herself unable to answer that question, all her preconceived ideas thrown up in the air.

But how did she begin to get herself out of the situation she had created because of her earlier prejudice...? More to the point, how did she avoid letting Ethan know of her earlier assumption concerning Andrea's paternity! Or did she avoid it at all? Wouldn't it be more honest on her part to own up to her mistake?

It might be more honest, she acknowledged, but she doubted it would be conducive to this being the harmonious Christmas Day Ethan wanted!

'Nothing to say?' he challenged at her continued silence.

Olivia moistened dry lips. 'Ethan, I—' She broke off, drawing in a shaky breath. 'I owe you an apology,' she burst out, before she had a chance to change her mind. 'It was presumptuous of me. I allowed my prejudice towards you to colour my judgement. I had no right to come to such a conclusion.' She was babbling! Worse than that, from the completely puzzled expression on Ethan's face, she was making no sense! 'I'm sorry,' she concluded heavily.

'Glad to hear it,' he accepted lightly. 'Now, would you mind telling me what it is you're sorry for?'

She winced. 'I thought Andrea— You see, Shelley didn't say— *You* didn't say—'

'Just a minute,' Ethan said slowly, frowning now. 'Correct me if I'm wrong, but until my comment a few minutes ago had you been under the misapprehension that I'm Andrea's father?'

Olivia's wince turned to a self-conscious grimace. 'It really was very presumptuous of me—' She broke off as Ethan began to chuckle, staring at him dazedly. 'It isn't funny, Ethan,' she told him crossly. 'I totally misjudged you—'

'Yes, you did,' he acknowledged with a grin. 'But don't you see, Olivia? To your credit, you kept coming back.'

'That was because of Andrea,' she admitted unhappily.

His expression softened at the mention of his granddaughter. 'She really is lovely, isn't she?'

'She is,' Olivia agreed. 'She's an absolute credit to her mother,' she added.

'I agree,' Ethan said. 'You really thought *I* was the one involved with Shelley?'

Olivia swallowed, knowing from his expression that now he had stopped laughing at her mistake he wasn't at all pleased by her assumption.

'She's only twenty years old, Olivia!' Ethan rasped.

'I realised that,' Olivia admitted. 'I just—I couldn't see any other explanation after she just left Andrea here with you,' she said defensively.

'Hmm,' he snorted. 'Well, as you've probably now realised, I am indeed a father. My son Andrew, who is only twenty-one,' he elaborated pointedly, 'was the one involved with Shelley a year ago.'

Andrea. Andrew. Shelley had named her daughter for the father... Surely that had to mean something?

'Andrew's mother and I were divorced years ago,' Ethan revealed. 'But Andrew and I have continued to have a very close relationship, nonetheless. I only met Shelley once, when he brought her here to dinner.'

He was telling her that that was how Shelley came to know him. And had known where he lived...

Olivia was feeling more and more foolish by the minute!

'And the reason Shelley, out of sheer desperation, brought Andrea here to me was because when she went to Andrew's flat she discovered he was away on a skiing holiday,' Ethan explained evenly.

Olivia's eyes widened. 'Your son lives in London?'

Ethan nodded. 'He's at university here. But don't be under the misapprehension that he's a student starving in a garrett,' he added dryly. 'Andrew lives very comfortably on the allowance I give him!' Too comfortably, his tone seemed to imply.

'You said he's on a skiing holiday?' Olivia prompted softly.

'Not any more,' Ethan assured her. 'I telephoned him early yesterday and told him to get himself back here. To his credit he was absolutely stunned when I told him the reason why. Apparently Shelley hadn't told him of her pregnancy when she broke off their relationship eight months ago.'

'Maybe she didn't know at the time...?' Olivia suggested lamely.

'Oh, she knew,' Ethan replied. 'But she had some misguided idea that she didn't want to force their relationship into something Andrew possibly didn't want just because of her pregnancy. So, instead, she chose to struggle on on her own.' He sighed angrily.

Misguided, perhaps, Olivia acknowledged, but as a woman she could see it from Shelley's point of view. If Andrew had shown no signs of wanting their relationship to be a serious one before the pregnancy, how could she possibly have told him about the baby without feeling she was pressurising him into something he might not want?

Olivia looked serious. 'They're both young...' She could only imagine Andrew's reaction yesterday, on learning he was a father—whether he was pleased or angry at the knowledge. In either case it must have been a shock to be told of Andrea's existence.

'Old enough to have a daughter,' Ethan countered. 'Besides, I was only Andrew's age when he was born.'

'But you've already said your marriage ended in divorce,' Olivia reminded him, determinedly shutting out her own memories of when she was twenty-one.

'*Touché,*' Ethan allowed. 'But I'm not proposing that the two of them should get married if that isn't what they want. Although I do know that Andrew was very upset when the relationship ended...' he amended thoughtfully.

'That might be a good sign,' Olivia agreed.

'Let's hope so,' Ethan replied. 'I picked Andrew up from the airport last night, and drove him straight to where I knew Shelley was staying. It wasn't exactly an auspicious meeting. Both of them were still too angry—with each other and themselves. But I've suggested that I continue to look after Andrea over Christmas while the two of them sit down and talk to each other. The least they can do is come to some sort of agreement about Andrea's future upbringing that won't result in a repeat of Shelley's recent feelings of desperation. I think that's fair enough, don't you?' He looked at Olivia intently.

What did it matter what she thought? None of this situation was really any of her business. Although that didn't mean she didn't have great admiration for the way Ethan was handling this delicate situation. In fact, she was starting to think he was a pretty wonderful human being!

She nodded abruptly. 'I think that's very fair,' she agreed, her admiration for him deepening by the minute. Not only had Ethan turned his own life upside down in order to look after Andrea, but he was also trying to help her young parents come to some sort of understanding over the situation.

'Good. At last I seem to have done something right in your eyes!'

Olivia stared at him. What could it possibly matter what she thought—of him or this situation…?

'Now, stop diverting my attention, woman,' Ethan said briskly. 'Let's go and prepare those vegetables!'

'You still want me to stay to lunch?' she said, amazed. Considering the strain he had been put under himself the last couple of days, her erroneous assumptions must surely have been the last straw as far as he was concerned?

He looked at her with mocking brown eyes. 'I'll let you know once you've peeled the potatoes,' he teased.

She had been let off lightly, Olivia acknowledged as she followed him through to the kitchen. Ethan had every right to feel absolutely furious with her for her presumptions, but he had chosen to explain the situation to her instead. If the circumstances had been reversed, Olivia knew she wouldn't have been so magnanimous...

Which, to her dismay, only served to prove to her how narrow-minded and self-opinionated she had become these last few years.

She had formed an opinion of Ethan Sherbourne based on...what? Her own assumptions, that was what. Well, she had been completely wrong concerning Andrea, so wasn't it feasible that she was probably wrong in most of her other ideas concerning Ethan, too?

Most of...?

There she went again, qualifying the positive with

an added negative. Why couldn't she just admit she had been wrong about Ethan, full stop? He—

'Stop beating yourself up, Olivia.' Ethan cut into her self-disgusted thoughts. 'If it's any consolation, I probably am most of the things you previously thought me.'

She sighed heavily. 'I somehow doubt that very much!'

'That bad, hmm?' He leaned back against one of the kitchen units to look at her assessingly.

'I'm afraid so,' she admitted self-disgustedly.

'Then that makes your being here all the more credible,' he told her warmly. 'Now, peel these potatoes.' He thrust the bag in front of her. 'I shall deal with the carrots and sprouts!' He turned back to take the other vegetables out of the fridge.

She swallowed hard. 'Don't you want to know what I thought?'

'I think I can guess most of it,' he said wryly.

Olivia couldn't even see the potatoes for the first few seconds she was peeling them, her eyes once again swimming with unshed tears.

She really was going to have to stop this, she decided firmly a few minutes later. Either she would have to sit down and have a really good cry, or she would have to get her emotions back under control. It was just that the latter was proving so hard at the moment!

'Olivia…?'

She turned slowly to look up at Ethan. He no longer made any pretence of working beside her, but stood looking at her instead. If, now having had time to think it through, he no longer wanted her to stay and spend Christmas Day with himself and Andrea, she would quite understand. After all—

Her self-berating thoughts came to an abrupt end as Ethan took her firmly in his arms and kissed her soundly on the lips!

An emotional sob caught in her throat as her arms moved convulsively over his shoulders, her lips parting as she began to kiss him back.

How long that kiss lasted Olivia had no idea. Her senses were reeling, every particle of her feeling totally alive.

Ethan pulled back slightly, looking down at her, his eyes dark and unfathomable. 'You are an extremely beautiful woman, Olivia,' he told her gruffly.

She gave a choked laugh, shaking her head. 'I'm narrow-minded. And opinionated. And—' She stopped speaking as Ethan put light fingertips against her lips.

Ethan shook his head. 'You're beautiful. Desirable. Intelligent. Warm. Caring—yes, you are, Olivia,' he insisted as she would have protested. 'Someone, or something, has hurt you very badly. But you can't hide your gentleness when you're with Andrea.'

'She's just a defenceless baby,' Olivia explained, still very aware of the hard strength of his body moulded against hers.

Ethan grinned. 'One you were obviously determined to defend from my inadequacies at baby-minding!'

'How was I to know you had done all this before?' Her voice rose indignantly.

Ethan looked rueful. 'Actually, I haven't—the fact that I didn't play enough of a role in Andrew's babyhood was one of the reasons my wife left me!' he admitted.

Olivia looked up at him quizzically. 'How long were you married?'

'Two years,' he acknowledged reluctantly.

'Two years!' she gasped incredulously.

He shrugged. 'Apparently I wasn't very good at it.'

'But even so—'

'How long were *you* married, Olivia?' Ethan interrupted, his gaze compelling now, his arms tightening about her waist as she would have pulled away.

She glared up at him as she found herself suddenly trapped in his arms. 'Let me go, Ethan!' she erupted.

'Not until you answer me.'

Her eyes became icy as they met his, her body

rigid within the confines of his arms. 'What makes you think I've been married?' she scorned.

'This.' He clasped her left hand and raised it into view, his thumb moving lightly over the third finger. 'Strange, isn't it, how the indentation from wearing a ring very rarely goes away, even when the ring is no longer being worn…?'

Olivia looked down at that hand too, easily able to see the indentation he referred to.

She snatched her hand back, pulling sharply out of his arms, breathing raggedly as she stepped away from him, her cheeks pale. 'I did slightly better than you, Ethan.' She spat the words out. 'My marriage lasted just over three years.' To her dismay—and her anger!—her voice broke over those last words. 'But at least I don't fill my life with a load of empty-headed male bimbos in order to make myself feel attractive and wanted!' She was breathing heavily in her agitation, glaring at him defiantly.

Ethan looked at her wordlessly for several long seconds, and then he drew in a harshly controlling breath. 'Peel the potatoes, Olivia,' he rasped.

Her eyes widened. 'I—'

'Before you say something you are definitely going to regret!' he concluded warningly, eyes narrowed to steely slits.

She had already said several things she deeply regretted! But Ethan had touched on a subject that, although almost ten years old, was still raw and painful.

But was that really a valid excuse for the insulting things she had just said to him...?

She shook her head. 'I really think I should leave,' she said flatly.

'For speaking your mind?' Ethan's brows rose, his expression surprised. 'God, Olivia, you don't know how refreshing it is to be with a woman who does exactly that!'

She looked at him. 'You really want me to stay?'

He nodded wordlessly.

Olivia looked puzzled now. 'But why?'

'Someone has to help me eat this huge turkey!' he returned teasingly, before turning back to the task of peeling the carrots.

Olivia could only stare at the broadness of his back, once again left reeling from his unexpected reaction to something she had said or done deliberately to insult and so ultimately antagonise him.

Deliberately because it was a form of defence that had always worked for her in the past. And yet Ethan refused to be offended...

He also kissed her whenever he felt like it. Deep, compelling kisses that made her knees shake and the rest of her body turn to jelly. Worse than that, despite the things she had said to him, she actually liked him. Perhaps more than liked him, she realised with increasing dismay...!

She had to get out of here before she fell completely under his spell!

'It's up to you, of course, to see that she doesn't leave,' Mrs Heavenly told Faith as she appeared beside her.

'I'm working on it,' Faith said, absolutely stunned at the older angel's appearance. Mrs Heavenly knew— She always— 'What are you doing down here?' Faith gasped her shock.

'I just love it here on Earth this time of year.' Mrs Heavenly looked across at the Christmas tree Olivia and Ethan had decorated so companionably earlier that morning, her cherubic features beaming with pleasure. 'It's a beautiful tree, isn't it?' she said happily.

'Yes, but— Mrs Heavenly, Olivia seems—special to you somehow, so if you would like to take over this assignment yourself, I really wouldn't mind,' Faith told her carefully.

'Don't be silly, my dear.' Mrs Heavenly gave another of her cherubic smiles. 'You're doing absolutely marvelously without any help from me.'

Which in no way answered the question of why Mrs Heavenly was taking such a personal interest in Olivia Hardy's future...

'I'll leave you to it, then, Faith,' Mrs Heavenly said.

For how long? Faith wondered as the image beside her shimmered and then disappeared...

CHAPTER EIGHT

'ETHAN, I really think—' Olivia broke off her excuse to leave as the doorbell rang out shrilly.

'Who on earth can that be?' Ethan exclaimed as he put down the knife he had been using and turned to go and answer the door.

Olivia's response was much more marked. It didn't matter who the caller was; it had to be someone who knew Ethan well enough to feel comfortable calling on him on Christmas Day—in which case she would very definitely be in the way!

She followed Ethan reluctantly from the kitchen, hanging back slightly as he moved to open the door.

'Dad...' A tall, dark-haired young man stepped forward to give Ethan a hug.

Andrew, she realised immediately. And standing beside him, looking extremely shy, was Shelley!

Olivia was very definitely in the way!

'Andrew!' Ethan stepped back at arm's length to look at his son. The similarity between the two men was obvious, despite the twenty-year difference in their ages. Both were tall, dark haired, and dark-eyed, though Andrew's looks were still boyishly handsome where his father's had honed down to carved teak.

'What are the two of you doing here?' Ethan asked quizzically.

'Neither of us could stay away from Andrea any longer.' Shelley was the one to answer, her eyes anxious as she looked past Ethan into the apartment, obviously searching for her baby.

Ethan stepped back. 'She's fast asleep in the bedroom on the left,' he told the young mother warmly. 'Go with her, Andrew,' he instructed his son huskily as Shelley hurried past him.

Olivia hung back in the kitchen doorway as she watched the young couple go into the bedroom together, Andrew's expression one of excitement mixed with awe. And no wonder; he was about to see his daughter for the first time!

She turned back to Ethan, able to see the expressions that flitted across his own face as he watched his son about to face fatherhood: love, pride, and lastly regret, for the fact that Andrew was no longer a child himself.

Olivia felt even more of an intruder as she so easily gauged those emotions.

She swallowed hard. 'Ethan…'

He instantly turned to smile at her, at the same time seeming to shake off those feelings of regret. 'It looks as if there might be four of us for lunch,' he said as he strode towards her.

Her eyes widened. 'You can't still want me to stay…?'

'Why can't I?' Ethan queried, bending to kiss her lightly on the lips as he passed her on his way into the kitchen. 'If things have gone as well as I hope they have between Andrew and Shelley then we can all have ourselves a real old-fashioned Christmas!' he added with satisfaction. 'You know—grandparents, parents and grandchild.'

It didn't take too many guesses to realise under which category he thought she came! 'Ethan, for one thing I'm not old enough to be a grandparent,' she began with embarrassment. 'For a second—' She broke off as Ethan swung round and took her in his arms. 'What—?'

'Exactly how old are you?' Ethan demanded to know, easily moulding her body against his.

She frowned up at him, totally stunned at finding herself in his arms yet again. 'Thirty-two. But—'

'Old enough to be the *partner* of a grandparent,' he assured her.

Olivia's eyes widened. 'But I'm not—'

'Dad, is it okay with you if—? Oh!' Andrew stopped abruptly in the doorway as he saw his father wasn't alone, and his euphoric expression turned to puzzled curiosity as he looked at Olivia.

Not just because Ethan wasn't alone, Olivia inwardly panicked, but because he was holding an unknown woman in his arms—unknown to Andrew that was!—in an obviously intimate way!

'It's okay, Andrew,' Ethan said as he turned to

face his son, releasing Olivia but still keeping his arm draped across her shoulders. 'You were saying…?' he prompted.

Olivia had never felt so embarrassed in her life, knowing from Andrew's speculative expression as he looked at the two of them that he was drawing his own conclusions concerning their relationship—and coming up with completely the wrong answer!

Andrew gave his father a knowing grin. 'Shelley and I were wondering if it was okay for us to spend the day here with you.' His grin turned to an uncertain frown. 'But obviously that was before I realised—'

'Of course you can all spend the day here.' Ethan cut briskly across his son's awkward glances in Olivia's direction. 'This is Olivia Hardy.' He smiled down at her warmly. 'A special friend of mine,' he added for his son's benefit.

'Olivia,' Andrew greeted.

'Andrew,' she returned, still reeling from Ethan's 'special friend of mine' claim.

'Have you and Shelley managed to sort anything out in the last twelve hours?' Ethan prompted sharply. Obviously the politeness of the introductions was over as far as he was concerned. 'Besides the fact that you both love Andrea, that is,' he added dryly.

That slightly dazed expression returned to

Andrew's youthfully handsome face. 'I still can't believed she's real,' he breathed.

'You will once you've done your share of walking up and down with her when she starts teething!' Ethan assured his son.

'I loved Shelley before, and totally disintegrated when she broke off our relationship, but this—! I've asked Shelley to marry me.'

'And?' Only the tightening of Ethan's hand on Olivia's shoulder betrayed his own tension.

Andrew went on, 'She's agreed to a six-month trial period. Just in case I want to change my mind. Which I won't,' he added firmly. 'I never wanted to break up in the first place, and now that I know the reason for it—! Be prepared for a wedding in six months' time!'

Looking at Andrew Sherbourne was like looking at Ethan as he must have been twenty years ago, Olivia realised. The younger man obviously had the same confidence and determination as his father, although, as far as she could see, Andrew had yet to develop his father's arrogance...

'Unless you were thinking of having one yourself before then...?' Andrew probed, thrusting his hands into the pockets of his denims as he looked speculatively at his father and Olivia.

Ethan looked down at Olivia as he felt her stiffen against him, his brown gaze openly laughing at the panic he easily read in her expression. 'I'll let you know if I do,' he answered his son evenly, those brown eyes continuing to laugh at Olivia's obvious discomfort.

'But don't hold your breath!' Olivia put in sharply, moving slightly so that she was no longer in the curve of Ethan's arm, able to breathe more easily, think more easily, now that she was no longer held against his warm masculinity. 'Now, if you'll all excuse me, I think it's time I went home and—'

'No way,' Ethan said firmly as he guessed what she was about to do. 'Andrew and Shelley have you to thank as much as me for looking after Andrea these last two days. We're all going to spend the day here together, Olivia,' he stated decisively, daring her to continue with her excuses to leave.

The prospect of spending the day with Ethan had been nerve-racking enough, but Olivia could imagine nothing more awful than having to be with his son, son's girlfriend, and baby granddaughter too. Almost, as Ethan had already pointed out, as if they were a family!

'Oh, please don't leave, Olivia!' Shelley had come out of the bedroom, baby Andrea nestled contentedly in her arms. 'For one thing I haven't had a chance to apologise to you for my rudeness the other evening,' she said. 'You must have thought I was awful, just leaving Andrea here in the way that I did—'

'Not at all,' Olivia instantly assured her warmly.

'Motherhood can be—overwhelming, can't it?' she sympathised.

'Yes,' Shelley acknowledged, glancing down at her baby daughter. 'But I've realised this last couple of days just how rewarding it can be too.'

Olivia swallowed hard as she saw the unconditional love in Shelley's face as she looked at her daughter, the emotional lump stuck in her throat preventing her from answering this last remark.

She was never going to get through an afternoon and evening of this!

She drew in a sharp breath. 'I really do have to go back to my own apartment for a few minutes, Ethan,' she told him firmly, not quite meeting his eyes, already knowing the censure she would see there.

'Would the two of you excuse us a few minutes?' Ethan spoke to Andrew and Shelley, but Olivia knew his gaze remained fixed on her.

'Please don't leave on our account, Olivia,' Andrew told her, before going into the sitting room with Shelley and their daughter, closing the door behind them.

Olivia kept her attention fixed on the third button down on Ethan's shirt. 'Perhaps you could take the opportunity of my absence to explain the real situation to Andrew and Shelley?'

'And what "real situation" would that be, Olivia?' he prompted.

She looked up at him now, blinking as she found herself caught in a feeling of dark warmth. 'That I'm just a neighbour, of course,' she said sharply.

'But you aren't,' Ethan told her softly.

Olivia stared at him searchingly, deciding that she really didn't want to know what he thought she was to him.

'Not to me,' Ethan continued. 'Any more than I believe that's all I am to you, either.'

The experience of caring for a very young baby had certainly broken down the barriers between them in a way that might otherwise have taken months to do—if ever. But that didn't mean Olivia wanted this situation to continue.

She stepped away from him, tilting up her chin challengingly as she looked at him. 'Ethan, I do believe you're allowing the Christmas spirit to affect your judgement,' she told him with deliberate mockery.

He looked totally unconcerned by her obvious sarcasm. 'I haven't had any Christmas spirit yet—but I intend to rectify that by opening a bottle of champagne as soon as you get back!' he said with satisfaction.

In other words, if she wasn't back within a reasonable amount of time he was going to come looking for her!

Damn.

'I'll try not to be too long,' she answered noncommittally. After all, she could always barricade herself in—she doubted even Ethan would go to the extreme of battering down her door in order to force her into spending the rest of the day with him!

'Five minutes,' he warned gently as she walked over to the door. 'After that I come looking for you.'

Olivia turned to give him a glare. 'I thought this was still a country with freedom of choice...'

'It is,' Ethan replied unconcernedly.

'As long as my choice fits in with yours!' she guessed.

He grinned across at her. 'You're learning.'

'Ethan, I have no intention of learning anything more about you than I already know. You—'

'Olivia—whoever he is, he isn't good enough to breathe the same air as you,' Ethan cut across her.

'*Who* isn't?'

'The married lover you hope has telephoned and left a message on your answer-machine?' he suggested.

'Married—!' She stared at him incredulously. 'What married lover?' she demanded; where on earth had he come up with this one? The only person who might possibly have left a message on her answer-machine while she was out this morning was Dennis Carter, and he was neither married nor her lover!

Ethan looked at her consideringly, folding his arms across the broadness of his chest. 'I've always wondered about you, Olivia—about the way you live alone, with very few friends visiting and no male visitors at all. But the more I've thought about it the last few days the more I've realised that it's the classic behaviour of a woman involved with a married man.'

Olivia was dumbstruck. Not just by his conclusion—wrong though it was!—but by the fact that Ethan had bothered to think about her in this way at all. She certainly hadn't given *his* private life the same consideration! Probably because his private life read like an open book. At least...she had thought it did...

This was incredible. She had lived her life quietly—reclusively, perhaps—these last ten years, not bothering anyone and not bothered by anyone, either, and yet still it seemed that people made conjectures, drew conclusions...that *Ethan* had drawn one particular conclusion.

'Statistics have proved that those sort of men very rarely leave their wife for the mistress,' Ethan continued gently.

She looked at him in shock. All this time he had thought—believed—! 'Maybe in this case you have that the wrong way round, Ethan—maybe it's me who doesn't *want* him to leave his wife,' she gritted—whoever 'he' might be!

'Like I said, whoever he is, he isn't fit to breathe the same air as you,' Ethan said.

Olivia gave him a pitying glance. 'I'll keep your advice in mind,' she told him tautly. 'Now, if you wouldn't mind, I think I'll just go and check for any messages on my answer-machine!'

'You have five minutes,' he reminded her.

Olivia was so angry as she left that it took every effort on her part to return Shelley and Andrew's smiles as she walked through the sitting-room to let herself out of the apartment.

She felt stunned as she stepped into the lift, hardly aware of its descent, of walking down the corridor to her own apartment, of letting herself inside.

But as she looked around the cool sterility of her own home—the home that usually offered her peace as well as sanctuary—comparing it with the warmth of Christmas that Ethan had so easily created in the apartment above, she felt a heaviness descend upon her, and dropped down into one of the armchairs to bury her face in her hands.

All this time Ethan had thought—

All the time he had been so kind to her, had kissed her, he had believed—

The life he had described for her—the fact that she lived alone, that few friends visited her, that no men came to her apartment at all—it all seemed so cold and empty after the warmth and laughter she had known with Ethan these last few hours. After the *kisses* she had shared with Ethan these last two days...!

Her face was still white with shock as she straightened, staring sightlessly ahead with huge grey eyes. She hadn't just enjoyed Ethan's company and kisses these last few days—she had fallen in love with him!

Yes, thought Faith as she saw the stunned disbelief of realisation on Olivia's face. Yes, yes, *yes!*

She looked around her for Mrs Heavenly, eager to share her euphoria with her, sure her mentor wouldn't want to miss Olivia's emotional awakening. But for once Mrs Heavenly hadn't appeared to offer her encouragement. Or congratulations.

Faith frowned as Olivia stood up like an automaton, moving woodenly into the bedroom, pulling open the bottom drawer of her bedside cabinet, taking out the photograph that lay there. The tears started to fall as Olivia held the photograph tenderly against her.

Then Faith knew exactly why Mrs Heavenly wasn't here to congratulate her on a job well done. Because this assignment was still far from over...!

CHAPTER NINE

'THE innocence of youth, hmm?' Ethan bent down to whisper in Olivia's ear as she sat in one of the armchairs.

She glanced across the room to where Andrew sat, his arm about Shelley's shoulders as she cuddled Andrea in her arms; they were all fast asleep.

'I thought a post-lunch nap was allowed on Christmas Day,' she said quietly, so as not to disturb the three.

Lunch had been extremely successful; the turkey had been cooked to perfection, as had the vegetables that accompanied it, and afterwards Ethan had brought a flaming, brandy-covered pudding to the table.

'For the oldsters, not the youngsters!' Ethan chuckled ruefully. 'Still, I suppose it *has* been rather an emotional time for them all,' he added with an affectionate smile for his son and his new family.

Olivia had been extremely reluctant to return to Ethan's after the revelation that had hit her earlier in her own apartment, but at the same time had known that if she didn't Ethan would do exactly what he had said he would, and come down to get her.

So she had returned, and to her surprise it had been a very enjoyable lunch, with baby Andrea's presence helping to make it the happy family day that it should be. But now Olivia felt it was time for her to return to her own flat.

'Do you think they'll make it?' Ethan was looking across at the young couple as he moved to sit on the arm of Olivia's chair.

She instantly felt herself tensing at his close proximity, a sudden tightness in her chest making it difficult to breathe too.

This was awful! For ten years she hadn't even looked at a man in a romantic way; how could she possibly have fallen in love with Ethan in only forty-eight hours?

Christmas was a time of miracles...

Now, where on earth had that thought come from? she wondered dazedly. Christmas might be a time of miracles, but what happened once Christmas was over and she was left with an ache inside her that would be her unrequited love for Ethan?

'Olivia...?'

She forced herself to look up at Ethan as she realised he was still waiting for an answer to his question. 'Why shouldn't they make it?' she replied. 'They stand as much chance as any other young couple embarking on a life together. More, probably, because they have Andrea, too,' she added wistfully.

Ethan looked down at her. 'Have you never wanted children of your own, Olivia?'

That tightness in her chest constricted painfully as she stared up at Ethan in disbelief that he could be saying these things to her.

Ethan reached out to cup her chin, his hand gentle, his thumb lightly caressing as he gazed down at her. 'You're so good with Andrea, Olivia. There's no doubt you would make a wonderful mother yourself.'

She drew in a harsh breath, knowing she had to put an end to this conversation—or she was in danger of breaking down again. She had already cried enough for one day.

'Are we back to the subject of my going-nowhere affair with a married man?' she taunted.

Ethan didn't move, but his face took on a hardness that hadn't previously been there. 'Did he telephone and leave you a message?'

There had been two messages on her answer-machine earlier: one from her parents, wishing her Happy Christmas before they went off to spend the day with friends, and a second from Dennis Carter, sorry that he had missed her but assuring her that he would call back later. Which was enough to make her want to leave the answering-machine on for the whole of the holiday!

She coolly returned Ethan's gaze. 'For a relative

stranger, you're taking an extraordinary interest in my private life, Ethan,' she derided.

His fingers tightened against her chin. 'We aren't strangers, Olivia.' He spoke gently. 'We never will be again. You—'

'I really don't think this is the time or the place for such a conversation, Ethan.' She glanced pointedly across the room to the sleeping couple and their baby before moving sharply away from him and standing up. 'I've had a lovely time, Ethan, but now—'

'We're way past the polite niceties stage, too,' he stated determinedly. 'And if you don't think this is "the time or place" for this conversation...' He stood up, crossing the room to take a tight grip of one of her wrists. 'We'll go down to your apartment and finish it,' he told her, pulling her along behind him as he marched forcefully towards the door.

'Ethan, stop this!' she hissed, desperately trying to free her wrist.

'Stop that, or you'll hurt yourself,' was Ethan's grim response to her struggles.

'*I'll*—*!* Ethan!' she bit out angrily, pulling even harder to free herself.

'Shh.' He turned briefly to silence her. 'You'll wake the children,' he said sardonically, before continuing on his way out of his apartment, pulling Olivia down the corridor and into the lift with him before pressing the button for the floor below.

'But—' Her protest was cut short as Ethan's lips came down forcefully on hers.

Her struggles ceased immediately, with a low groan of surrender in her throat as she gave herself up to the pleasure of that kiss. Her arms were released and she entwined them about Ethan's neck, her body pressed warmly against his.

Ethan was breathing hard by the time he raised his head as the lift came to a halt. 'I'm not going to allow you to retreat back behind those steel bars, Olivia,' he told her fiercely, his hands tightly gripping her upper arms as he stared down at her intently. 'Do you understand me?' He shook her slightly.

She moistened suddenly dry lips before answering him. 'I understand you, Ethan.'

It would be a useless thing to try anyway; loving Ethan in the way she did meant that she had nowhere to hide!

Once again her apartment seemed cold and uninviting in comparison with the warmth she had so recently known in Ethan's home. Would it always feel this way to her now, simply because Ethan wasn't in it? Oh, she hoped not!

She swallowed hard, not knowing what to say now they were completely alone. It might have been hard for her to be in the company of the young couple and their baby most of the day, but being alone here with Ethan was even more uncomfortable!

'I'm in love with you, Olivia.'

She became very still as she stared across the room at him, her blood feeling as if it had turned to ice in her veins. He couldn't really have just said—

'I said I'm in love with you, Olivia,' he repeated harshly.

He *had* said it! But why? What possible reason could Ethan have for saying something like that?

She swallowed again. 'Don't you think you're taking this idea of saving me from myself a little too far?' Did that strange-sounding voice really belong to her?

'Damn saving you from yourself,' Ethan rasped scathingly. 'I want to save you *for me*!' He moved restlessly about the room. 'This last couple of days have been—wonderful. So much so—'

'Wonderful?' Olivia echoed, staring at him incredulously. 'Ethan, you've had baby Andrea left on your doorstep, discovered that you're a grandfather, had your life turned upside down by having to care for her—'

'Andrea was a surprise, yes,' he agreed. 'But she isn't the one who's turned my life upside down,' he assured her, his eyes a warm chocolate-brown as he looked pointedly at her.

Olivia felt the ice melting under the warmth of that gaze, shaking her head to dispel the heat that seemed to be spreading through her body. 'Ethan, what I'm trying to say is that you're disorientated by all that's happened to you the last few days. You've been—forced to distance yourself from—from your normal way of life.' She couldn't quite meet his eyes now, hating even having to mention those other women she knew were in his life.

'Let me get this straight,' he said slowly, looking at her through narrowed lids. 'You think that because I've been unable to see any of my empty-headed bimbos—I think you once called them that?—I've somehow misjudged what's been happening between us?'

'Nothing has been happening between us, Ethan,' Olivia said evasively. 'You—'

'Is that what you think, Olivia?' Ethan persisted.

'Yes!' she answered forcefully.

He began to smile. 'But even *I'm* allowed time off from work over Christmas.'

'Time off from work…?' she repeated. 'But—' She broke off as the telephone began to ring, her heart immediately sinking as she thought she knew who the caller might be. This was definitely not the time for Dennis to call her back!

'Aren't you going to get that?' Ethan prompted as Olivia could only stare across at the telephone in fascinated horror.

'No! I— Yes!' She realised that perhaps she had better, or else Dennis would simply wait for the answer-machine to take over and leave her another message. One that Ethan would hear. Not a good idea, in the circumstances!

'I'll get it,' Ethan told her sharply, calmly picking up the receiver before Olivia could get to it. 'Yes?' he responded coldly. 'No, she isn't. No, she can't come to the phone,' he added hardily. 'Yes, I'll tell her.' He ended the call as abruptly as he had begun it. 'Dennis says to tell you hello, and that he'll see you after Christmas,' he told Olivia, arms folded challengingly across his chest now, as he looked at her.

She shook her head exasperatedly. 'Dennis is a work colleague—'

'I had a feeling he might be,' Ethan replied.

'And just what do you meant by that?' Olivia bridled.

'It's usually the way it works, isn't it?' he said wearily. 'Conversations about how his wife doesn't understand him, how his children all take him for granted, how even the cat ignores him—'

'You're being totally ridiculous now,' she cut in disgustedly. 'For your information Dennis doesn't have a wife, children—or a cat!'

Ethan looked at her with steely eyes. 'Then why isn't he here with you?'

'Because I don't want him to be!' she said agitatedly. 'Because he *is* just a work colleague! To me, at least,' she concluded awkwardly as she remembered Dennis's fumbled kiss at the party.

'Ah!' Ethan pounced knowingly.

'Make your mind up, Ethan.' She sighed her frustration. 'Either Dennis is or is not this married man I'm supposedly having an affair with!'

'It appears that…he isn't,' Ethan admitted. 'That perhaps he isn't the answer at all,' he continued consideringly.

'Back to the drawing board, hmm?' Olivia scorned.

'I'm not going back to anything, as far as you're concerned, Olivia,' he assured her firmly. 'I've told you I'm in love with you.'

'You don't even know me!' she replied exasperatedly.

'As well as you know me,' he returned sardonically.

'Which isn't very well!' she insisted.

'No?' Even as he spoke he took a step towards her, his arms slowly encircling her waist as he gently pulled her against him, her body fitting perfectly to his. 'I know you, Olivia,' he told her. 'And you definitely know me, too,' he added, as her breasts hardened against his chest.

'You're talking about physical compatibility,' she told him desperately, very much afraid that no matter what she might say her body was betraying her instinctive response to him.

She had never known anything like this before. She had loved Simon, spent some wonderful years with him, and yet she could never remember feeling this breathless need for him, this complete awareness of another human being, this physical ache for possession that she knew every time Ethan touched her...!

Ethan went on, 'I'm talking about love, Olivia. The burning need to be with a certain person, the ache to love and protect her for the rest of your lives. The wanting to make her your wife.'

Her gasp was one of surprise. 'You told me you've already tried being married, that you weren't any good at it,' she reminded him breathlessly.

'I was twenty-one years old. What the hell did I know then of lifelong love, let alone the commitment of marriage?' he said self-disgustedly.

Olivia looked up at him, tears swimming in her eyes. 'But you think you know about those things now?'

His mouth tightened as he heard the mockery in her voice. 'I don't think it at all—I know it.'

She shook her head, blinking back the tears. 'There's some things about me that you need to know before you go any further with this conversation.'

His arms remained like steel bands about her waist as he refused to let her go. 'Olivia, nothing you can say is going to change the way I feel about you.'

She wanted so badly to melt in his arms, to say yes to whatever he wanted from her, to never have to be without this man ever again. But she had so much emotional baggage, so many things that Ethan just didn't know…

'Let me go, Ethan,' she told him strongly, easily releasing herself as he relaxed his hold, stepping back determinedly. 'I—'

'I don't remember seeing this here last night…' Ethan bent to pick something up from the coffee table.

Olivia paled as Ethan straightened and she saw the photograph he now held in his hands. How had that got there? She had looked at the photograph earlier, just to remind herself before she went back up to Ethan's apartment. She didn't remember leaving it here when she left…

But she must have done. How else could it have got from her bedroom to the sitting-room…?

How else, indeed? Faith wondered, frowning.

'I put it there.'

Faith turned slowly to Mrs Heavenly, no longer surprised at the way the elderly angel kept appearing like this. But she *was* surprised at what Mrs Heavenly had just said concerning the photograph…

'I don't understand,' Faith responded.

That wasn't exactly accurate. She understood completely what Mrs Heavenly had just said to her; what she didn't understand was the way Mrs Heavenly had taken things into her own hands. Didn't she think Faith was capable—?

'You're more than capable, my dear,' Mrs Heavenly assured her as she easily read Faith's troubled thoughts, her blue gaze very direct as she looked at Faith. 'I just...' She sighed. 'I shouldn't have interfered, I know that. It's just that—I was unsuccessful in helping Olivia ten years ago,' she added heavily. 'I would hate us not to succeed a second time simply because of Olivia's lack of faith in herself.'

'You—?' Faith gasped, glancing at the troubled Olivia before turning back, wide-eyed, to Mrs Heavenly. 'But I thought this was the first time Olivia had sent up a prayer like this...' It was the impression Mrs Heavenly had given her, at least...

The elder angel smiled shyly. 'I wasn't always in the position you see me in now, my dear. Ten years ago I was the angel assigned to help Olivia in her despair,' Mrs Heavenly told her sadly. 'I failed her—failed to convince her that there is a time and a purpose for everything. Her prayer for help two days ago answered one of my own prayers, too,' she confided. 'One that I've had for so long I was the one who was beginning to despair. I only hope that at long last they're both going to be answered.' Her gaze was intense as she turned back to look at Olivia.

Faith stared at her mentor. Somehow she had never imagined Mrs Heavenly as being in the same position as herself. Or that Mrs Heavenly could ever have failed in one of her own assignments…

But if Mrs Heavenly had failed ten years ago, Faith wondered, what chance had she of succeeding now—even with Mrs Heavenly's help…?

CHAPTER TEN

OLIVIA watched Ethan frown darkly as he looked down at the photograph he held, knowing exactly what he would see there, no longer needing to look at it herself. The image was burnt inside her head, to be conjured up whenever she needed it.

He would see a young man, boyishly handsome, with a six-month-old baby held securely in his arms, both of them laughing at the camera. Both of them laughing at *Olivia* as she took the photograph...

'My husband Simon and my son Jonathan.' Olivia spoke woodenly, her eyes deep grey orbs in the paleness of her face.

Ethan didn't move, simply raised his gaze to look at her searchingly. 'What happened to them?'

'They died,' she said harshly, forcing herself to meet his searching gaze. 'Ten years ago. In a road accident. I—I survived.' She spat the last detail out fiercely.

Ethan put the photograph down to give her a considering look. 'Did you?' he finally asked gently.

She drew in a sharp breath. 'Of course I—'

'Somehow I don't think so, Olivia.' Ethan slowly shook his head, his dark gaze unfathomable as he continued to look at her. 'Oh, physically you may have survived,' he conceded. 'But, unless I'm mistaken, you let the spirit that is Olivia Hardy die along with them.'

She had heard all this before. *Life has to go on, Olivia. You mustn't bury yourself along with them, Olivia. You're still young enough to find love again, Olivia.* And finally, exasperatedly, *We can't help you if you aren't willing to help yourself, Olivia.* Oh yes, she had heard it all before—it was the reason she was now estranged from her own parents.

They meant well; she knew that. Knew that they loved her too, that it had hurt them deeply when she'd begun to distance herself from them all those years ago, until their relationship became the strained one it now was. But she just couldn't bear to hear those things from them any more—knew that nothing anyone could say to her could ever bring back the two people she had loved so dearly.

Except…against all the odds…she was now in love with Ethan Sherbourne!

She looked at him now, a shutter down over the emotions in her eyes. 'I can't love anyone ever again, Ethan,' she told him bleakly.

'Can't?' he repeated. 'Or won't?'

She flinched at the challenge in his voice. 'What difference does it make which it is?' She turned away. 'The conclusion is still the same—you're wasting your time loving me, Ethan. If, indeed, you do,' she added dismissively.

'Oh, I do. And it's my time to waste,' he murmured close behind her, the warmth of his breath warming the nape of her neck.

Her hands clenched into fists at her sides as she forced herself not to flinch at his closeness. 'I would like you to leave now.'

'No.'

She did turn to face him then, frowning incredulously. 'I want you to leave,' she repeated tensely.

Ethan stayed where he was. 'And I said no. The rattle you showed Andrea this morning—it was Jonathan's, wasn't it?' he probed gently.

'Ethan—'

'Wasn't it?' he persisted forcefully.

'Well…yes. But—'

'The first of any of his things you've ever given away?' Ethan continued his probing.

She swayed slightly, closing her eyes, instantly seeing those two big brown boxes in her second bedroom that contained everything that had ever been Jonathan's; she had never been able to bear parting with any of it.

'Olivia!' Ethan was breathing shakily as he once again took her into his arms. 'I can't even begin to imagine what losing the two of them did to you.' He spoke into her hair. 'Nor can I blame you for wanting to shut yourself away emotionally these last ten years—if only so that you could never be hurt in that way again. But don't you see, my darling, that it's too late to think you can carry on doing that any longer? By giving Andrea that toy this morning, perhaps without realising what you were doing, you began the painful process of letting go—'

'Rubbish!' Olivia denied heatedly, trying to escape Ethan's arms—but failing as he simply tightened his hold on her. 'It was only a teething ring, for goodness' sake!' She glared up at him.

'It was Jonathan's teething ring,' he insisted evenly.

Olivia's anger towards him deepened. 'Well, he's hardly going to need it again, is he—? I can't believe I just said that!' she groaned emotionally, burying her face in her hands. 'He was so beautiful, Ethan. So young, and sweet—such a happy baby.' She shook her head. 'And ultimately so utterly vulnerable…!' She began to cry then, deep heartrending sobs, the tears falling like hot rain down her cheeks.

Ethan's arms tightened about her as he lifted her up and carried her over to one of the armchairs, sitting down with her cradled in his arms, her head resting on his shoulder as he let her continue to cry.

How long they sat like that Olivia had no idea, only knew that finally she felt exhausted by her own grief. And so very aware of Ethan's closeness…

She shook her head. 'I can't love you, Ethan,' she told him gruffly.

'As I said—can't or won't…?' he returned softly.

She raised her head to look at him. 'Does it matter which?'

'Of course it matters,' he said.

Olivia gave a scathing snort. 'Don't you already have enough women in your harem without trying to add me to their number?'

Ethan remained unmoved by her deliberate attempt to alienate him. 'I'm a fashion photographer, Olivia. Sometimes I work from home.' He shrugged. 'There is no woman in my life. Only you. Each and every one of those women you've seen coming to my apartment has been there for one reason only— so that I can photograph them. Remind me to show you my studio in the second bedroom when we go back upstairs,' he said, as she continued to look sceptical.

He was *that* Sherbourne…! Why had she never thought of such a simple explanation for the comings and goings to Ethan's apartment of those numerous women? Because it had been easier to think of Ethan as a rake and a womaniser, and not a world-famous fashion-photographer, came the instant answer to that question!

'I'm not going back upstairs with you—'

'Oh, yes, you are,' he assured her. 'Can't you see, Olivia? It's too late. For both of us. I wasn't exactly looking for love myself, you know,' he added teasingly. 'I've spent the last twenty years perfecting the art of the brief, meaningless relationship,' he said.

'But you, with your huge expressive eyes, that ethereal beauty, the snappy dialogue you've developed to hide your own vulnerability—you've crept under my defences, Olivia. And, although I may not have been looking for love, I do not intend turning my back on the gift now that it's been given to me.'

A gift... Yes, love was a gift. Could she really take the risk of loving someone again, of perhaps losing them?

But, as Ethan had said, did she really have a choice, when she was already in love with him? Was denying him now, ejecting him from her life, going to make any difference to the way she felt about him?

She wasn't seriously thinking of accepting his proposal, was she...?

To spend every day and night with Ethan... To wake up beside him in the morning and know that he loved her as much as she loved him... To come home to him each evening and know that he had simply been counting the hours, as she had, until they could be together again... To have dinner with him every night... To lie in his arms every night... To do all the simple day-to-day things together, like shopping, and preparing food...

All the things she had once done with Simon...

'Would Simon have wanted you to spend the rest of your life alone?' Ethan's arms tightened about her as he seemed to sense the drift of her thoughts.

'Would you have wanted that for him if he had been the one left behind?'

'Of course not,' she gasped, her face paling as she realised what she had just said. 'I loved Simon very much,' she told Ethan defensively—but realised even as she did so that she had used the past tense...

'Of course you did,' Ethan agreed. 'And loving me doesn't mean you have to stop loving him,' he assured her firmly. 'I'm going to ask you again, Olivia.' He straightened in the chair, looking her fully in the face now, his gaze intense. 'Will you marry me? Will you let me love you? Will you love me in return? Will you marry me so that we can spend the rest of our lives together?'

Olivia swallowed hard, her heart leaping at the words, her cheeks flushed, her pulse beating erratically in her chest.

Could she do that? Could she make what was, after all, a leap of faith?

'Will she?' Faith groaned, chewing worriedly on her bottom lip as she watched Olivia and Ethan together.

'Shh,' Mrs Heavenly admonished impatiently. 'Or we'll miss her answer!'

EPILOGUE

'OLIVIA…? Darling, I'm home!' Ethan called out. 'I've got the tree.' He barely paused as he put his car keys down on the tray in the hallway. 'But I'll need some help bringing it into the— Oomph!' He groaned breathlessly as Olivia ran from the kitchen to launch herself into his arms. 'Hello, my darling.' He grinned down at her before kissing her soundly on the lips. 'Mmm, you smell good.' He buried his face in her shoulder-length hair.

'I've been preparing and steaming the Christmas pudding this afternoon.' Olivia laughed happily. 'With a little help from my friends, of course,' she added indulgently, barely having time to move out of the way as two small tornadoes came hurtling down the hallway.

'Daddy!' the duo cried together, even as they launched themselves into their father's waiting arms.

Olivia's smile widened as she watched their small daughters snuggle up to Ethan, one in each arm, the two of them giggling happily as their father tickled them by blowing lightly on their chubby necks.

At two years old, Emily and Daisy were as alike as two peas in a pod—dark-haired, brown-eyed little charmers. Much like their father, Olivia thought indulgently as she gazed lovingly at her husband.

'Did you make a big Christmas pudding?' he was teasing his daughters now. 'We have Nanny and Grandad coming to spend Christmas with us this year.' He smiled at Olivia with this mention of her parents. 'And Andrew, Shelley and Andrea.'

Olivia never ceased to wonder at the transformation there had been to her life these last three years: her reconciliation with her parents, her marriage to Ethan, their move to this large house in the country, Andrew's marriage to Shelley, the birth of the twins a year after their own wedding...

Although it was her love and marriage that she cherished the most. Ethan was a wonderful husband—caring, considerate, loving her so completely she could never doubt their future together.

It truly was a marriage made in heaven...

Mrs Heavenly, smiling from above, with tears of happiness in her eyes, could only nod silently.

CHRISTMAS PASSIONS

Catherine Spencer

CHAPTER ONE

AVA was neither looking nor feeling her best. Chilled to the bone, her hair hanging around her face in semi-frozen rats' tails, her hands and nose so numb they might just as well have been amputated, she huddled in the barn and watched Leo disappear into the swirling night.

"Wait here," he'd told her. "I'll go raise someone at the farmhouse and persuade them to take pity on us."

The occasional stamp of hooves and warm animal smell told her there were horses in the stalls behind her. Somewhere beyond the paddock, on the other side of the fence, Leo's Ford Expedition nestled nose-down and up to its rear axle in a snowdrift. And no more than fifteen miles away, her parents were waiting to welcome her to her first Christmas at home in over three years.

A horse barn, however well-kept, was no more part of the plan than finding her one-time idol Leo Ferrante waiting to meet her flight when it touched down six hours late at Skellington Airport. He was supposed to be wining and dining his lady-love, not stranded up to his knees in snow with her best friend.

Ava's first reaction when she saw him towering head and shoulders over the sparse crowd at the arrivals concourse had been that he probably wouldn't recognize her; her second, the fervent *hope* that he wouldn't since, the last time they'd met, she'd been all of sixteen and so horribly ill-at-ease in her too tall, too skinny body that she'd given new meaning to the word "ungainly." She liked to think she'd improved somewhat in the intervening twelve years and now commanded a presence so elegantly cosmopolitan that he'd look right past her in search of a more homely specimen.

He'd dashed any such hope by striding forward the second he caught sight of her, and pinning her in a smile that sent a remembered skewer of pain through her heart. "Ava, I'd have recognized you anywhere!"

Oh, terrific! she'd thought, crushing that belated and completely inappropriate stab of adolescent hero worship. He was Deenie's lover—soon to be her fiancé, from everything she'd written in her latest letters—and Ava had come home for Christmas with her family, not to make a fool of herself by lusting after a man she couldn't have.

So she'd smiled a lot during the thirty mile drive to Owen's Lake, and made polite small talk, and congratulated herself on projecting the image of chic professional taking time out from her adventurous life overseas to make a flying visit home. Until they'd had to abandon his vehicle mid-journey, that was, and slog their way across a windblown paddock, and her once-elegant leather shoes had been reduced to frozen blocks encasing her feet.

Noticing the way she was floundering to keep up with him as he forged ahead, he'd clamped an arm around her shoulders and attempted to shield her with his body from the worst of the weather. The honed perfection of him beneath his sheepskin jacket had felt solid and safe and wonderful. His thigh brushing hers at each step had peeled away all her layers of acquired sophistication and left her palpitating with awareness of how deliciously masculine and strong he was: a world-class athlete-cum-movie idol dressed up as a small-town lawyer romancing the girl next door.

He had never kissed Ava, never held her hand. Never by so much as a word or a glance intimated that he had the slightest interest in anything she did. She'd been nothing to him but the *other* girl who lived six houses away on upscale Charles Owen Crescent; the one who sometimes came with her mother and father to his parents' place when they hosted a summer barbecue around the pool, or an open house at Christmas. The one who, with her friend Deenie, used to giggle and blush and whisper behind her hand whenever he put in an appearance.

Cowering now in some stranger's barn, it struck Ava as supremely unfair that, in less than an hour, he could compress all her accomplishments into a mere blot on her résumé, and reduce her once again to an unprepossessing heap of flesh beset by futile wanting.

"Don't go there, Ava!" she admonished out loud, slamming shut the door on such traitorous nonsense. "Leo Ferrante has never been more off limits."

A horse poked its head out of the nearest stall, gave a snuffling whinny, and regarded her reproachfully, as though to say, *We're trying to sleep in here, if you don't mind!*

"Sorry if I disturbed you, handsome," she crooned, moving close enough to stroke the long, velvety nose. "If it makes you feel any better, I'll be gone soon."

"Don't go making promises you can't keep," Leo advised her, letting himself into the barn just in time to overhear. "I'm afraid we're stuck here for the duration."

She didn't like what that implied. "And how long is the duration expected to last?"

He shrugged. "Until daylight, at the very least."

"And you're saying we have to spend the intervening time in *here?*" She stared in disbelief at their surroundings which, while unquestionably luxurious for horses, hardly amounted to much in the way of human comfort. "Wasn't anyone home at the house?"

"Only the very nervous young mother of a colicky baby. Seems her husband's off helping a neighbor with a sick animal, and even if she'd been willing to admit a couple of strangers past the front door, her guard dogs weren't."

"I'm sure if you'd explained—"

"I did." He pulled off his gloves and touched his

hand to her cheek, a lovely, too brief contact. "Not exactly the welcome home you were expecting, is it, Ava? But at least I persuaded her to phone your folks and let them know you're safe."

Actually, what she'd expected was taking a taxi from Skellington to the grand old house in Owen's Lake where she'd been born, and finding her parents waiting to ply her with hugs, cocoa and questions. She'd envisioned the garden transformed into a fairyland by hundreds of coloured lights threaded among the trees and shrubs. She'd pictured the railing of the wraparound porch trimmed with pine branches held in place with red ribbons and silver bells.

She'd looked forward to the scent of wood smoke, and the warm reflection of flames flickering over the cool white marble fireplace in the living room, and the ceiling-high Noble Fir Christmas tree filling the big bay window.

She'd counted on having time to prepare herself to face the happy couple without betraying the envy eating holes in her heart. On being dressed to the nines in her smart Thai leather suit that was as soft and pale as whipped cream, or swaying into a room in the beaded silk dress she'd found in Hong Kong. In other words, she'd planned to be in command of herself and her situation, and look like a million dollars on the outside, regardless of how she might be feeling inside.

Instead, she was being forced to spend the night

with Leo. In a stable. And looking like something no respecting dog would dream of dragging in.

It was enough to make her wish she'd accepted the marriage proposal offered through an intermediary by a grateful tribal chief whose son she'd nursed through a health crisis. At least he'd rated her on a par with his most prized water buffalo! From the way Leo was surveying her though, she might have been the bearded lady from a traveling sideshow!

"You don't look so great," he remarked, as if she hadn't already figured that out for herself.

"Thanks, Leo," she said, peeved. "I really needed to hear that!"

"What I mean is, you're practically blue with cold. You'd better get out of those wet clothes."

"And do what?" She tried to laugh—no easy task when her teeth were chattering like demented castanets. "Climb under a horse blanket and pray for deliverance?"

He didn't even crack a smile. "There's a tack room at the other end of the stable which we're welcome to use, and yes, Ava, horse blankets and hay are going to be the best this hotel can offer."

"And where will you spend the rest of the night?"

He raised his altogether stunning eyebrows, as though he couldn't quite believe she'd asked such an idiotic question, and said, "With you, of course. Where else?"

Her heart should have sunk. Instead, it soared.

When she was old and grey and lying on her death-bed, she'd be able to boast that, just once, she'd slept with Leo Ferrante. It almost made her present predicament worthwhile.

Almost. Thankfully, she wasn't entirely bereft of common sense or decency. "If you think I'm going to strip for your entertainment, think again," she said flatly.

"You might have lived in Africa for the last three years, but you're still a nurse, Ava, and as such ought to know better than anyone the dangers of hypothermia." He steered her firmly toward a door at the far end of the barn, thrust it open and shoved her into a room lined with horsey equipment. "I'm not suggesting you take off everything, but at least get rid of the wet shoes and stockings, and the coat. They're not doing you any good, anyway, and you aren't going to be much help to Deenie if you wind up in bed with pneumonia."

"Why on earth does Deenie need my help? She's the most self-reliant person I know."

"Deenie," he said succinctly, "is a mess right now and *everyone* is counting on you to deal with her. Whatever it is that's bugging her isn't something she's prepared to talk about."

He sounded more like an exasperated father than a besotted lover. "It could be simply a matter of adjusting," Ava said. "Exchanging the world of international ballet for small-town life can't be easy for someone who always swore she'd never settle for the kind of domestic bliss the rest of us thrive on.''

Oh, great! She came across more like an aging aunt who'd buried four husbands, rather than a twenty-eight-year old who'd yet to exchange the single life for matrimony.

Not that he cared, one way or the other. Apparently tired of the subject, he shrugged and made for the door. ''Whatever! Right now, I'm more interested in grabbing a couple of hours sleep. Why don't you get rid of the wet clothes while I round up some hay for a mattress?''

What the devil was wrong with him, that he'd complain to Ava Sorensen of all people? There were no secrets between her and Deenie. From what he could tell, they'd been joined at the hip practically from birth and shared everything. *Everything!*

He hefted a bale of hay and grimaced at the painful twinge which shot through his lower back. For Pete's sake, the stuff couldn't weigh more than thirty pounds, and six months ago he could press nearly two hundred without breaking a sweat. Could run five miles and swing a golf club, too. Now, thanks to an out-of-control snowboarder using him as a braking device, he was limited to brisk walks, strengthening exercises, and spending too much time with Deenie who was cute and amusing. Yet despite plenty of opportunity and a certain amount of flirtatious bantering, they hadn't come close to any sort of intimacy.

"A fine pair we'd make!" he'd said, making light of it the one time she'd told him she wouldn't mind a little sex on the side to relieve the tedium. "Between my back spasms and your sore shoulder and ankle, we'd both likely wind up back in physiotherapy. We're better off sticking to gin rummy and cribbage."

He'd been relieved when she'd let the idea drop without further comment. Mightily so, in fact— which made him wonder if more than just his spine had been cracked in the accident. What if he'd suffered other injuries which had gone undetected? What if he'd lost interest in sex forever?

Cripes, talk about a guy's life spinning out of control! He needed to put a halt to things, and fast, beginning with the insane hints flying around that he and Deenie were an ideal couple and should be making what her mother so unsubtly referred to as "plans." There *were* no long-term plans for him and Deenie. They were friends, and that was all.

Shouldering the hay, he trudged back to the tack room and rapped on the door. "Are you decent in there, Ava?"

"As much as can be expected."

He found her perched on a stool with her knees drawn up under her chin and her bare feet poking out from under the poncho she'd fashioned from a horse blanket. Her toes were straight and unscarred, with perfect nails painted the colour of cranberries, and he thought how much prettier they were than

Deenie's which had become almost deformed from years of dancing *en pointe.*

"You're looking better already," he said, spreading the hay on the floor and tossing a couple of blankets on top. "You want to hop down from there on your own, or do you want me to give you a hand?"

"I can manage," she said hastily, which was just as well. If he couldn't have lifted Deenie at five foot two, he didn't have a prayer of playing hero to Ava who stood at least seven inches taller.

Clutching the poncho around her, she scurried across the cement floor and dropped down on the makeshift mattress, but not so swiftly that he didn't get an eyeful of her legs. Long and tanned, they were as elegant as her narrow feet, with sweetly curved calves and finely turned ankles. She might have been too tall for ballet, as Deenie had said, but she'd be a knockout in a Las Vegas chorus line.

"Why didn't Deenie come with you to meet me?" she said, glaring at him as if she'd caught him peeking up her skirt.

"She was planning to, but she begged off when we heard your flight had been delayed. Claims she's had too many late nights recently. But she wants you to give her a call as soon as you're up and about in the morning. She said something about getting together with you for lunch."

He removed his jacket and pulled off his boots, which sent her scooting to the far corner of the mattress with fire in her eyes. What did she think—that he planned to get buck naked and flaunt himself at her? "Relax, Ava," he said, choking back a laugh. "This is as far as it goes. I'll even keep my socks on, just to make sure our feet don't get too intimate."

She bit her lip and blushed a little, and he wondered if she had any idea how charmed he was by everything about her. Comparisons were odious, he knew, but he couldn't help thinking that if Deenie had been the one forced to bunk down in a stable for the night, especially after being in transit for over eighteen hours, she'd have raised hell and put a lid on it. Could be that's why she and Ava had remained such close friends all these years: the old "opposites attract" syndrome.

"You're nothing like Deenie, you know," he said, crouching next to her.

"I've always known that, Leo," she replied coolly. "And I stopped trying to be, years ago."

"Good." He spread another blanket over her, took a couple for himself, and stretched out. "The world's not big enough for two like her."

"She *is* special. I've always known that, as well."

Her eyes, big and beautiful and grey as summer thunderclouds, all at once had such a bereft look to them that he knew a crazy urge to fold her in his arms and tell her she was special, too, and that she shouldn't assume what he'd said about Deenie was necessarily a compliment.

Leaping up to turn off the overhead light before he did or said something really stupid, he felt his way back to the makeshift bed and made a point of stuffing a wad of blanket between him and her. "I think anyone who meets her recognizes she's different and always has been. According to her mother, she was still in diapers when she decided she was going to be a prima ballerina, and she's never once deviated from the path of that ambition which, by itself, makes her something of a rarity."

"Exactly," Ava said, her voice flowing over him in the dark like sweet, heavy ice wine. "So tell me, Leo, how is it that two months around you was enough to persuade her to give up the adulation of sold-out audiences in Europe and settle down in sleepy old Owen's Lake?"

CHAPTER TWO

Snow batting against the paned window marked the silence ticking by as he tried to come up with an answer. "I guess," he finally said, "it began with our both being sidelined by injuries that kept us away from our regular routines. We were housebound former neighbors who met at the physiotherapy clinic one morning, gravitated towards each other by mutual sympathy and boredom, and...one thing led to another."

"You make it sound as if you drifted together by default," Ava accused.

"Don't get me wrong," he said, wishing she hadn't managed to pinpoint matters quite so accurately. "Deenie's a lovely, intelligent woman and I'd have gone stir crazy if she hadn't been around to keep me entertained. But I'd be lying if I said our...relationship left me deafened by violins or dazzled by stars. I'm not programmed to react like that. I don't know any lawyers who are."

The hay rustled softly as she shifted to a more comfortable position. Or was it her silky underwear sighing against her skin—a possibility which sent heat prickling down his torso to threaten areas best left undisturbed.

"You might not be a romantic, Leo," Ava said, "but Deenie is, which brings me back to my original question. What made her decide to stay in Owen's Lake?"

"I think," he said, striving to maintain a lofty perspective despite the lecherous urgings of his body, "her injuries made her face up to the fact that her performing career isn't going to last indefinitely. You were a dancer yourself when you were younger, Ava, albeit an amateur. You know how much punishment your body took. Multiply that a thousand times and you get a pretty good idea of the wear and tear on Deenie, both physically and emotionally. She knows that although she'll probably make a full recovery this time, she'll be forced into retirement much sooner than most women—probably within the next five years. So she's trying to compromise."

"That doesn't sound like the Deenie I know."

"What can I say? People change. Maybe being a prima ballerina isn't enough to satisfy her anymore. Maybe she wants to have something else to turn to when her dancing days are over."

"And she's convinced she'll find that 'something' with you?"

Cripes, the question suggested the notion that he and Deenie were on the brink of marriage had spread farther than he feared! "I certainly wouldn't go that far," he said neutrally, "even though her family does seem to think we're a match made in heaven.''

Ava turned toward him. He could tell because her breath sifted over his face, fragrant as sun-warmed peaches. It brought to mind the lush, smooth texture of her lips and left him wondering if she'd taste as sweet as she smelled. Even as a teenager, she'd had a mouth that begged to be kissed and from the little he'd seen, time had only added to its appeal.

''From everything she's told me, Deenie seems to think so, too.''

''Don't read too much into what she's told you, then,'' he replied, irritated as much by his reaction to her proximity as by her probing questions. ''I'm a thirty-seven-year-old lawyer who's handled enough divorce cases to know that if people were more realistic about what makes a relationship work, and less prone to fantasizing, I might not have quite such a fat bank account but I'd have a hell of a lot more free time to devote to other pursuits.''

Ava, dogged to a fault, wasn't about to get side-tracked. ''I'm not interested in a run-down of your financial assets, Leo. Deenie and I are as close as sisters and I don't want to see her hurt. So what I'm waiting to hear you say is that you're not leading her on, and that you share a clear understanding of how things really stand between you. Can you give me those assurances?''

A hollow gloom descended on him, one with

which he'd become all too familiar in recent weeks. Usually it attacked first thing in the morning, filling him with a sense of foreboding before he was awake enough to wrestle it into submission with pragmatic reason.

It stemmed, he'd told himself, from the frustration of enforced idleness; to the knowledge that while he followed doctor's orders, his partners in the Skellington law firm were doing double duty picking up the slack created by his putting in half days only at the office. But Ava's continued cross-examination bared a truth he'd been unwilling to face. The real cause of his discontent sprang not from professional frustration, but from the uneasy suspicion that he'd somehow lost control of his private life.

"Well, Leo? That wasn't such a difficult question surely, so what's taking you so long to answer?"

"If you must know," he snapped, feeling like the cornered rat he undoubtedly was, "I'm tired of other people assuming they have the right to poke their noses into matters which are none of their concern."

"I see. Well now that you've got that off your chest, let me ask you this. What do *you* want from the immediate future, Leo?"

"To get back to work full time. To be on top of my case load. To return to normal, for Pete's sake!"

"Does 'normal' include making time for Deenie?"

"Cripes, Ava!" he exploded. "You never used to

be such a pain in the butt, so where's all this coming from now? Are you jealous because she's got a man to keep her company, and you haven't?''

The question sliced through the night like a blade and he knew from the utter silence which greeted it that he'd drawn blood. ''Oh, jeez!'' he muttered. ''Ava, I'm sorry. I had no right to say that.''

Her breathing flitted across to him, jerky and uneven. ''No, you hadn't.''

''Are you crying?''

''No,'' she said, her voice swimming in tears.

Awkwardly, he reached for her, planning to give her shoulder a comforting, brotherly pat. But he misjudged the distance between them and instead made contact with her hair. It looped around his fingers like damp strands of silk and snagged in the metal band of his watch.

''Oh, hell,'' he said softly. ''Don't try to pull away, Ava. We're all knotted up.''

It should have been a non-incident; *would* have been if she hadn't ignored his request and, in trying to disentangle herself, moved her head in such a way that her mouth blundered against his.

He didn't exactly kiss her. He just sort of…let his lips rest against hers while he worked with his free hand to unsnarl her hair.

She'd spent the better part of two days in a plane. She should have reeked of stale aircraft food and recycled air. Instead, she tasted delicious. Peaches again.

"Your perfume is driving me wild," he said against her mouth.

A tremor raced over her. She brought her hand up to cover his, to push it and him away. "Please don't—!" she began.

"I won't," he said.

But he did. This time, he kissed her, and no two ways about it. He cupped her head and took advantage of her gasp of shock to trace his tongue over the silken inner lining of her lips. And just for a nanosecond, she responded, curving her body to fit against his and angling her mouth to give him greater access.

Big mistake! The violins and stars he'd denied experiencing with Deenie made a belated appearance, seeming not to care that they'd shown up for a woman he hadn't seen in years, and there was no telling what he might have tried next if Ava hadn't come to her senses. Which she did with a vengeance, by hauling off and cracking her palm across his cheek at the same time that she reared back and yanked her hair free from his watchband.

"You had no right to do that!" she spat.

"I know," he said, prepared to shoulder the blame. "I'm sorry."

But he wasn't. He was dazzled. Dazed. Exhilarated.

"Then why did you?"

He shook his head, less to refute her question than to clear his mind. "Search me! Temporary insanity?"

She drew in a hissing breath. "Make a joke of it if you like, but I don't mind telling you, your behaviour disgusts me."

"It didn't a minute ago," he said, ticked off by her holier-than-thou attitude. "If anything, you seemed to enjoy it."

"In your dreams, Leo Ferrante! If Deenie had any idea…!"

"Who's going to tell her? You?"

"I should," she said. "She has a right to know—"

"What? That I kissed you and you liked it?" He flopped onto his back and sighed wearily as common sense replaced his brief euphoria. "Look, Ava, I made a mistake and you didn't exactly rebuff me, but it won't happen again. Let's not make more out of it than that."

He thought he'd put the matter to rest and was almost dozing off when she said in a small voice, "I feel so ashamed. I don't know how I'll ever face her without blushing. It's not just that we kissed, it's everything you've told me—about not being madly in love with her, and all that. You never should have said such things."

"Probably not. But there's something about lying

next to you in the dark that makes me do and say things regardless of the consequences.''

"You *definitely* shouldn't be saying that!''

He shouldn't be touching her, either, but the mattress was too narrow to allow for the luxury of distance and no matter how he tried to preserve an illusion of decency, some part or other of him—his leg, his hip, his shoulder—kept rubbing up against her.

Pretending the contact was meaningless didn't carry a whole lot of weight with his hormones coming to a slow boil and him no more able to stop than he could put an end to the storm raging outside. So much for a dead libido!

As for Ava—hell, she could deny it all she liked, but she was far from oblivious, as well. He could hear the rapid, unnatural rhythm of her breathing. Sense the brittle tension stretching her nerves so tight they were ready to snap.

"Is there some guy waiting for you, back in Africa?'' he asked, hoping like blazes she'd say yes.

"No,'' she said on a faint breath of despair.

"Why not?''

She shrugged, a fatal error of judgement on her part because it provided yet one more reminder of how little stood between them. Or, more accurately, it made him aware that what stood between them had taken on a life of its own even though it had no business standing at all! "I just haven't met the right man yet."

"How will you know when you do?"

"It will feel right," she said, sounding winded.

He reached for her. May God forgive him, he couldn't help himself. "But this feels right, Ava," he murmured, stroking his hand over her jaw and down her neck, "so there must be more to it than that."

She trembled under his touch. "How can you say that, when we both know that what you're doing and saying is completely unacceptable?"

It was the politically correct response he expected, but the indignation which would have given it substance became lost in a sigh of defeat. He rapped gently against her temple. "Knowing up here is one thing. Accepting it as truth here..." He drew his hand down her face, her throat, and didn't stop until his palm lay snug and flat beneath her left breast. "Ah, Ava, that's quite another. And knowing I shouldn't kiss you again isn't doing a damn thing to make me want it any less."

"Don't, Leo!" she begged—another politically correct answer, but even as the tortured plea escaped, her mouth bumped against his again.

"Our being here at all is totally inappropriate," he said, charged with awareness that if he moved his hand just a fraction, her breast would nestle against his palm. "We both expected we'd be spending the night someplace else. But it doesn't change the fact that we're lying side by side, there's no one here to monitor what we say or do, and that, if I could live with myself afterward, I'd make love to you.''

She didn't come up with any smart rebuff this time. Instead, she grew so perfectly still that he'd have said she froze—except that implied bone-chilling cold, and even though the temperature had dipped to well below freezing outside, the currents swirling around that unheated tack room were suddenly stifling.

When the beating silence became more than he could tolerate, he moved his open hand and brought it to rest, fingers splayed, between their two bodies. ''Ava?''

He knew she couldn't see the gesture, but surely she sensed it, and recognized the question it asked?

Seconds ticked by, measured by the heavy thud of his heart. Then, when he was just about ready to give up hope that she'd respond, her much smaller hand settled on top of his, aligning itself as best it could, palm to palm, thumb to thumb, finger to finger.

He found it the most profoundly erotic touch he'd ever experienced. More moving than a kiss. More arousing than the most intimate commingling of flesh between a man and a woman. And not nearly enough to satisfy the surge of desire boiling through his blood.

Decency be damned! If she'd let him, he'd have taken her with all the speed and fervour at his command. Locked himself deep inside her and let the devil take the hindmost. Sold his soul for the thrill of bringing her to orgasm, and then, when she was helpless and liquid around him, filling her with the rush of his own release.

He didn't because, even as he rose up and over her in the dark, she said in a small, sad voice, "I know. And we can't."

Defeated, he fell back to the hay, the explosive hiss of his escaping breath betraying more eloquently than words what it cost him to ignore the rapacious demands of a body never more vibrantly alive, and submit instead to the belated tug of conscience.

"No," he said glumly. "We can't. But if we could, I'd love you all night long. And the next time someone asked if there's a special man in your life, you wouldn't say you're still waiting for him to show up, because—"

"Leo, please! I'm so confused…so tired…."

"Yeah, me, too." He expelled another breath and felt it balloon above his face in chilly condensation. Now that the heat of the moment had passed, the air was penetratingly cold. Sliding his arm over her waist, he tugged her close enough that she was molded against him, thigh to thigh, hip to hip, breast to chest.

She burrowed her head against his shoulder and uttered a little moan. Of protest? Misery? He couldn't be sure. The only certainty was that it was colder than a witch's thorax in that room, and horse blankets and hay alone weren't enough to ward off the creeping chill of winter.

"Your virtue's safe," he said, "but if we don't conserve body heat, we'll both wind up dead before morning. Cuddle up, sweetheart, and try to get some sleep or you'll look like hell tomorrow."

She supposed she did—get some sleep, that was— because after some initial skittishness, a great feeling of calm overtook her and the next time she became aware of her surroundings, a pale, cold light filtered through the square of window on the far wall. The second thing she noticed was that her legs were snugly pinned by Leo's, and his blue eyes were watching her with the shuttered expression of a man not about to reveal a hint of what he was thinking.

But if the workings of his mind remained a mystery, she was left in little doubt about her own. Embarrassment and guilt swept over her in equal measure. How could she have allowed him to kiss her—to come disgracefully close to making love to her? And how would she ever again face Deenie without cringing?

"No need to look so stricken, Ava," Leo said. "Neither of us surrendered to our baser instincts in sleep. If anyone asks, you can truthfully say you upheld your scruples in the face of adversity."

"And what will you say, should anyone ask you?" she retorted, immeasurably ticked off that he sounded so unruffled when she was all of a-dither at finding his thigh flung over her hip and the lovely warm length of his torso pressed up against hers.

"That you snore," he said blandly.

"I certainly do not!"

"How do you know? Did you ask the last man you slept with?"

"That's none of your business," she said, not about to admit that the closest she'd come to "sleeping" with anyone was in the back seat of her prom date's car when she was eighteen—a disastrous, fumbling affair which had ended when he'd suffered the humiliation of premature ejaculation before he'd divested her of her bra—and a couple of semi-hot dates with an ambulance driver when she was in nursing school.

"No," Leo said. "I guess it's not." He lifted the blankets and let a gust of cold air sweep away the cosy warmth between their bodies. "And lying here speculating won't get my vehicle out of the ditch."

He rolled cautiously to his feet, stretched guardedly, and reached for his sheepskin jacket. "You planning to spend the day down there, Ava?'' he inquired, when she didn't rush to join him.

''No,'' she said, eyeing her pantyhose which sprawled wantonly over a saddle rack. ''I'm waiting for you to leave so that I can dress without an audience.''

''Dress?'' To her horror, he picked up her stockings and dangled them from one hand the way a husband might. With intimate familiarity. ''If you're talking about climbing into these, you might as well forget it. They're still soaking wet. And your shoes,'' he added, peering at the pitiful things which lay side by side on the floor like two drowned rats, ''aren't any better. You'll have to throw yourself on the mercy of the lady of the house—always assuming she's more charitably disposed toward us this morning than she was last night.''

The lady of the house proved more than accommodating, as did her husband. She sent a pair of socks, boots a size too large, and an invitation to breakfast, while he hooked a tractor to Leo's vehicle and hauled it out of the ditch. By ten o'clock, Ava and Leo were on their way, fortified with home-cured ham and farm fresh eggs, and with nothing to show for their overnight mishap but the faint whiff of horses clinging to their clothing.

That, and a smothering air of disquiet.

CHAPTER THREE

"As *I* understand it, coming home for the holidays is supposed to be a happy time," Leo observed acidly, as they approached the outskirts of Owen's Lake. "Unless you want to arouse the suspicions of everyone from the family dog to the town mayor, I recommend you trade in the look of long-suffering misery for something a little more cheerful and upbeat."

Ava shot him a poisonous glare. "Forgive me if I'm not as adept at covering up my sins as you appear to be!"

"A minor indiscretion hardly amounts to sin, Ava. Stop blowing last night out of proportion and focus on today. If anyone's to blame for what happened back there in the stable, I am. So leave me to deal with it."

Easy for him to say! He didn't harbour a secret passion for someone who was strictly off limits. He wasn't the one who'd been ready to abandon his scruples *and* betray his best friend for the dubious pleasure of one night of illicit love. "And if I can't?"

"You will if you concentrate on enjoying the kind

of good, old-fashioned Christmas you've been missing for the last three years.''

It wasn't fair that, despite having spent the night on the floor in a stable, he managed to exude an aura of masculine sexuality so appealing that she went weak at the knees. Turning to stare out of the window before she forgot herself so far as to start drooling, Ava saw that he had a point. Owen's Lake was decked out with a vengeance for the season. Last night's blizzard had given way to blue skies and the cold clear brilliance of a northern winter sun, as different from Africa's molten heat as diamonds from rubies.

Platinum glittered from icicles draping the eaves of the grand Victorian homes typical of Owen Heights, the exclusive neighborhood where she'd been born. Huge holly wreaths hung on wrought-iron gates. Illuminated reindeer pulling sleighs romped across lawns buried under a thick quilting of snow. Lampposts sported miniature fir trees draped in sparkling lights.

Half a mile farther along the boulevard, Leo turned the Expedition onto Charles Owen Crescent and a few minutes later pulled into the long driveway leading to her parents' home. ''Time to start smiling, sweetheart,'' he muttered. ''Here comes the family, all set to welcome home the nomadic daughter.''

Indeed, the SUV had barely come to a stop under

the *porte-cochère* before her parents and Jason, their golden retriever, shot out of the house in a tangle of legs and excitement. Her father yanked open the passenger door and, slithering to the ground in her too-big borrowed boots, Ava found herself wrapped in a bear hug which took her breath away.

"Your mother's had me up since dawn and just about driven me mad with her pacing back and forth," he said. "And now that you're here, she's crying her eyes out. I tell you, Ava, I'll never understand what makes a woman tick."

"Oh, hush up, you big softie," her mother sobbed happily, wading between him and Jason's thrashing tail and reaching for Ava. "Who was so impatient to see his little girl again that he was ready to strap on skis and piggyback her home last night, so that she could sleep in her own bed instead of a stranger's house? Come here, darling, and give your mom a kiss. It's wonderful to have you home again."

Her mother smelled of cinnamon and mincemeat and almond paste—lovely nostalgic reminders of Christmases past, when life had been full of simple, innocent pleasures, and affection freely expressed. That this year's was clouded with guilt and secrets when it should have been the most joyful of all, filled Ava with a regret so intense that she, too, started to cry.

"This is supposed to be a happy time," Leo reminded her, with pointed emphasis.

"That's why they're both in tears." Blithely unaware of the hidden undercurrents swarming through the cold air, her father gave Leo one of those man-to-man slaps on the back meant to convey masculine amusement at the vagaries of women. "They cry when they're sad, when they're happy and when they're mad. And just for good measure, they cry when they get married, so better get used to the sight, Leo, because from what I hear, you'll be learning that firsthand before much longer. Here, let me give you a hand with that luggage, then come on in and join us for morning coffee."

The mere idea of Leo Ferrante cosying up for a visit under her parents' roof was enough to dry Ava's tears on the spot. "He can't possibly!"

"Why not?" her father said. "It's the least we can do, to thank him for meeting your flight—and for taking such good care of you last night."

Oh, if he only knew the direction that care had taken!

"Thanks," Leo said easily, running a hand over his jaw, "but although coffee sounds good, a shower and shave sound even better."

He looked, Ava thought, as eager to be gone as she was to be rid of him. "We absolutely understand," she said, with what she feared must seem like insulting relief. "Goodbye, and thank you for...everything."

He leveled a satirical blue gaze her way. "Glad I could help."

Help? Averting her eyes, she bent to fondle Jason's silky ears. Ye gods, things had been bad enough to begin with. How much worse they'd become was something only she and Leo would ever fully understand, and she didn't appreciate his pitiful attempt to turn the situation into a joke!

"Perhaps it's just as well he didn't stay," her mother said, ushering everyone inside the house as he drove off. "Deenie plans on taking you out for lunch, so I'm kind of glad to have you to myself for a bit before you get caught up in all her Christmas plans. Go warm yourself up by the fire in the library, darling, while I pour the coffee and your father takes your bags up to your room, then we'll all sit down for a nice long chat."

Yesterday, Ava would have liked nothing better. Now, the knowledge that she'd have to face Deenie before the morning was out cast a pall over her homecoming that no amount of rationalizing could dispel.

I think he's going to propose and give me a ring for Christmas, Deenie had written. But nothing Leo had said pointed in that direction, so whose version was closer to the truth?

"Is everything all right with you, Ava?" her father asked, eyeing her as she pulled off her borrowed boots.

"Of course," she said brightly. "Why wouldn't it be?"

"I'm not sure. But I do know that, for a woman who claimed she couldn't wait to come home again, you don't look particularly pleased to be here."

"Oh, I am!" she exclaimed, aghast that her parents might think they were the reason she wasn't brimming over with festive cheer. "I always miss you and Mom, but especially at this time of year."

"So why all the strain and tension, honey? Did you Leo have some sort of falling out?"

Falling in, was more like it! "No," she said, too quickly, and almost jumped out of her skin when the phone rang.

"That's probably Deenie again," her father remarked, still watching her thoughtfully. "She's called twice already this morning, and I must say, you make quite a pair. She's wired tighter than a drum and you're as jittery as a cat on hot coals. What's with the two of you?"

"I'm not jittery," Ava said.

But denying the obvious didn't carry much weight when she promptly put the lie to her allegation by giving another start as her mother called out from the kitchen, "Phone's for you, Ava. It's Leo. Take it in the library, why don't you?"

She waited until her father had trudged upstairs

with her suitcases and she heard her mother hang up in the kitchen, then cradling the telephone receiver furtively, whispered into the mouthpiece, "What do you think you're doing, calling me here?"

"Where else do you suggest I call in order to get in touch with you?" Leo inquired, and even the sound of his voice was enough to send an unlawful tingle of excitement down her spine.

"You shouldn't be phoning me at all," she snapped, taking refuge in umbrage. "What if my parents were to overhear?"

"What if they did? I hardly think they'd take exception to my letting you know I found your watch on the floor in my vehicle."

Not believing him, she pulled back the sleeve of her sweater and saw that her watch was, indeed, missing. "Well, how did that happen, do you suppose?"

"Search me," he said equably. "Maybe it fell off when you tried wrestling me into the back seat so you could have your wicked way with me."

Fuming, she spat, "I'm glad one of us finds this whole situation so amusing!"

"Actually, I don't, but it beats the way you're reacting."

"And how is that?"

"By donning sackcloth and ashes, and bleating to the whole world that you're a fallen woman."

"I am not bleating—and nor, for that matter, am

I a fallen woman, though that's hardly something you can take credit for!''

"Sweetheart," he said, his patience clearly flagging, "no one's going to buy that argument for a minute unless you stop acting as if our farmer hosts caught us stark naked and rolling around on the stable floor having sex."

"I am *not* your sweetheart."

"No, you're a pain in the butt, but it being the season of goodwill toward men and all that, I'm trying my damnedest to be charitable." He didn't sigh exactly—he wasn't the sighing type. "Look, Ava, the watch is obviously expensive and I thought you'd want to know it's safe, that's all. And since I intend giving it to Deenie to pass on to you when you see her later on, I also thought you'd like to be prepared for the event, rather than be caught by surprise and overreacting to a perfectly innocent occurrence—which, by the way, is what you're doing now."

"I suppose you're right," she admitted. "And thank you. It *is* an expensive watch."

"Solid gold, from the looks of it."

"Yes."

"Souvenir of your exotic travels?"

"Yes."

"Then I'm glad it didn't fall off when you were trekking through the snow, or it'd be lost for good."

"Me, too."

"Enjoy your lunch with Deenie."

"Thank you. I'll try."

"You'll do better than that, and we both know it. She can't wait to see you."

She'd never imagined there'd come a time when she wouldn't feel the same way. As it was, when Deenie phoned about ten minutes later and made arrangements to pick her up at half past noon, Ava knew only a sickening sense of dread.

"You look wonderful, you know! So tanned and healthy and glowing. And I love the way you're wearing your hair." Deenie, who hadn't once stopped talking from the second she'd arrived to pick up Ava at the house, plopped herself down at a window table in the Owen's Lake Country Club dining room. "Have I said that already? I'm sorry. It's just that I'm so glad to see you, Ava."

But she didn't look glad. She looked drawn and painfully thin. Her smile was too fixed, her nerves too taut. She'd always been highly strung, but the restless agitation that kept her jerking like a poorly controlled marionette was pitiful to behold.

"What shall we order? Let's have champagne cocktails. To celebrate your coming home."

"How about to celebrate our both being home at the same time again?" Ava suggested.

"Oh, that!" Deenie waved a dismissing hand and turned to stare out at the lake, covered at this time of year with ice thick enough for people to skate on—but not before Ava caught the shimmer of tears in her eyes. "We'll do that tomorrow."

"What's happening tomorrow?" Ava pretended not to notice the tears, and wondered how it was that years of complete trust and sharing between her and her dearest friend could splinter into the shallow chit-chat of mere acquaintances. Was it her fault? Had her manner alerted Deenie to the fact that something amiss had occurred the night before?

"Didn't your mother tell you?" Deenie's smile was back in place again, dazzling and totally superficial. "My parents are throwing their usual pre-Christmas bash, and combining it with a family and friends' reunion. Our house is bursting at the seams with relatives I haven't seen since I was in diapers and Leo's expecting company, too, but his parents winter in Florida now and aren't flying in until Christmas Eve, so the only person he'll be showing up with is some dotty old woman he calls 'duchess' because one of her many husbands was some displaced European aristocrat, or so she claims. She's a nutcase, if ever there was one."

I'd say, from the way you're acting, you're not far off from that yourself, Ava thought, watching her. "Then it's to be a big party, I take it?"

"About forty people. Big enough." Deenie rearranged her cutlery, moved her water glass a fraction of an inch to the left, and picked a wilted leaf off the potted poinsettia in the middle of the table. "Doesn't the clubhouse look wonderful? I love all the wall hangings and the way they've done up the tree in the foyer. Did you see it? It must be twenty feet tall and have about a million lights on it."

"I don't care about the Christmas tree in the foyer, Deenie," Ava said, reaching across the table to still those restive hands. "I care about you. How are you, really?"

"Really?" Deenie let out an overwrought giggle. "I'm a walking disaster, can't you tell? Thanks to my dance partner, I'm recovering from a torn muscle in my shoulder and damaged tendons in my ankle. I suppose I should be grateful he only dropped me. If he'd landed on top of me, as well, I'd probably be dead."

"He must feel dreadful about it."

"Oh, I wouldn't go that far. Marcus isn't a man to waste a lot of time on guilt."

Taken aback by the venom in Deenie's tone, Ava said sharply, "But it was an accident, wasn't it?"

"Let's just say that's the conclusion everyone reached."

"What are you implying?" Aghast, Ava stared at her. "That he dropped you on purpose?"

"I think he wanted to see his latest protégée dancing the lead in *The Nutcracker,* and having me sidelined with injuries came at a very convenient time."

The contempt with which she spat out "latest protégée'' spoke volumes. Stunned, Ava said, "Oh, Deenie, were you personally involved with this Marcus? Did he cast you aside for her?''

Deenie looked up, eyes bright with angry tears. "Yes, to both questions.''

"But you always said you'd never—''

"So I broke my own rules and fell in love with a colleague. Sorry if I've disappointed you, but we can't all be as morally high-minded and disciplined as you.''

Ava reared back in her chair, shocked as much by her friend's bitterness as by her own ongoing sense of shame. "I'm the last person to judge you, for heaven's sake!'' she exclaimed, feeling as if she'd just kicked a puppy in the teeth. "I'm just so sorry you were hurt.''

"Not anymore, I'm not! I've moved on to bigger things.''

"And you're happy?''

Again, that too bright smile which stretched the skin over Deenie's cheekbones until she looked almost skeletal. "Wouldn't you be, if you were dating Leo?''

Heavenly days, yes! "We aren't talking about me, Deenie. It's how you feel that matters.''

"I already told you—like celebrating. Which reminds me, I want you to come shopping with me for something to wear to the New Year's Eve dinner dance here at the club. There's quite a smart little boutique downtown—very upscale for a backwater town like this. Designer labels and the works, with all kinds of neat accessories. Say you'll come.''

''Well, sure. I'm always game to go shopping, you know that.''

''Great. Not tomorrow, though, because I'm expecting guests from out of town and have to meet them at Skellington Airport, but maybe the day after that?''

''Fine.''

''And before I forget, here's your watch.'' Deenie groped in her bag and slid the watch across the table. ''Now, let's get down to some serious celebrating.''

With a snap of her fingers, she brought a waiter hurrying over. ''Two champagne cocktails, please,'' she ordered, then abruptly changed her mind. ''Better yet, just bring a whole bottle and have done with—whatever you've got on ice will do.''

As the man raced off to do her bidding, she glanced defiantly at Ava and said, ''What are you looking so sour about? I thought you'd be happy to get your watch back.''

''This isn't about my watch, and I'm not looking sour! Surprised, maybe. I'm not used to downing a whole bottle of wine at lunch and the last I knew, you weren't, either.''

''Oh, stop being so po-faced! You're my friend, not my mother, and it's Christmas, for heaven's sake! What's wrong with living it up a bit when a woman's future's looking so rosy?''

But the speed with which she knocked back two glasses of champagne resembled someone desperately seeking escape from today, rather than one in happy anticipation of tomorrow.

''Are you sure you're headed in the right direction with Leo?'' Ava asked her cautiously. ''I know you mentioned in your last email that you and he were serious, but has he actually said anything about getting married?''

''Not in so many words, perhaps, but he will. It's only a matter of time.'' Deenie swigged down another mouthful of champagne and smirked suggestively. ''A man's actions often speak louder than words, if you get my drift!''

There was hardly any missing it! ''If that's the case, why are you so…twitchy? Is it the idea of a wedding?''

''No. It's the bit which comes *after* that's worrying me.''

''You mean the honeymoon?''

Deenie laughed tipsily. ''I mean the marriage, dopey! I mean facing Leo across the breakfast table every morning, and ironing his shirts, and being the gracious hostess when he invites his colleagues over for dinner.''

''Aren't they what marriage is all about?''

"For types like you, perhaps. But I'm not cut out to be a small-town *hausfrau.*"

"In that case, why are you even *thinking* about becoming engaged to a man like Leo?"

"Because a girl's got to do what a girl's got to do." Deenie hiccuped and regarded Ava owlishly. "You know what they say about the means justifying the end, right? Sometimes, you have to play hardball to get what you want. Well, guess what! I'm playing hardball."

Despite the mixed metaphors and slurred words, there was nevertheless a certain steely determination in her voice that left Ava very uneasy. "You're up to something, Deenie," she said, "and I want to know what it is."

Deenie shook her head—let it flop foolishly from side to side, actually. "No. S'too late for true confessions."

"It's never too late, Deenie."

"Yes, it is," she said, with exaggerated solemnity. "Let's have another drink."

"Forget it! You need food." Ava wasn't sure if Deenie really meant what she was saying, or if the champagne was to blame for the disquieting confessions spilling out of her mouth. But she did know that trying to hold a rational conversation with someone close to falling-down drunk was a waste of time. Sober, Deenie might be singing quite a different tune.

On the other hand, *in vino veritas…!*

Flagging down their waiter, Ava ordered club sandwiches with French fries. Not the most healthful meal on the menu by a long shot, but at least the carbohydrates would soak up some of the wine.

"And bring us another bottle of champagne," Deenie said, tripping over the words.

"Bring us coffee instead," Ava countermanded. "A very large pot of it, please."

"You've spent so long overseas tending to the poor and underprivileged, you've forgotten how to have fun," Deenie pouted. "You're being a real party pooper, Ava."

"No. I'm being your friend."

But a good friend, a *real* friend, would hear what Deenie wasn't saying, and would give her the kind of unselfish, unbiased advice she obviously needed. *Don't take up with one man when you're still in love with another,* she'd say. *Don't use Leo. He deserves better than that.*

Trouble was, her own motivation was too murky to allow her to speak so plainly. Because the truth was, she'd like nothing better than to throw a monkey wrench in the works and set Leo free to pursue a relationship with her.

And what kind of friend did that make her?

CHAPTER FOUR

HE AND Ava were avoiding each other. Beyond exchanging a flickering glance of acknowledgement when she arrived at the Manville's home for the dinner party, she'd behaved as if he were just another piece of highly polished furniture, and he'd gravitated to the other end of the room to take up his post next to the glittery artificial Christmas tree.

"Who's that lovely, long-legged stork of a gal?" Cousin Ethel inquired, sidling up to him as the pre-dinner cocktail hour began to wind down.

"Which one?" he asked, gazing vacantly around the room at the mob of guests, and doing his utmost to look properly puzzled.

Playing dumb with the duchess had never worked. She was too smart, too observant and too outspoken for her own good, and the fact that she'd just turned eighty-four—she wasn't actually *his* cousin, but his father's several times removed—didn't impair her faculties in the least.

"This might be my third martini, boy, but I'm a long way from being plastered," she declared, chewing on her olive. "You know very well which one, given that she's the reason you're lurking behind this appalling tree so you can ogle her through its silly artificial branches.''

''Oh, *her!*'' he said, removing a skein of tinsel festooning his left ear, and feeling as big a fool as he no doubt must look. ''She's just the daughter of one of the neighbors.''

Not to mention the sexiest creature in the western hemisphere. In her sleek retro dinner dress, Ava might have stepped out of some classic 1930's drawing room drama. ''Elegant'' was the word which most immediately sprang to mind, although other, less intellectual parts of him stirred with an even greater appreciation for what lay beneath that shining length of slinky black satin.

''Then she's a friend of the diminutive Deenie's?''

''That's right,'' he managed, on a strangled breath as Ava shrugged one shoulder and sent ripples of reflected candlelight shimmering down her torso.

''Aha! Introduce me.''

''What?''

Ethel knocked back the rest of her martini and eyed him balefully. ''Something wrong with your hearing, Leo, or has joining the sleaziest profession on God's earth addled your brains to the point that you can't understand simple English?''

Caught squarely between amusement and annoyance, he tucked her hand in the crook of his arm and cruised her over to where Ava leaned against the grand piano, sipping champagne and chatting altogether too cosily with some imported suit wearing too much jewelry.

"Hi," he said, striving to appear unmoved by the sight. "Someone here wants to meet you. Ethel Whitney, this is Ava Sorensen. And...?"

"Bret Turner," the suit supplied, flashing a mouthful of perfectly capped teeth. "Charmed to make your acquaintance, madam."

Ethel nodded. "No doubt. Go amuse yourself with someone else, young man, and leave me to get acquainted with this enchanting lass. Not you, Leo," she commanded, snagging him by the elbow just as he was about to make his escape. "I'm talking to Mr. Turner. *You* stay put and be sociable."

His problem, Leo decided, stifling a groan, had less to do with the fact that Ethel was a domineering dowager used to doling out orders with imperial disregard for the wishes of others, than it had with his having been brought up to show respect toward the elderly regardless of how unreasonable their demands might be. So, like a dog highly trained in obedience, he remained rooted to the spot even though his every instinct told him to hotfoot it away with all due speed.

Ava offered her hand. "How do you do, Ms. Whitney? I'm delighted to meet you."

Ethel inspected Ava's short oval nails, painted the same rich cranberry colour as Leo had noticed on her toenails two nights previously, and the slim, capable fingers. "Good hands as well as good manners," she pronounced with satisfaction. "Good bones, too. Are you a model, child, or merely a model child?"

Ava laughed, a low rich ripple of amusement which further captivated Ethel. "Neither, I'm afraid. I'm an ICU nurse, and my mother blames me for all her grey hairs."

"A nurse? The hell you say! And was Leo your patient when he injured his back?"

"I was never in ICU, duchess," he said, almost breaking out in a sweat at the thought of Ava giving him a bed bath.

Simultaneously, Ava said, "No. For the last three years, I've worked in Africa, but I came home on leave to spend Christmas with my parents and to spend some time with my friend Deenie. We don't often find ourselves in the same place at the same time, these days."

With mounting approval, Ethel scrutinized her from head to foot. "You and she are very close, are you?"

"Very." Ava's smile grew a tad strained and she shot a defiant glance Leo's way before continuing, "We've been best friends since our mothers enrolled us in the same ballet academy when we were four. We might not be blood sisters, but the bond between us is as strong as anything identical twins might know.''

"Yet unlike twins, you aspire to different ambitions.''

"Yes, although, at one time, becoming a prima ballerina was my dream, as well. But even if I'd had the talent—which I didn't—I grew to be much too tall. At five nine in my bare feet, I'd have towered over most male dance partners when I was *en pointe.* So I exchanged my tutu for a uniform, my ballet slippers for white Oxfords, and enrolled in nursing school in Vancouver at about the same time that Deenie, who was both supremely gifted *and* petite, flew to Britain to train at London's Royal Ballet School.'' Her smile this time was more genuine. "'Teenie Deenie', Madame Antonia, our teacher, used to call her.''

"How nauseatingly quaint,'' Ethel snorted. "And what did she call you, my dear?''

"I didn't rate a pet name.''

"Praise the Lord! Now let's talk about you and Leo.''

"There's nothing to talk about, duchess!'' he blurted, nearly swallowing his tongue. Cripes, if she ever got wind of the other night, she'd be blackmailing him for the rest of her days—and his!

"Au contraire, mon cher,'' Ethel decreed, regarding him with the fond contempt of one being pestered by a beloved but tiresome child. "However, if

we're boring you, consider yourself free to go peddle your funny papers elsewhere.''

Ava choked on her champagne and tried to cover it up with a polite cough. And he, who hadn't blushed since he was in diapers more than thirty-five years ago, felt his face redden.

''If I'd known you were going to give Ava the third degree like this,'' he muttered, ''I'd never have introduced you in the first place!''

Ignoring him, she fixed Ava in a benevolent gaze. ''Tell me how you came to know Leo.''

''We used to live practically next door to each other. I've known him as long as I've known Deenie.''

''I see. And do you consider him a close friend, too?''

Involuntarily, Ava's glance locked again with his, and this time a flush stained the smooth golden perfection of her cheeks. ''Not exactly. He was older and we didn't share much in common.''

''I'm sure you didn't—at least,'' Ethel said, after a significant pause, ''not back then. Try though I might, I can't picture Leo in tights, looking as if he's got a purse full of loose change stuffed in his—''

''*Ethel!*'' This time, he roared. Loud enough for heads to turn all over the room.

Alarmed, Gail Manville, Deenie's mother, came fluttering over, her rope of pearls swinging like a hula hoop around her well-toned neck. "Is there a problem, Leo?"

Hell, yes! And it was compounding by the minute! "My cousin's a little hard of hearing, especially with so much background noise," he improvised, taking grim satisfaction in Ethel's affronted gasp. "Of course, at her age, it's to be expected."

"Poor old dear!" Failing to recognize the scorn with which Ethel regarded her, Gail patted her arm consolingly. "I quite understand, Mrs. Whitney. My mother's rather ancient, too, and has the same problem. But we'll be sitting down to dinner shortly and I think you'll find it easier to follow what's being said then because instead of trying to cram everyone into the dining room, I've had the caterer set up tables for four throughout the conservatory, and we'll change dinner partners with each course. It'll be *such* fun, and you'll get the chance to meet people a few at a time, which I'm sure you'll find a lot less confusing."

"Great balls of fire, the woman'll be organizing us into teams and having us play spin the bottle before the evening's out!" Ethel fumed, loudly enough that Gail must have heard.

But if she did, she gave no sign. Instead, she drew Ava aside and said, "Deenie disappeared to take a phone call in her room about half an hour ago and hasn't been seen since. Would you mind getting her down here, dear? Dinner's about to be served, but we can't very well start without her.''

''I can,'' Ethel declared, as Ava made tracks for the stairs and Gail hurried to confer with the chef beckoning to her from the butler's pantry. ''If I don't get something solid in my stomach soon, I'm likely to keel over.''

''And if you don't start behaving yourself as of right now, I'll be shipping you out of here before you're even halfway through your soup,'' Leo threatened. ''Are you deliberately trying to land me in hot water?''

''You don't need my help to do that, dear boy,'' she said, all sunny smiles. ''You're doing a splendid job of it all by yourself—with a little help from the lovely Ava.''

He didn't ask what she meant by *that* remark. He didn't want to know.

When she finally ran her to earth in her *en suite* bathroom, Ava saw at once that Deenie had been crying. ''Talk to me,'' Ava begged, handing her another tissue and scooping the soggy wad already heaped on the vanity into the waste-basket. ''Good grief, Deenie, you know there's nothing you can't tell me.''

But the old Deenie, who'd have poured out her heart in a flash, had been taken over by a secretive stranger. ''It's nothing,'' she sniffed. ''I'm just feeling…'' Her voice quavered briefly. ''…a little let-down. Someone I'd hoped would come to his…um, tonight's shindig, isn't going to make it, after all.''

''I'm sure that's very disappointing, but it doesn't change the fact that there's a roomful of hungry guests downstairs raring to start dinner, and your mom would like it if you'd put in an appearance. It doesn't look good for the only genuine home-grown celebrity to go AWOL.''

''Have you seen Leo?''

''Oh, yes!'' Ava replied, with more feeling than she'd intended. Between him and Ethel, she'd seen plenty! ''I imagine *he's* wondering what's keeping you away, as well.''

''I'd be surprised if he even noticed I was gone.'' Deenie's lower lip trembled ominously.

Recognizing another bout of weeping was imminent, Ava said bracingly, ''All right, Deenie, the pity party's over. If you're this uncertain about your relationship with Leo, for heaven's sake say so now, and put us all out of our misery.''

''Leo isn't the problem, I am.''

''That much I already figured out. The question is, why?''

''I'm overtired and stressed out and…'' She rotated her shoulder, flexed her injured ankle and winced. ''Sore.''

''In that case, take an analgesic for the pain, and

make a point of getting to bed early. You'll be surprised what a decent night's sleep will do for you.''

"You're not dishing out orders in ICU now, Ava, and I won't be spoken to like that,'' Deenie said peevishly.

"And you're not starring in your own tragic ballet, so get rid of the superstar attitude! You're dating a wonderful man, not facing lethal injection on death row.''

Deenie's head drooped like a faded blossom on her slender neck. "Being stuck in this backwater over Christmas feels like a death sentence. I'm not exactly a poster child for small-town living, in case you haven't noticed. I'm used to bright city lights and action.''

Ava blew out a long, frustrated breath and headed for the door. "You're imparting that little gem of news to the wrong person, old friend. Why don't I go get Leo and you can tell him to his face what you really think about settling down with him?''

"Don't you dare do any such thing!''

"Why not? If you're so certain he's buying you a ring for Christmas, don't you think he has a right to know how you feel *before* he shells out his hard-earned money?''

"No.'' Deenie snatched up another tissue, gave her face a final scouring, and searched in the medicine cabinet for drops to take the red out of her eyes. "Just blowing off steam to you is enough to make me feel better."

Ava wished she could say the same. But for the first time ever, her loyalty was torn between her oldest, dearest friend, and a man to whom she was so powerfully drawn that it was a wonder sparks didn't fly when she found herself in the same room with him. That both he and Deenie were separately ambivalent about their liaison added yet another wrinkle to the dilemma.

"Don't look so worried," Deenie said, inspecting herself one last time in the mirror. "You ought to know me well enough by now to realize I'm not nearly as suicidal as I sound. Leo's a darling and I don't need you or anyone else to tell me I'm the luckiest woman in the world to have run into him again when I did."

"I agree," Ava said glumly.

"All right, then! Let's go join the party. Did you get to meet many people earlier?"

"A few. An investment banker named Bret was very attentive, and those out-of-town guests you mentioned, the ones whose flight you met yesterday."

"Ah, yes, Paul and Lynette Markov. They're two other principals from our dance company, en route to Santiago for the spring tour, but they took a little side-trip to see me before heading south." Deenie's expression grew almost crafty. "Did you happen to notice if they spent any time at all chatting with Leo?''

"No," she said shortly. "I had better things to do than keep tabs on him. But he did introduce me to the duchess.''

"Oh, you poor thing! I warned you evil Ethel's a royal pain in the rear—and a scary sight in all that silver lamé, don't you think? Looks as if someone tried to shrink-wrap her in aluminum foil!''

"That's cruel, Deenie!'' But Ava laughed anyway, glad to see the old familiar Deenie had vanquished the distraught stranger of a few minutes ago.

CHAPTER FIVE

THE Manvilles' conservatory, a soaring masterpiece of glass architecture reminiscent of the Victorian era at its most splendid, had been transformed into a Christmas wonderland. Hundreds, perhaps even thousands, of miniature lights draped the tropical foliage. Underwater flood lamps spot-lighted the stone fountains. Glimmering white pillar candles clustered cheek by jowl with banks of scarlet and pink poinsettias. And as a final festive touch, a live fir tree sparkling with antique glass balls stood in the middle of the atrium, tall enough that its topmost branches brushed the peak of the pagoda-shaped roof.

Already famous for their lavish parties, this time the Manvilles had really outdone themselves. Georgian sterling, pearly French china and Austrian crystal graced tables cloaked in starched hunter-green linen. To the baroque guitar strains of "The Holly and the Ivy," mimosa salad followed sherried consomme. "Good King Wenceslas" heralded the arrival of crayfish bathed in Pernod-flavored cream sauce. "The Twelve Days of Christmas" accompanied partridge stuffed with wild rice and spiced crab apples. "Here We Come A-Wassailing" kept company with palate-cleansing lemon sherbert served in fluted dishes no bigger than a thimble. And so it went, culminating in a flaming plum pudding stuffed with silver favours, and a dessert and cheese buffet which not even the most calorie-conscious diner could resist.

And at every opportunity, Deenie flirted outrageously with Leo, and flaunted him in Paul and Lynette Markov's faces as if he were a trophy she'd bagged on safari. Ava bore up as well as her private misgivings and misery would allow, but by the time coffee and liqueurs were offered, the sullen throb symptomatic of one of her rare migraines had taken hold.

Knowing it marked the end of the evening for her, she waited until Deenie's father ushered everyone into the music room for a finale of carol singing, then slipped away from the crowd and took refuge on a bench surrounding the trunk of a huge potted palm at the far end of the conservatory.

"I can't take any more of this," she moaned softly, pressing her fingertips to her closed eyes, and almost had a heart attack when a hand squeezed her shoulder and a voice she recognized only too well murmured, "Me, neither, Ava."

Appalled, she sprang to her feet. "How did you know where to find me?"

"I saw you leave," Leo said, "and followed

you." He inspected her narrowly. "You don't look so well."

"I have a headache."

It was a woman's oldest and lamest excuse since the beginning of time, but he accepted it without protest. "Then I'll take you home. It'll give me an excuse to escape this shindig, as well as be alone with you."

She flung a furtive glance around before meeting his gaze. "You shouldn't be here!" she whispered, shaken. "If anyone were to see us together...or hear what you've just said...!"

Ignoring her attempts to evade him, he massaged his thumbs over her temple in small, comforting circles. "Don't flatter yourself that anyone gives a rap, Ava. Hell, the way the booze has been flowing, we could hide out in here for the rest of the night and no one would care."

Miraculously, the pain was leaching away and leaving her almost drowsy with pleasure. "Deenie might, if she knew," she said, doing her level best to resist the drugging seduction of his touch. "And both her family and mine certainly would!"

His fingers slid around her neck, warm and strong and intimate. "The question is, do *you* mind, sweetheart?"

"Please don't call me that," she whispered weakly. "And don't ask me such questions. Don't make me *care* about you. It isn't right."

"Right be damned!" he muttered, drawing her into his arms. "The truth is, you already *do* care for me, Ava—maybe as much as I'm beginning to care for you."

She was quivering all over, so confused she barely knew what she might say or do next. So wanting that, for all she wished she could look away, she continued to feast her eyes on him. How beautiful he was with those high, aristocratic cheekbones and smooth olive skin, and that hair like midnight touched with just a glimmer of frost.

This was a man to turn heads, to make a woman wish for things she couldn't have. "You should be saying these things to Deenie," she said, in a low, trembling voice. "She's the one you're supposed to be dating."

"We were never 'dating' in that way."

"And what way is that, Leo?"

"Seriously. The way I'd date you, if you'd give me half a chance."

"Odd," she said, steeling herself against the temptation to believe him. "That's not exactly the impression you've given Deenie. She seems to think you're very serious. About her."

"Then she's mistaken."

"Really." She laughed bitterly, remembering Deenie's coy insinuation at lunch the other day. *Sometimes, a man's actions speak louder than words.* "I wonder how that happened?"

He buried a sigh. "Sometimes, people deliberately mislead themselves and others, then have trouble finding a way to extricate themselves gracefully. I suspect that's where Deenie's at now. But just because she's lying to herself is no reason for me to compound matters by letting her get away with it. Turn away from me all you like, Ava," he said, when she tilted her face to the side, "but you can't turn away from the facts. I'm no more the right man for Deenie than she's the right woman for me. The pity of it is that it took meeting you again to really bring that message home."

"Are you saying this…this *mess* is my fault?"

"No," he said, stroking his palms down her spine and bringing them to rest with shocking familiarity against her hips. "If anyone's to blame, I am, for allowing too many people to jump to too many false conclusions."

"I don't see how they could have done that if you hadn't given the wrong impression in the first place."

He let fly with a pent-up oath of frustration. "Okay, I admit it. For a very short while when we first met up again, I let circumstance and proximity fool me into wondering if Deenie and I might have found something lasting, when the most we ever shared was a passing attraction. And if she were to be really honest, I think she'd agree. Events conspired to bring us together, when it should have been passion. Now events are driving us apart, and there's no doubt the fallout is going to upset a few people.'' He inched her closer. ''I'd have to be blind not to see that it's upsetting you.''

Pity for her friend tore at Ava, making her own misery seem small and insignificant by comparison. How did a woman face the embarrassment of being tossed aside by the man she'd boasted was on the verge of proposing? Never mind that she appeared less than enthusiastic about her impending engagement; being ''dumped'' was never anything but humiliating. ''How are you going to tell her?''

Letting go of her, Leo stepped away, but before he could answer, high-heeled footsteps clipped over the terracotta tiles and Mrs. Manville appeared. ''We missed you, Leo, and your cousin mentioned that she saw you headed this way,'' she said, her glance swinging from his impassive face to Ava's which, Ava knew, was flushed with guilt. ''Why are you lurking out here with Ava? Is there a problem of which I'm not aware?''

''Yes,'' he said, taking charge of the situation with admirable calm. ''Ava's not feeling well, and I'm trying to persuade her to let me take her home.''

''I'm sorry.'' But Mrs. Manville sounded more suspicious than sorry. ''Exactly how are you not feeling well, dear?''

''A headache.'' That much, at least, was true. The

migraine, which had subsided to bearable levels, had come roaring back with a vengeance.

"Then you should have turned to *me,* not Leo. I could have given you an aspirin."

"I don't think an aspirin's going to do the trick," Leo said. "Look at her, Gail. She can barely see, she's in so much pain."

"I'm afraid Leo's right," Ava said, terribly afraid that she might be sick if she didn't soon find some relief from the hammers pounding inside her skull.

"You have turned rather pale," Gail Manville allowed. "Perhaps it might be best if someone took you home. Wait here and I'll go alert your parents."

"Don't do that."

Leo's peremptory tone had Mrs. Manville raising her eyebrows in annoyed surprise. "And why not, Leo?"

"Because it'll disrupt the party and put a damper on the whole evening, which would be a shame, considering all the trouble you've gone to to make it a success.

A burst of distant laughter lent emphasis to his words. Mrs. Manville tapped a manicured forefinger against her pursed lips, clearly caught between not entirely trusting the situation and not wanting her gala evening spoilt by something as trivial as a migraine attack. "Perhaps you're right. Well…since you've already offered to play chauffeur, would you mind…?"

"Not a bit," he said, with what struck Ava as unnecessary enthusiasm. "I'll bring my car around to the back entrance."

"No." Ava waved a feeble hand. Being alone in a car with him would only exacerbate a situation already threatening to run amok. "Our house is only four doors away, and a walk in the fresh air might help."

"Then I'll come with you to be sure you make it home safely." Overriding her protests, he pressed her down on the bench again. "Stay put, while I get your coat and boots."

When he was gone, Mrs. Manville inquired with only a veneer of sympathy, "Do you need a doctor, Ava?"

"No. I have medication at home which will help."

"You never used to get headaches." She made it sound like an accusation. "What brought this one on?"

"I'm afraid it was the mousse at the dessert buffet. I never touch chocolate as a rule, but I couldn't resist it tonight. Please don't be concerned, Mrs. Manville. The medication kicks in very quickly."

"Then I'll wish you good night and hope you feel better in the morning." On the verge of leaving, Deenie's mother paused. "I hope I don't have to remind you that Deenie has already laid claim to Leo's attentions, Ava," she said, over her shoulder.

"Please don't impose on his time any more than is absolutely necessary."

"Deck the Halls" was the song of choice belting out of the music room as he searched for the coat and high leather boots Ava had described, and a particularly boisterous *Fa-la-la-la-la!* camouflaged his footsteps when he returned to the conservatory. But nothing, Leo decided, could mask the chill in Gail Manville's voice as she leveled her final directive at Ava.

"If I didn't know better, I'd think she didn't like you," he said, kneeling in front of Ava and cradling her elegant feet prior to sliding them into the boots. "Considering she's known you practically all your life, she's not exactly gushing warm concern."

"She likes me well enough—as long as I don't threaten Deenie's place in the spotlight."

"Meaning what?" he asked, trying to quell his jolt of awareness when she raised one leg to ease her foot into its boot. But a man needed to be made of sterner stuff than he possessed to remain unmoved when the skirt of her dress slithered over his hands in cool, satiny whispers to reveal a delectable hint of sleek, silk-clad thigh.

Oblivious to her effect on him, she said, "She's always been very ambitious for Deenie. We— Deenie and I, that is—weren't much more than babies when we began taking ballet classes together, but right from the start Mrs. Manville viewed me as potential competition. If I was chosen to perform a solo at the annual dance recital, she saw to it that Deenie performed two. It wasn't until I started to grow like an ungainly weed and clearly would never make my mark as a prima ballerina at any level that she relaxed enough to let my friendship with Deenie flourish on its own merit.''

Ungainly weed, my left foot! He had no recollection of Ava as a small child, nor was he much given to flowery comparisons. But if what he'd just heard was true, small wonder Gail was practically frothing at the mouth. Because there was little doubt that the ''competition'' had blossomed into a woman more exquisite than anything blooming in the Manville conservatory.

''Given such poor growing conditions, I'm surprised your friendship thrived at all,'' he said, wishing the same was true of his nether regions which, at that glimpse of feminine thigh and contrary to his most earnest efforts, showed a lively interest in sprouting past socially acceptable proportions. ''But that hardly explains why Gail was so flinty-faced with you just now.''

''She's a mother, Leo, and she's no fool. She sensed there was more going on between you and me than there should have been. She's afraid for Deenie.''

''She should be,'' he said, ''but not for the reasons you're implying. Deenie's badly off-balance, and it has nothing to do with you, nor, I'm beginning to think, with me. Something else is going on with her, and I'm hoping like hell she'll have the guts to spill it out before...."

"Before what?" Ava's gaze, big, grey and beautiful anytime, widened so much that her upper lashes almost touched her elegant brows.

"She goes completely over the edge. Right now, though," he said, helping her into her coat and escorting her through a side door to a path leading down to the lakefront walk, "I'm more concerned about getting you home. You look about ready to pass out."

"Actually, I'm feeling a bit better," she said, inhaling deeply of the sharp night air. "The headache's subsided to a dull roar again."

"What brought it on to begin with?"

"Mrs. Manville asked me the same thing. I told her the chocolate mousse was to blame."

"And was it?"

"No. I didn't have any." She lifted her shoulders in a shrug. "I suspect it's just a tension headache. And don't bother to ask the reason for that, when we both know full well why."

"Don't *you* take on my problems and make them yours."

"How can I help it?" Her hair, as she swung a glance at him, gleamed in the moonlight. "I'm supposed to be Deenie's dearest friend, yet I find myself wishing...."

"What?" he asked, when she dwindled into silence.

"That I didn't care about her so much. Because then my conscience wouldn't be bothering me the way it is."

He heard a world of misery in her voice; a potent regret. "Don't blame yourself," he said, pinning her arm in the crook of his elbow and catching her hand in his. "What was, at best, a superficial attraction between Deenie and me floundered long before you came on the scene. You're not the one who took the bloom off the rose."

He knew that to be true, but *she* wasn't buying it. "Yes, I am," she said brokenly. "If I weren't here, she might have come to the realization that things between you weren't working out, and ending it would have been mutual. As it is now, you're using me as the excuse to break off with her, and even if she can forgive me, I'll never forgive myself—or you for putting me in the middle of it all."

They'd reached the bottom of her garden by then, and were shielded from the houses on either side by a stand of pines. Slipping free of his hold, she unlatched a wrought-iron gate set in the low stone wall enclosing the property.

The night was clear, with a million stars and a cold-faced moon. The lake lay glassy and still beneath a thick layer of ice. But a fitful wind had sprung up, nipping and plucking at Ava's hair like a puppy with a toy. Unable to help himself, he reached out and snagged a wayward strand in his bare fingers.

"Three wise men followed a star and found a saviour," he said, tugging her back to face him. "Do you suppose I could be as lucky?"

"It all depends." Her voice quivered, as if it, too, were at the mercy of the wind. "What is it you want to be saved from?"

"Myself," he said. "And you."

Her gaze flared in the gloom, so wide that he saw the pinprick reflection of the starlight in her pupils. "Oh, Leo, stop playing with me! Stop trying to make me believe one thing and letting Deenie believe another. It's wrong."

"Wrong?" He drew her to him. Slipped his hands inside her coat and shaped the pattern of her body, committing to memory the sweet indentation of her waist, the gentle flare of her hips. "How can this be wrong?" he murmured against her mouth. "You tell me that, Ava."

CHAPTER SIX

AVA'S heart missed a beat. "Let me go," she pleaded, her eyes too full to hold back the tears.

But he wasn't listening. Or if he was, he chose to ignore an entreaty she knew to be half-hearted at best. Because although she was saying all the correct and proper things, her body was betraying her with bold impropriety. Yearning toward him. Finding refuge in the warm, solid strength of him. And just by the way it curved against him, giving him explicit permission to go ahead and kiss her.

Which he did. And if, that first time—in the dark, in the stable—their mouths had blundered together by accident, this time they came together with slow and sensuous deliberation.

And if there weren't celestial trumpets sounding from the heavens, there should have been, because *something* tumultuous and jubilant drowned out the feeble protests of her conscience. *Something* drove her not to care about anything but the stolen ecstasy of the moment.

Under cover of her coat, a heavy black velvet lined with quilted scarlet satin which swirled around to cloak them in intimacy, his hands stole from her hips with brazen urgency and cradled her bottom.

"Come to me," he begged against her lips, and she knew what he meant.

Knew because, even as he asked, he pulled her closer until her pelvis swayed in tandem with the bold, rocking rhythm of his hips, and the liquid pull of her own desire pooled between her thighs at the proud thrust of his arousal pressing against her belly.

A wild tension thrummed within her, so intense that if he'd lifted the hem of her dress and pulled down her panties, she'd have parted her legs and let him take her there and then, and never mind that the temperature hovered some fifteen degrees below freezing. Or that the two of them could have been discovered by anyone happening along the lakefront walk. Or that her betrayal of her best friend grew more despicable with every second which passed.

For the space of a blissful minute or more, she was a creature possessed. So receptive to his advances that her mouth opened in invitation without his having to resort to persuasion. So hungry and desperate to belong to him—in his heart, where it really mattered; and know that he belonged to her in the same way—even if it was just for now and he'd have changed his mind by tomorrow, just as he had with Deenie—that she was beyond shame. So wanting and aching and willing that she didn't care that, in the morning, she'd despise what she'd become and what she'd done.

Sadly—or perhaps not!—he lived by a less flexible code of ethics. Like a man suddenly waking from a nightmare, he lifted his head and thrust her away from him so abruptly that if the gate hadn't been at her back, she'd have missed her footing on the snow and gone sprawling.

"What the devil am I doing?" he exclaimed hoarsely, swiping the back of his hand across his mouth. "Ava, forgive me!"

"There's nothing to forgive," she whimpered and, depraved weakling that she was, would have flung herself again into his arms if he hadn't fended her off with both hands.

"Oh yes, there is!" he said, the horror and disgust in his voice impossible to miss.

"Leo…!"

"Listen to me, Ava." His voice shook with the force of the emotions at war within him. "I want you about as badly as any man *can* want a woman. But not, God help me, like this. Not like some out-of-control teenager groping around under cover of dark. And most of all, not furtively, as if we have no right to desire one another."

The bitter night air shot into her lungs and put paid to the recklessness which had clouded her mind. Repelled by her own wantonness, shamed that he was the one with conscience enough to call a halt to their deplorable behaviour, she retorted sharply, "A better reason might be, not as long as another woman's under the impression you're about to ask her to marry you.''

"If that's what Deenie's told you, she's delusional!'' he said flatly.

"Is she? Or is it closer to the truth to say you're enjoying playing both ends against the middle?''

"If that's what you really believe, then you don't know me at all.''

"Perhaps not, but this much I do know. I'm not about to enter into a tug of war over any man, and I'm definitely not interested in someone who's as cavalier about his relationships as you appear to be. You didn't mind using Deenie when nothing better presented itself, and it seems you have no qualms about ditching her now that you think you'd rather have me.''

"For what it's worth, Ava, I never 'had' Deenie.''

...a man's actions can speak louder than words...! "So you say!''

"Yes, I do,'' he agreed, with deadly calm. "But if my word carries so little weight with you, perhaps I'm wasting my time trying to convince you I'm neither toying with her affections nor coming on to you because I'm ready for a change of pace.'' He tugged up the collar of his overcoat and turned away. "My apologies for having overstepped the mark with you. It won't happen again.''

"I was starting to worry about you,'' her mother remarked, when Ava straggled into the kitchen just after ten o'clock the next morning. "Gail mentioned that you left the party early because you were tired, but even so, it's not like you to sleep so late. And if you don't mind my saying so, honey, you still look a bit peaked."

In fact, Ava had been awake through most of the night, plagued by doubts. Had she judged Leo too harshly? Was Deenie playing some sort of game whose rules were known only to her? Was it really possible that after all the years they'd known each other and all the confidences they'd shared, Deenie had deliberately set out to deceive her supposed best friend?

"It's just the jet lag catching up with me," Ava told her mother. "It'll pass before the day's out. Is there any coffee left?"

"Plenty. I just made a fresh pot." Her mother filled a cup and passed it across the breakfast bar. "Deenie phoned to remind you you're going shopping together this afternoon to find gorgeous outfits for New Year's Eve."

"Oh...." Gloomily, Ava leaned on one elbow and stirred her coffee. "I'd forgotten about that."

"She suggested picking you up here around two, but you mentioned wanting to buy a couple of Christmas gifts, and since I have to run a few last-minute errands as well, I thought it would be nice if we went into town together. We can do what we have to do, then get together for lunch before you meet Deenie at The Soiree Boutique, which is where she wants to shop. How does that sound?''

''Lovely,' Ava said, striving to inject a little enthusiasm into her voice. Not that she didn't want to spend time with her mother, because she did, but the thought of keeping up a cheerful front with Deenie appealed not at all.

''Lovely!'' Her mother came around the breakfast bar and gave her a hug. ''That's what we'll do, then.''

Christmas was only two days away, and Owen's Lake town center, as always, looked picture-postcard charming. That morning, the air was so crystal clear, it almost rang. The snow huddled purple-blue in the shadows of the steep courthouse roof. In the middle of the square, some prankster had crowned the marble statue of Charles Owen with an evergreen wreath. It hung tipsily over one eye, hilariously at odds with the founding father's air of timeless dignity.

Not far away, Stuart Shultz, who had to be eighty if he was a day and whose long white beard was real, sported the same red felt Santa Claus suit he'd worn for as long as Ava could remember, and did a roaring business selling hot chocolate and roasted chestnuts from his decorated stall.

On the corner, his wife Violet, dressed as Mrs.

Claus in a long green skirt and lace-trimmed blouse under her red-checkered apron, doled out fresh-from-the-oven gingerbread men to the children passing by her shop while, from Saint Martha's church at the other end of the square, came the sound of the boys' choir practicing "Silent Night" for the Christmas Eve carol service.

This was what Christmas should be all about, Ava thought, swallowing the sudden lump in her throat. Not stealthy kisses and clandestine trysts with a man she wasn't sure she could trust, but the pure, soaring voice of a boy soprano, and the wide-eyed innocence of children as a kind old couple who'd never had babies of their own put on a show that made even adults half believe in Santa Claus.

Her mother, waiting for her in the dining room of The White Horse Inn, at a table set between the fireplace and a window overlooking the lake, noticed at once that something was amiss. "We both need this," she said, pushing one of two glasses of sherry toward Ava and raising the other in a silent toast, "and then you're going to explain why you're looking as if you've just lost your best friend. And don't bother telling me I'm imagining things, because I know you too well."

"I can't talk about it," Ava said, but the sherry loosened her tongue and she found herself spilling out her heart to the one person in the whole world who'd continue to love her, no matter how far she fell from grace. "Oh, Mom, I might well have lost my best friend, and it's all because of Leo."

"Leo Ferrante?" Her mother set down her glass and blinked in surprise. "Good gracious, what's he done?"

"It's what I've done." No use blaming Leo, after all. He'd never have put the moves on her if she'd taken the moral high road to begin with, instead of throwing herself at him.

"I understand he walked you home last night," her mother said. "Is *that* what this is all about?"

"Not really. It began before that." Ava blotted her mouth with her napkin and heaved a sigh. "When Deenie first told me she was thinking of settling down with him, I was surprised because she'd always said she was married to the ballet. But she convinced me she was making a change for the better. She insisted she'd never been happier, that I'd love Leo, that he hadn't changed a bit from when we both mooned over him in our teens, and that he was the perfect man for her."

"Well, has he? Changed, I mean?"

"No," Ava said, staring hopelessly out of the window at the sun-washed gloss of the frozen lake. "Unfortunately, neither have I, Mom. That's the trouble."

"Good heavens! Are you saying that you're still smitten with him?"

"That's one way of putting it, I suppose. But I'm afraid my feelings go deeper than that."

"Oh, Ava!" Her mother's distress was palpable. "Honey, you're overreacting. Think how embarrassed you and Leo both would be if he had any inkling—"

"He knows."

"You told him?"

"Not in so many words. I didn't have to. But that's not the worst of it. He…."

Comprehension dawned, leaving her mother temporarily at a loss, but she recovered quickly. "Oh, my stars! Ava, are you trying to tell me he returns your feelings?"

"He's…intimated as much. Or if not that exactly, then he's made it pretty clear he's never been serious about Deenie."

"But that can't be true! Gail Manville as good as told me he's giving Deenie an engagement ring for Christmas!" She shook her head, bewildered. "This isn't like you, Ava. I know how much you hope to marry and have children someday, but you're not a teenager anymore. You're twenty-eight years old, widely traveled, an expert in your field of nursing."

"None of which exactly qualifies me for the young-and-foolish category, and certainly doesn't excuse my stealing another woman's man. I know, Mom. You don't have to hammer the point home. But it doesn't change what I feel."

"Which is pure infatuation. The kind of love a marriage is built on doesn't strike out of the blue like this."

"It did with you and Dad. You've said so many a time."

"So I have." Her mother's shoulders sagged in defeat. "If Gail gets wind of this," she said mournfully, "she'll string you up by the thumbs! She confided to me only last night that she's hopeful there'll be wedding bells for Deenie and Leo by Easter."

"I'm more concerned about how Deenie might react. You know how close we've always been, and this is killing me. If I'd had any idea...."

But how could she have known that she would indeed love Leo—not, as Deenie had presumed, in a sisterly way, but with all the passion and depth and longing of a woman who'd long outgrown her schoolgirl crush? How could she have known the realization would strike her the minute she laid eyes on him at the airport? That all the time she'd been roaming the world hoping to meet Mr. Right, he'd been waiting on her back doorstep at home? How could she have known she'd be so susceptible to him?

"I wish I'd stayed away," she said miserably. "I wish the pair of them would just disappear in a puff of smoke. At least then, I wouldn't be torn in half like this."

"If he's telling you the truth and Deenie's misunderstood his intentions—and I have to say, Ava, Leo's never struck me as a man who'd lie about anything, let alone something as serious as this—*wishing* isn't going to change a thing. You have to deal with what *is*."

"And how do I do that, Mom? How do I justify getting involved with him, if he ends things with Deenie? What sort of friend does that make me?"

"Well...." Her mother looked past Ava and scanned the room at large as she debated the question. But whatever advice she'd been about to offer suddenly shifted direction as her gaze settled on something beyond Ava's view. Face creased with dismay, she leaned forward and said urgently, "Oh dear! Better put this conversation on hold for now and paste a smile on your face, honey. Deenie just walked in the door with those two dancer friends of hers, and they're headed this way. One look at you, and she'll know there's trouble in the air, and this is certainly not the time or the place to air it."

Setting an example, her mother beamed brightly as the trio came abreast with the table. "Hello! How nice to see you again, Mr. and Mrs. Markov, and what a coincidence, running into you here, of all places."

"Not really. I phoned your house and Mr. Sorensen told me where you were meeting for lunch." All smiles, Deenie slung an exuberant arm around Ava's shoulder. "Listen, there's been a change of plan. Lynette and Paul are catching the four-thirty flight out of Skellington this afternoon, so I'm taking them on a bit of a sightseeing tour of Owen's Lake before they leave. We've got a limo waiting outside and—''

''I quite understand,'' Ava said, a huge wave of relief washing over her. ''Please don't worry about canceling the shopping trip. It can wait until another day.''

''Who said anything about canceling?'' Deenie trilled. ''Of course we'll still go shopping! Just not as early as we planned, that's all, because I've also made an appointment to see a house I'm thinking of renting—I need a place with a room I can set aside as a dance studio, you see,'' she said coyly, ''and Leo's apartment isn't nearly big enough.''

''No,'' Ava's mother murmured, in the awkward pause following that remark. ''I can see that it wouldn't be.''

''Exactly!'' Deenie bathed Ava in a winning smile. ''So instead of meeting me at the boutique, I wonder if you'd mind picking me up at the rental property, instead?'' She pulled a slip of paper out of her purse. ''Here's the address. It's out at the far end of Lakeshore Drive and since that's on the Skellington side of town, we'll wind up our tour there, and the limo driver can drop me off before he heads out to the airport with Lynette and Paul.''

Ava hesitated, wishing she could come up with a

very good reason to refuse. She didn't want to spend time alone with Deenie. She particularly didn't want to look at a house Deenie implied she'd be sharing with Leo.

Seeing her reluctance, Deenie produced another dazzling smile. "Pretty please?" she wheedled. "Say in about an hour and a half? That'll still give you time to enjoy a nice long lunch with your mom."

How could she refuse without seeming churlish, or worse yet, arousing Deenie's suspicions?

CHAPTER SEVEN

IT TOOK longer than she expected for Ava to find the property. Located in a cul-de-sac and hidden from the road by a dense hedge, the house had been built at the turn of the twentieth century by one of the well-to-do families who'd settled the area.

There was no sign of the limousine, but a car she assumed belonged to the leasing agent stood parked at the front door. *Probably the Markovs have left already,* she surmised, ringing the old-fashioned pull bell, *and Deenie's inside, inspecting the rooms.*

But to her utter consternation, Leo answered the door. And from the grimace which passed over his face, not to mention his decidedly hostile greeting, he was no more pleased to see her than she was to see him. "What the devil do you want, Ava?"

"I came to pick up Deenie."

"Well, she's not here, and I ought to know. I've been hanging around for nearly half an hour, waiting for her to show up."

"You?" Ava said disbelievingly. "She's supposed to be meeting the agent showing this house."

"Bull!" he shot back. "She asked me to pick up the keys and meet her here because she wanted me to look over the lease before she signed anything."

More of Deenie's games? Ava wondered, dragging her gaze away from Leo who looked good enough to eat in a very lawyerly grey suit and dark tie, and staring instead at the snow-draped shrubs edging the garden. Or was she being unfair? Now that she thought about it, Deenie never had actually said she was meeting the leasing agent, merely that she'd made an appointment to see the house.

"Well?" Leo said, as the silence between them lengthened. "Cat got your tongue, all of a sudden, darlin'? Aren't you going to accuse me of some dastardly plot to get you and her in some hidden, out-of-the-way spot, and indulge in a three-way orgy?"

"No," she snapped, feeling a flush ride over her face. "I'm wondering why you're not driving your own car."

"Because it's in for servicing and this one's a loaner. Any other questions riding around in that suspicious little mind of yours?"

"No," she said again, feeling more of a fool with every second that passed.

"Then perhaps you'd tell me why Deenie needed you to pick her up, instead of driving herself here in the first place."

"She took her ballet friends on a limo tour of town and was supposed to be dropped off here before the driver took them to the airport." She shrugged. "I guess they're running a bit late."

He scowled, his displeasure mounting. "What next, for Pete's sake?"

"Well, don't take your frustration out on me!" Ava shot back, her own temper more than a little frayed around the edges. "I'm just catering to the diva's wishes, but since you're here anyway, *you* can drive her back to town. And tell her I'm not going shopping for dresses, either, while you're at it!"

The sparking anger in his blue eyes softened slightly. "Oh, what the hell! Now you've driven all this way, you might as well come in and take a look around. I've only walked through the downstairs rooms so far, but it's enough for me to see it's quite a show-place. Come on, Ava," he coaxed, when she shook her head and turned away. "Let's at least try to behave like the mature adults we're supposed to be."

Would she have acquiesced so easily, had the request come from any other man? Would her heart have leaped so erratically when he caught her arm and said with a rueful smile, "Hey, I'm sorry. I know none of this is your fault."

Of course she wouldn't! But it wasn't any other man; it was Leo. And that being the case, her resentment melted like butter left out in the hot desert sun. Defeated, she allowed him to draw her over the threshold and relieve her of her heavy coat.

The entrance hall was magnificent. Graced by a

branched staircase of mellow oak, it could well do double duty as a small ballroom, and her first thought was that Deenie would be in her element playing hostess in such a setting.

Leo's mind ran along a different track, though. "I bet those banisters have known more than their share of kids sliding down them," he remarked. "This place was made for a large family. You ever thought about having children, Ava?"

"Um..." She gulped, unnerved by the question. Having babies wasn't something she could discuss composedly with Leo Ferrante.

Appearing not to notice her discomposure, he cupped her elbow and steered her toward a door on the right. "This is the dining room. See what I mean? You could seat twenty people around that table, and still have room to spare."

"Does the place come furnished?" she babbled, desperate to change the subject.

"It's one of the options in the lease."

She ran a finger over the glossy surface of a rosewood sideboard. "That's convenient for Deenie."

"I guess." He raised his shoulders in a mystified shrug. "But I can't see why she'd be interested in a place this size unless she plans to start her own dance school."

"Actually, there is supposed to be a room somewhere which would do as a studio."

Leo scanned the sheaf of papers in the folder he

carried. "Must be the games room over the garage, then. Says here it's thirty feet by twenty. Let's go take a look—unless you want to see the kitchen first? It's quoted as being 'a gourmet affair, recently updated with top-of-the-line appliances.'"

"No," she said. "I don't want to see the kitchen."

He shrugged again. "Why not? Isn't it supposed to be the heart of every home?"

Don't talk to me about heart! she wanted to cry. *Mine's aching too much already. If things were different, you and I might have been looking at this house with the idea of us living here together and planning where we'd put the Christmas tree next year, and where we'd hang the stockings when the babies came along. Then, of course I'd want to see if the refrigerator's big enough, and if there's counter space enough for me to roll out cookie dough, and which room we'd use as a nursery!*

But the confusion and mistrust brought about by the last few days was such that the only thing she'd likely be tempted to do in the kitchen was stick her head in the oven!

"I wonder what's keeping Deenie," she said, peering out of the stained-glass window next to the front door.

"Who knows? She enjoys being fashionably late. On the other hand, given her mood swings lately, it's just as likely she's changed her mind altogether about renting the place and not bothered to let us know.'' He slapped the folder closed and threw it down on the table. ''Let's check out this room she's interested in, and if you don't think it'll serve the purpose, we might as well lock up and leave. I don't know about you, but I've got better things to do than waste what's left of the afternoon hanging around here.''

He loped up the stairs, leaving her hard-pressed to keep up with him, and had thrown open a door on the left by the time she reached the landing.

''Well, will you take a look at this bedroom!'' he said, giving a low whistle of appreciation.

''You take a look,'' she told him shortly. ''I'm only interested in the games room.''

Clearly baffled by her attitude, he gestured to a wide, paned window running the width of the landing. ''You'll be telling me next you're not impressed with the view, either. What's the matter, Ava? Isn't this your kind of house?''

It was so much her kind of house, it hurt! The late-afternoon sun bathed the old stone exterior in pale golden light and turned the ice-covered lake into a dazzling opalescence. The high ceilings, the airy, gracious rooms visible through other open doors farther down the upper hall, the deep carved moldings and smooth oak floors—they called out to her so urgently, she could have wept.

''What does it matter?'' she cried. ''I'm not the

one who'll be living here! Stop quizzing me at every turn, Leo. What I think is irrelevant.''

''Not to me,'' he said quietly, reaching for her. ''I've tried telling myself what you think isn't important and I don't need the complications you've brought into my life, but despite what I said last night about not bothering you again, I'm having a hard time sticking to it.''

That great, beautiful house teemed with the ghosts of former couples who'd loved and lived under its roof. The echo of past laughter, the deep and measured breathing of shared passion between a husband and wife, the sound of a mother crooning to her baby, haunted the air. They pulled at Ava, drawing her into Leo's arms as if trying to tell her she belonged with him, and that *they* were the ones to inherit that legacy of joy.

''Don't!'' she begged feebly, feeling herself drowning in the searching intensity of his gaze.

''I can't help myself,'' he said, his mouth cruising over her eyelids, her cheekbones and along her jaw until it found her lips.

No man should be able to kiss with such mastery—like an angel, able to make a woman lose all sense of self-preservation and live only for the rapture of the moment. Like a devil, wielding such unholy power that she uttered inarticulate little sounds of surrender deep in her throat when, all the time, she knew she should be giving vent to outrage.

He was taking unpardonable liberties. Persuading her with a suggestive nudge of his hips to move into the seclusion of the big bedroom with him and then, when he'd succeeded, inching the door closed so that they wouldn't be discovered. Cushioning her between him and the wall, and leaving her half blind with desire at the pressing, urgent weight of him.

His hands skimmed down her throat. Brushed fleetingly at her breasts, just enough to arouse her nipples to tingling awareness—but not nearly to satisfy it. Paused at her hips to raise the hem of her sweater and then, with stunning audacity, pulled her satin camisole free from the top of her skirt.

He touched her waist, lightly, beguilingly. Awoke a thousand sensory pinpoints of pleasure on her exposed skin. "Come with me," he said, his words caught between a plea and a groan. "Let me take you away from here to somewhere quiet and undisturbed by all the insanity coming between us...to someplace where we can confront our feelings for one another openly. Stop fighting the inevitable, Ava."

She yearned to agree. Felt the tug of physical longing join forces with her surging emotions—a potent combination beside which conscience and integrity struggled to survive.

"Hang Deenie out to dry, you mean?" she managed, her heart breaking.

"Leave Deenie out of this," he said, cradling her

waist in both his hands. "Do you really think that throwing her name into the mix is going to make me forget what it's like to hold you in my arms, or kiss you and feel you respond to my touch? Will it make *you* forget?"

"No. But she believes—"

He shook her; not roughly, or ungently, but with a desperate urgency. "Listen to me, Ava! It doesn't matter what she believes! I *don't care* what she believes!"

"How can you say that?" she cried softly. "Don't you love her at all?"

"No," he said.

"She thinks she loves you."

He closed his eyes. "I doubt that that's true. But even if it is, I don't return her feelings. I'm sorry if that sounds harsh and unfeeling, but you're smart enough to know that love's not something any of us can dish out on command. We love because we can't help ourselves."

"Stop trying to confuse the issue!"

"I'm not. I'm trying to confront it head-on." He cupped her chin and forced her to meet his troubled gaze. "You love your parents, I love mine, and we both love our work. But we both know that what we feel for one another is a whole world removed from those other loves. They're safe, comfortable. This isn't. It's wild and greedy and overwhelming. And ignoring it isn't going to make it go away. So tell me, Ava, what do I have to do to make you face up to that?''

She tore herself away from him and backed toward the door. ''There's nothing you can do,'' she said. ''The only person who can alter the outcome of events in a way that I'd ever find acceptable is Deenie herself. As long as she wants you—or thinks she does—you're off limits. So don't come near me again. I don't want to be alone with you. I don't want you smiling at me, or talking to me in private, or making knowing eye contact. And most of all I don't want you touching me. I'm hurting enough already.''

CHAPTER EIGHT

FRUSTRATED, Leo stared around the room. Judging from its size and furnishings, it had to be the master suite. Set at right angles to the window, so that its occupants could look out at the lake, stood a great big bed. The kind where, in the old days, mothers gave birth, then leaned against the headboard and nursed their babies.

In his mind's eye, Leo could see Ava there, his child at her breast, her lovely face flushed and tender, her dark hair spilling over one shoulder. But day-dreaming about it wasn't enough to make it happen. More positive action was called for, a point Ethel had driven home with her customary bluntness when he'd taken her out for lunch that day.

"When are you going to do something about that sweet gal?" she'd wanted to know.

"I assume you're referring to Ava," he said blandly, just speaking her name enough to remind him of the black satin creation she'd worn the night before. Of how it had slipped through his fingers like cool spring water—and how later, in the small hours, he'd dreamed of stripping it off her and woken in a fine state of arousal.

"Of course. Why would I waste breath on that

other creature? The only thing she needs is a good slap on the behind, but I doubt her father has the *cajones* for the task. And quite frankly, boy, I'll be wondering about yours if you continue evading the subject like this. You're clearly so smitten with Ava that I fail to understand why you don't come straight out and tell the obnoxious Deenie to take a hike, instead of pandering to her neurotic need to be the centre of attention all the time."

"Deenie's an *artiste*. It's the nature of the beast to enjoy the spotlight, on top of which she's in a pretty fragile state right now."

"Fragile, my hind foot! She's self-centred, shallow, and utterly oblivious to the feelings of the people around her. If she weren't, she'd see that you and Ava were made for one another, and do everything in her power to bring you together, instead of preying on your time and attention like a black widow spider."

"That's a bit harsh, surely?"

"I don't think so!" She'd snorted with disapproval and drained her martini. "Take this business of dragging you out to some house this afternoon to look over a lease when you've got a perfectly good office in which to conduct business, and she could just as easily have come there. She's up to something, Leo, and if you can't see that, you're not the man I always took you to be."

"Regardless of what you think of my testosterone

levels, duchess,'' he'd said mildly, ''I do know how and when to take a stand. I also know when to back off—and Ava made it pretty clear last night that she doesn't welcome my advances.''

Sure she had! And he'd assured her he'd received the message. But all that had gone by the board when he'd found himself alone in this room with her. In fact, if it had been up to him, he'd probably have had her underneath him on that bed and made thorough and complete love to her, and never mind who might come in through the front door at any given moment!

Deenie's voice, sharp and petulant outside on the landing, yanked him out of idyllic introspection and back to irritating reality with a jolt. ''Why are you lurking around up here, Ava, and where's Leo?''

''Right behind you,'' he said, stepping out of the bedroom to find Deenie and her friends clustered on the landing. ''Is there a problem?''

Ava, looking stricken, hovered at the top of the stairs. Upon seeing him though, Deenie was suddenly all sunny smiles. ''Hello, darling!'' she cooed, rushing up to hug him. ''Sorry we're a bit late, but the Vancouver flight has been delayed an hour, so we took a little detour!''

Despite his attempt to shrug her off, she latched on to him like a barnacle. *Oh, cripes!* he thought, recognizing her overly demonstrative response with sinking dismay. *She's on-stage again, right down to the melodramatic 'darling'!*

Ava had noticed, too, but with a different interpretation. He saw the flash of pain she couldn't hide; the brief but telling glance of mistrust she leveled at him before averting her gaze. "I'll wait for you in the car," she told Deenie, and went swiftly down the stairs, her spine poker-straight.

"Sure." Deenie waved her away as if she were of no more importance than a gnat. "Leo, darling, tell me what you think of the house."

Wrenching his gaze from Ava's departing back, he said, "It's far too big for what you—"

"Perhaps. But would you be willing to pay the rent they're asking for it?"

"I'm not the one—"

Once again, she interrupted him. "I know what you're going to say. It's up to me to decide, but you're the one with the lease." She fluttered over to her friends. "Isn't he adorable? Do you know any other man who'd be so accommodating? So sensitive to my needs?"

Resenting the implied intimacy of her remarks, he said abruptly, "I want to have a word in private with you, Deenie. There are a few things we need to get straight."

He must have looked as grim as he felt because she spun around like a wind-up china doll, ushered the Markovs toward the stairs, and exclaimed, "My goodness, I had no idea how late it is! Say goodbye to Lynette and Paul, Leo darling. It's time they were on their way.''

"Indeed," he said, and would have offered his hand if she'd allowed him to get within spitting distance of the couple. "Safe journey, both of you, and good luck with your upcoming tour. Deenie, I'll wait for you downstairs.''

She waggled her fingers in acknowledgement and hurried the Markovs away. He waited until they'd gone, then went back for a last regretful look around the bedroom. Yeah, he could definitely see himself living here with Ava. After thirty-seven years, carefree bachelorhood had lost its charm, big time! All he had to do was convince her of it.

He heard a car door slam closed and the purr of a departing engine. And then, immediately after, another car leaving. *So, she's sent Ava on her way, too,* he thought, heading downstairs. *Just as well! By the time I've had my long-overdue say, Miss Deenie isn't going to be fit company for anyone.*

He'd returned to the dining room, picked up the key where he'd left it next to his briefcase, and stowed the lease before it occurred to him that Deenie was taking a hell of a long time to come back inside and face the music. Pacing to the entrance hall, he pulled open the front door and looked out.

The driveway was empty. The little witch had left with Ava!

"You've been had again, you dumb schmo!" he growled, smacking his forehead with the heel of his hand.

He should have known better than to think she'd play straight with him. She didn't know the meaning of the term!

"Leo seemed awfully crabby just now," Deenie remarked, as they drove away. "Did something happen between the two of you before I showed up?"

"Happen?" Ava felt the blood drain from her face and pool weakly around her ankles. "Happen how?"

"I don't know. A disagreement, perhaps? Did you tell him you hated the house, or something?"

"I loved the house," she said, grateful that on that subject at least, she could speak freely. "I think it's gorgeous."

"Oh, Ava!" Deenie chortled. "Despite that smart cosmopolitan veneer you've acquired, you're still just a small-town girl at heart. You'd probably be quite happy to settle down and spend the rest of your life in Owen's Lake if nothing better presented itself."

"I don't know why that strikes you as so amusing, given that it's exactly what you're proposing to do," she retorted.

"But I'm not," Deenie said. "Not really. I was just playing a little game."

"For whose benefit?"

"Well, whose do you think? For mine, of course!"

"Why, Deenie?"

The question, uttered as it was in a tone laced with reproof, would have been enough to spark indignation in the old Deenie. But this new, secretive incarnation merely said, "For reasons you can't begin to understand, Ava, and which I can't begin to explain."

"Then a lot's changed between us, because we never had a problem communicating in the past. Half the time, we both knew what the other was thinking or feeling without a word being spoken. But now...." Ava tightened her grip on the steering wheel, a very real regret coursing through her. "We're like strangers, Deenie. Something's been out of whack between us ever since I got home. And it makes me very sad."

"Perhaps it's because I'm not the only one with secrets," Deenie said darkly. "You're keeping a few of your own, and don't think I haven't noticed."

Stunned, Ava sputtered, "I don't know what you think you've noticed!"

"You've got man trouble, Ava, and don't bother denying it because I recognize the signs only too well. Yet I don't hear you confiding in me. If our being open and honest is all that important, why are you being so reticent? Are you ashamed of him?''

Without stopping to think how she might be incriminating herself needlessly, Ava blurted out, "No! That's not it at all!"

"Is he married, then? Are you having an affair with someone else's husband?"

Perspiration needled her skin. "No," she said again, but this time with a lot less conviction.

"Then it must be unrequited love." Deenie patted her knee with empty sympathy. "I've been there, too, kiddo. It's no fun, is it? But the way you get over it is to dive into an affair with another man and flaunt it in the bastard's face. Make him sorry he passed you up for someone else."

"In other words, use one man to punish another?" Ava shuddered inwardly. "When did you become so cynical and unfeeling, Deenie?"

"When I realized that if I don't look out for myself, no one else will. Pull over into that parking spot, why don't you? The boutique's only half a block away."

"If it's all the same to you, I'm going to pass on the shopping. I lost my enthusiasm for trying on dresses. In fact, I doubt I'll even bother going to the club on New Year's Eve."

"Good heavens, you really are out of sorts, aren't you? No matter. Just drop me off at the door—I'll be fine on my own—and we'll get together…well, let's see." She dug in her bag for her diary and flipped open the pages. "Tomorrow's Christmas Eve and I'm pretty much tied up all day, then the twenty-fifth's set aside for all the relatives, so probably not before the twenty-sixth or -seventh. I guess the gift exchanging will have to wait until then."

Ava slid the car to a stop outside the dress shop, let her passenger out, and pulled away before Deenie changed her mind again.

She should have been disappointed. After all, spending time with Deenie had been high on her agenda when she'd first arranged to come home. But things had changed in the days since, and all Ava could think now was, *Two whole days of not having to deal with you or Leo? Well, hallelujah! Maybe Christmas won't be such a wash-out, after all.*

The snow began again late in the afternoon of the twenty-fourth. Ava, listening to carols on the radio as she helped prepare the bouillabaisse her mother traditionally served for Christmas Eve dinner, didn't hear the doorbell ring and was caught totally off guard when her father pushed open the swing door to the kitchen and announced, "You've got a visitor, Ava. It's Leo. You want to see him in here?"

"Of course she doesn't," her mother scoffed, sending her a knowing glance. "For heaven's sake, Gary, show the man into the living room and pour him a drink."

"Why's he here at all?" Ava said in an under-tone, when her father had gone.

"Only one way to find out." Her mother pushed her aside and took over the stirring of the stew. "Off you go, honey. Whatever this is about, I'm sure you'll find a way to deal with it."

If only! But good intentions and firm resolve were no match for her thudding sweep of reaction at the sight of Leo standing deep in thought before the fire. He wore navy cords and shirt, with an off-white sweater—a casual, ordinary combination which on any other man would have been unremarkable.

"Ordinary" and "unremarkable" didn't belong in Leo Ferrante's world, though. He looked...he looked....

She swallowed in an effort to unglue her tongue from the roof of her mouth. He looked sleek and tantalizing and utterly irresistible. Even his thick grey socks—he must have left his boots at the front door, she decided, staring at his feet because it was a lot safer than looking at that superbly molded face—were sexy.

"Hi," he said, his husky baritone overriding the background sound of the carols drifting from the speakers at the base of the tree. "Thanks for seeing me."

"I'd have preferred not to," she said.

"I know. You made your feelings about me very clear yesterday."

She raised her eyes and found him watching her. His gaze was sombre, his mouth unsmiling. He was, she thought on a painful breath, the most beautiful man she'd ever seen, and the most troubled. "Then why are you here?"

"Because I want you to hear it from me that before any more misunderstandings or assumptions occur, I intend to make it abundantly clear to Deenie that she and I are nothing but platonic friends. And if spelling it out plainly puts an end to the friendship, I can live with that, and she'll have to, as well. I've tried to be patient with her erratic behaviour and put the most charitable interpretation on it, but enough's enough."

From the speakers, a children's choir caroled "Joy to the World!" And for a brief, uncharitable second, joy did indeed possess Ava. It sprinted through her blood, then died just as quickly as the import of his words hit home. "Oh!" she exclaimed softly. "Oh, poor Deenie! After everything she's been telling people, she'll be so humiliated!"

"Poor Deenie nothing!" he countered. "Her willful distortion of the facts has gone on too long and caused enough trouble. It has to come to an end."

"I suppose it does," she said. "But why are you telling *me* all this?"

"Because I also want to make it clear that this has nothing to do with you or what might have been between you and me. You should feel no guilt or responsibility for any of it.''

In other words, *Don't leap to the conclusion that with her out of my life, I'll be inviting you into it.* ''Then why bother telling me at all?''

''Because you're probably the person she'll turn to, and I felt it only fair that you be prepared ahead of time to cope with her. You know how she is. Most of the time, her actions and reactions are over the top. I don't flatter myself that she'll be heartbroken when I clear the air with her, but she'll probably feel she must act as if she is.'' He gave a rueful smile. ''We both know drama is right up her alley— the tragic princess, and all that.''

''On stage, perhaps,'' Ava said sharply. ''But don't assume her emotions are quite that shallow in real life.''

''I'm not. All I'm saying is that they never went very deep with me in the first place. I was a convenient understudy: a stop-gap solution to a problem I suspect she's still not willing to address. In any event, please don't let yourself get carried away with guilt if she cries on your shoulder. As I said at the start, you play no part in any of this. *None at all.* So go ahead with a clear conscience and be the good friend to her you've always been.''

''When do you intend to speak to her?''

''Tonight, I hope.''

"*On Christmas Eve?* Couldn't you have timed it a bit better than that?"

Clearly exasperated, he said, "I've tried. I asked her to stay behind at the house yesterday and she took off with you. I tried to see her last night, but she begged off, claiming she wasn't feeling well. And today she's pulled a complete disappearing act. Her parents claim they have no idea where she's gone or when she'll be back. If it weren't contrary to everything she's said and done lately, I'd think she was deliberately trying to avoid me."

In other words, more of Deenie's erratic behaviour. "Well, she hasn't confided in me, if that's what you're wondering. But if she does get in touch, I'll let her know you're looking for her." Ava regarded him expectantly, wishing he'd leave, and at the same time loath to see him go. "Is that all you came for?"

"That, and to say goodbye in case I don't see you again before you head back overseas. When do you leave?"

"January the fourth."

He scanned the room, taking in the brass bowl of holly and clove-stuffed oranges on the coffee table, the cedar swag draping the mantelpiece, the Noble fir standing tall and proud in the window alcove. And finally, reluctantly, brought his gaze to bear on her. "How much longer do you plan to be away?"

"My present contract expires in March, but I've

been offered a promotion which would keep me there another two years.''

"Will you accept it?"

"Probably," she said, dreadfully afraid he'd see how close to tears she was. It didn't help any that "Chestnuts Roasting on an Open Fire" happened to segue into "Winter World of Love" just then, filling the room with nostalgia and foolish notions of romance. "There's nothing to bring me back here in a hurry."

"There's your family."

"Oh, I'll visit. Often."

"Maybe we'll run into each other the next time you're here, then."

"It's possible."

"Ava—"

"I think you should go, Leo," she said. "I really don't see that we have anything further to say to one another."

But he wasn't done torturing her quite yet. Reaching into the pocket of the jacket he'd thrown over the arm of the sofa, he pulled out a small box wrapped in gold paper. "I have something for you."

"I don't want it," she said, her throat swelling with emotion. "Please, Leo, just go. Leave me alone. You've done enough."

"It's nothing much, a token of friendship, that's all. Something to remind you of Christmas back home when you're baking under the hot desert sun next year at this time.''

There it was again, that word ''friendship'' which could mean everything—but in this case meant not nearly enough.

He held out the gift. Came closer.

But she shied away, her composure so fragile she could almost hear it splintering.

Accepting her rejection, he shrugged and placed the package on top of the others already stacked under the tree. ''Just in case you change your mind,'' he said, then turned and left.

CHAPTER NINE

AVA couldn't face attending Christmas Eve service at Saint Martha's in her present mood, not when she knew that everyone on the street would be there, including Leo. So as soon as her parents left for the church, she changed out of her silk-wool dress into warm slacks and a sweater, borrowed her mother's down-filled jacket, and took Jason for a walk along the lakefront. The overcast sky had cleared somewhat, reducing the snow to an occasional flurry and allowing glimpses of moonlight to flit between ragged streamers of cloud. The air had an unmistakably northern bite to it, sharp and pine-scented.

This was Owen's Lake as she'd always known it, the place where she'd always thought she belonged. This was Christmas, pristine and perfect, just as she yearned to experience it when she was thousands of miles away and living in a culture which didn't recognize the traditional celebrations she'd grown up with. And she could hardly wait to get away from both!

I hate you, Leo Ferrante! she thought balefully, as she passed the big white house where he'd grown up. *You've spoilt everything that mattered to me. Home, the holidays, and my friendship with Deenie.*

But he hadn't done it alone, and that was what grieved her the most. She'd been his accomplice, every step of the way, as much the instrument of her present misery as he was. More so, really. Because he couldn't have taken over her heart so easily if she hadn't let him in to begin with.

A few yards farther along the curving path and just as she drew level with the Manville home, she heard a sound.

"Psst!"

Startled, she glanced up and saw nothing but the pale gleam of moonlight on the picket fence running along the bottom of the garden. The house itself was in darkness, except for the winking lights strung along the back porch and one window on the upper floor.

Deciding her imagination was playing tricks on her she hauled Jason up short on his leash and was about to turn back the way she'd come when a shadow, blacker than the rest, emerged from the bulk of the neighboring hedge. "Psst! Ava!"

"Deenie?" she exclaimed, recognizing the voice. "What on earth are you doing?"

"Waiting for you. I saw you coming along the lakefront."

"So you thought you'd hide out in the bushes to ambush me? Aren't you a bit past the age for playing such games?"

"I don't want anyone to know I'm here." As if

that wasn't already clear enough, she tugged Ava into the shelter of the hedge. "Listen, something's happened, I need a really, really big favour from you, and I don't have much time to talk about it."

"What is it?" Ava asked warily, wondering if Leo had dropped his bombshell.

But, far from sounding or acting as if she'd just received a dressing-down, Deenie seemed charged with restless energy and a brittle kind of excitement. Casting a furtive glance over her shoulder, she plucked again at the sleeve of Ava's jacket and said, "Can we go back to your place? No one will think of looking for me there."

Not waiting for a reply, much less agreement, she followed up the question by towing Ava and Jason along with her as she scurried like a hunted rabbit over the snow-packed path to the Sorensens'.

Only when she was safely ensconced in Ava's room, with the door locked and the blinds drawn, would she elaborate further. "Brace yourself, girlfriend," she began, curling up at one end of the bed, the way she used to when they were teenagers trading adolescent secrets. "What I'm about to tell you is going to come as a bit of a blow. I'm running off to get married."

"No, you're not," Ava said flatly. "I already spoke to Leo. I know he's not in love with you."

"Leo?" Deenie's eyes grew wide with astonishment. "What's he got to do with any of this?"

''Nothing. That's my whole point.''

''But I didn't say I was marrying *him,* silly!'' Her face lit up in a dazzling smile and she hugged herself in unfeigned delight. ''Oh, Ava, the most incredible, wonderful thing has happened! Marcus and I are together again. He phoned me yesterday afternoon from La Guardia to tell me he was catching the red-eye to Denver, and from there to Vancouver, and that he'd be landing at Skellington Airport at eleven-forty this morning.''

''So that's where you were!''

''Huh?''

''You disappeared without a word to anyone, Deenie. Your parents were worried.''

''They'd have been more worried if they'd known what I was up to! My mother's going to throw a hissy fit when she finds out I'm marrying Marcus. She doesn't think male dancers make good husband material.''

''I see. So what's this huge favour you want of me?''

''Well, we're eloping tonight. We'll fly to Las Vegas to get married, then join the rest of the company in Chile next week.'' She grasped Ava's hands in the first show of genuine delight since their reunion. ''We're going to be partners again, in every sense of the word. As soon as the company doctor gives me the all-clear on my ankle, we'll be dancing together again—but as man and wife this time.''

"And?"

"And I want you to explain to my parents. You'll do it so much better than I will."

Ava let out a squeak of stunned laughter. "You must be joking!"

"No," Deenie said in an injured tone. "I've never been more serious. Look, Ava, this isn't a decision I've made on the spur of the moment. Marcus and I have been in touch constantly over the last week or so. Remember the night of the dinner party, when you came looking for me in my bedroom? I'd been on the phone with him then."

"What I remember is that I found you in tears."

"Because he'd been phoning nearly every day, begging me to come back to him, but never once offering me the kind of commitment I wanted, and I was afraid he never would."

"So you used Leo as a bargaining chip?" Try though she might, Ava couldn't mask her dismay.

"No more than he used me—perhaps not as a 'bargaining chip' as you so quaintly put it, but certainly as a diversion to relieve the boredom of being laid up with a bad back for so long."

"And the Markovs?"

She made a face. "Okay, so I used them, too."

"And that whole business of looking at the house yesterday was just another part of the plan? You conned Leo into meeting you there, then showed up with people you knew would run to Marcus with the tale of how you were on the brink of setting up house?''

"What do you want me to say? I'm used to giving a convincing performance."

"You're a brat, Deenie, and I'm furious with myself for having let you string me along like this."

"Well, there wouldn't have been much point in putting on an act if I went around telling people that's all it was, now would there?"

"Rationalize your behaviour any way you like. My answer remains the same regardless. I absolutely will not act as the go-between here. You'll have to tell your parents the truth yourself."

"I can't. My mother will weep copious tears and my father will look as if I've driven a stake through his heart. But you've always been so good with words and with people's feelings, Ava. It's why you make such a fabulous nurse."

"Buttering me up isn't going to work, Deenie. I won't do it, and you have no right asking me to. For once in your life, you're going to have to clean up your own mess."

"Perhaps," Deenie said, a distinct chill entering her voice, "I haven't made my position clear. My lover—my *true love*—is waiting for me in the departure lounge at Skellington Airport. I came too close to losing him once already. I don't intend to risk having it happen again by missing our flight."

"If he was half the man you think he is, he

wouldn't be lurking in the next town and letting you face this alone. If he really loved you—''

''The way you love Leo, Ava?'' Deenie's eyes narrowed. ''Oh, please! Spare me the naïve, wide-eyed stare! Do you think I haven't noticed the way you are around him, circling like some timid animal afraid to get too close, and either blushing like a rose every time he looks at you, or practically falling into a dead faint?''

''You always did have a vivid imagination, Deenie,'' Ava retorted, feeling the betraying blood surge into her cheeks.

''And you always were a rotten liar, though why you feel you have to fib to me I can't imagine. Listen, maybe you care about him, and maybe you don't. That isn't the real issue, is it? What matters is that you and I have been friends for too long to let anything or anyone come between us. So please, do this one thing for me and I'll never ask you for another favour as long as I live.''

''No.''

Deenie studied her in silence for a moment, then said, ''I really hate it when you get that look on your face. You're not going to budge, are you?''

''No.''

''Not even if I grovel?''

''No.''

''I half expected you might take this attitude.'' She sighed and pulled an envelope out of her bag.

"Will you at least give them this, then? Tomorrow, after I'm gone?"

"No." She was tired of being put in the middle. Tired of trying to accommodate everybody else at the expense of her own sense of decency.

"It's just a letter explaining—"

"I don't care. Give it to them yourself. They're your parents, for pity's sake! Show them some consideration—some compassion."

"Good grief, whatever made me think I could count on you?" Deenie flounced off the bed and planted her fists on her hips. "You've changed, Ava. All that desert air has dried up your sweet nature and left you miserable as an old prune."

"I'm sorry if I disappoint you," Ava said, sadly. "But the truth is, we've both changed. Our values are different. We want different things out of life."

Deenie glared at her a moment, then burst out crying. "I know," she sobbed, flinging herself into Ava's arms and hugging her fiercely, "and I can't stand it. But I can't help who I am, either. I'd find living in this town about as interesting as watching paint dry. But Marcus and I are two of a kind. We belong on a wider world stage. So please be happy that we've finally found our way back to each other."

"If he really is the right man for you, then I am," Ava said, returning the hug before asking, "As a matter of interest, does Leo know about any of this?''

''Oh yes!'' Deenie rolled her eyes in mock dismay. ''I told him this evening after he collared me just before dinner and read me the riot act for letting people think our relationship amounted to more than it really was. He can be a real pain when he puts his mind to it, spouting off about moral integrity and such. Why do you ask?''

''I just wondered.'' *Wondered if he'd followed through on his decision to speak up, or if he'd slithered out from under the responsibility when he learned Deenie had set her sights on someone else and thereby spared him the aggravation of having to play the heavy.*

''He's much more your type than he is mine, you know.''

''Perhaps.'' Ava steered her to the door. ''Listen, Deenie, the church service must be just about over. Go home and wait for your parents and do the decent thing. You've got plenty of time before you need to leave for the airport.''

''I suppose you're right.'' She scrubbed at her face and pulled on her coat. ''We'll be in touch?''

''Of course.''

But it was a bittersweet goodbye, even though neither of them came right out and said so. Because they both knew things would never again be the same between them. Too much deception had eroded the openness and trust which formed the cornerstone of their friendship.

Christmas Day passed quietly. Word that Deenie had eloped with her dance partner percolated through the neighbourhood and added a little extra spice to the roast turkey and plum pudding. Her mother threw the predicted hissy fit and her father hid in the solarium with his orchids.

"Would you be terribly disappointed if I went away for a few days?" Ava asked her parents, after dinner that night.

"Not a bit," her mother said. She'd seen the unopened gift from Leo still sitting under the tree. "We understand perfectly."

"Your mother might," her father declared, "but I don't. Where would you go?"

"I'd like to drive up to Topaz Valley Resort and do some skiing."

"On your own?" Her father didn't look impressed. "Doesn't sound very exciting to me, spending Christmas with strangers."

Nor to me, Ava thought miserably. *But it beats hoping Leo will show up at the front door, vow his undying love, and ride off into the winter sunset with me thrown over his shoulder—something which clearly isn't in the cards.*

As if she could read Ava's thoughts, her mother

said sympathetically, ''It'll be a nice change. You'll meet new people, make new friends.''

''You won't find accommodation,'' her father grumbled. ''You're talking about Zach Alexander's place, and it's always booked solid over Christmas.''

''There was a cancellation. I spoke to him in person this afternoon, and he assured me I can rent one of the cabins for the week. I know you'd rather I stayed here, Dad, but I need to be by myself for a while.''

Her father scowled. ''Will you at least come home for New Year's Eve?''

Would six days be enough to get over the ridiculous urge to bawl her eyes out, and pull herself together? Hardly! But the disappointment in her father's eyes tugged at her heartstrings. ''Yes. I'll be home for New Year's Eve.''

Leo spent Christmas Day with his parents and Ethel. Inevitably, the conversation turned toward the gossip buzzing around town that Deenie Manville had run off with a man in tights.

''That girl never was happy unless she was in the spotlight,'' his mother observed, wading through her turkey-with-all-the-trimmings dinner. ''Nothing like that nice Ava Sorensen. Now *there's* a girl with breeding!''

''You always did have a soft spot for her,'' his

father said, with a smile. "Not that you really believe any woman's quite good enough for our son, but if Leo were to get married, she's the one you'd have him choose."

"Is it any wonder? She was genuinely lovely, inside and out."

"She still is," Leo said, with enough feeling to make his father sit up and take notice. "I'd even go so far as to say she's improved with age."

His mother sighed into her plum pudding. "I hope we have a chance to see her before she leaves town again."

Not nearly as fervently as he hoped *he* would! If truth be known, he hoped like the devil that she wouldn't be leaving town at all!

As for Deenie, setting the record straight with her had taken a load off his mind. He hoped she really had found her true love—and that he hadn't left it too late to find his.

CHAPTER TEN

FOR three days, Ava rose with the sun and except for a half-hour break at lunch, skied until the lifts closed. Then, exhausted, she trudged back to her little guest house, stoked up the fire, loaded a disc into the CD player, slipped into something comfortable, and had a meal delivered to her door.

The staff and other guests tried to include her in the holiday program, inviting her to join them for *après-ski* cocktails in the main lodge, or the nightly dinner-dance in its elegant dining hall. But the hurt she suffered went deeper than sore muscles unused to the strenuous downhill slopes. She ached inside, in a place neither a whirlpool spa nor kindly strangers could reach.

A relationship she'd treasured all her life had crumbled. And if that weren't bad enough, she'd fallen in love with a man who might be attracted to her but who appeared not to be interested in any sort of lasting commitment. The knowledge left her so sodden with grief, for a lost friend and a lost love, that it strangled the life out of any pleasure she might otherwise have taken in the Topaz Valley Resort. She simply couldn't drum up the energy to put on a cheerful front for people she'd never see again, once her respite there was over.

So when a knock came at her door, just after seven on the evening of the thirtieth, she assumed it was the busboy delivering the sandwich and soup she'd ordered. Probably the Christmas music playing on the stereo had drowned out the sound of his motorized cart drawing up outside.

But it wasn't the busboy, it was Leo. Leo in blue jeans and a dark red sweater with a navy racing stripe down the side, a black canvas sports' bag slung over one shoulder, and a pair of skis balanced on the other.

Leo, looking like an ad for a posh European ski resort. Like a god making a brief visit to earth to see how mere mortals like her were faring. Leo, looking so mouth-wateringly gorgeous that saliva pooled under her tongue.

For long, tense, unsmiling seconds, he simply drank in the sight of her. Probably because he couldn't quite believe what he was seeing, she thought glumly. Probably because, if he opened his mouth, he'd start laughing and wouldn't be able to stop!

She was wearing yellow fluffy slippers and a long, voluminous flannel nightgown so circumspect that even her great-great Victorian forebears would have approved it. She'd tied her hair up in pigtails, rag-doll style, for pity's sake! The injustice of it all was enough to give her the heaves.

Finally, when the silence was stretched so taut that she could almost hear the stars wink, she found the courage to ask, "What do you want?"

There wasn't so much as a hint of amusement in his tone when he answered. "You," he said, his voice a caress.

Hearts don't actually stop for things like that, she'd once told a friend who'd happened to find herself alone in an elevator with a man she had a crush on, and had been afraid she'd die from the thrill of it when he unexpectedly kissed her.

But Ava had been wrong. At that moment, hers stopped completely, and left her hanging in a limbo poised equally between heaven and hell.

"May I come in, darlin'?"

Trance-like, she opened the door wider. He stepped across the threshold, disposed of his bag and skis, and bent to remove his boots. The scent of him—an alluring blend of cold mountain air and clean, wind-chilled skin to which a trace of aftershave still clung—tormented her unbearably.

She longed to touch him; to lay a hand on his hair and absorb its thick, springy texture. To feel the warmth and vitality of him beneath all that winter clothing.

Then he straightened, and she realized how little room there was for two people in the tiny capsule of an entrance hall. His breath winnowed over her face, clean and sweet. The width and height of him blocked an escape. Not that she was looking for one. His nearness, when she'd thought she wouldn't see him again for years or even never, was a gift which might cost her dearly in the long run, but which, for now, was too tempting to withstand.

He stood close enough that she could distinguish each long, dark lash framing those heartbreaker blue eyes. Close enough to detect the tiny nick left by his razor that morning—there, at the hint of a dimple in his chin. Close enough that if she'd raised herself up on her toes, she could have touched his lips with her own.

"You're probably wondering how I knew where to find you," he said, forcing her to abandon her spellbound preoccupation with his looks, and address the reasons behind his sudden appearance.

"I assume my parents told you, since they're the only ones I told."

"Your mother, actually, but only after a great deal of persuasion on my part, and on the understanding that my coming to see you wouldn't cause you any more grief than you've already suffered."

"Why did you want to see me? I can't imagine we have anything left to say to each other."

He hesitated and glanced past her to the main room of the guest house. "I have a great deal to say, and it's going to take some time, so do you think we could talk in there? Maybe have a drink together?'' He hefted the tote and smiled for the first time. "I came prepared. There's a bottle of very good Bordeaux in here.''

Other women might have succumbed to the promise of good wine, but she fell under the spell of that smile. "If you like,'' she practically gasped.

"Oh, I like,'' he replied, eyeing her up and down, nightgown, pigtails, and all. "I like very much.''

"You didn't like enough to come and find me sooner,'' she accused, marching back to the living room in high dudgeon.

"I most certainly did,'' he said, the vehemence of his reply devastating her puny efforts to remain distant. "I'd have been beating a path to your door first thing Christmas Day if I'd thought you'd let me in. But in case you've forgotten, you were pretty steamed with me the last couple of times I saw you. So I thought I'd give you some time to cool off.''

"And you're sure that's all it would take to have me falling into your arms, are you?''

"No,'' he said soberly. "I'm sure of only one thing and that is that I couldn't let you leave the country without pleading my case one more time.''

He took her hand and drew her down next to him on the sofa in front of the fire. "I'm fully aware your homecoming wasn't everything you hoped it would be, Ava. I know your friendship with Deenie has been put to the test and come out of it a lot the worse for wear. I realize it burdened you with feelings of guilt and disloyalty which spoiled your holiday. And I'm not so clueless that I don't realize I'm partly to blame.''

"You're right. You are,'' she said, noticing that he was still holding her hand and trying not to read too much into it, even though her heart was almost fibrillating with sudden hope. ''In fact, I'd even go so far as to say you're mostly to blame!''

"How?'' he asked her, somehow loading the question with such undertones of intimacy that she quivered inside.

"You know how!'' she said feebly.

"By putting an end to all the misunderstandings and rumors about my relationship with Deenie, you mean? Well, as far as that's concerned, I had no choice, and at the risk of sounding unfeeling, I'd have been a lot blunter a lot sooner if she hadn't seemed so emotionally brittle.''

"Not that,'' Ava said. ''I know you weren't at fault there. She came to see me before she left town and admitted she wilfully misrepresented your intentions for reasons of her own.''

"What, then? For falling in love with you? Hell, that wasn't something I planned or expected—nor even something over which I had any control. But I can tell you it made abiding by your rules not to come near you, or look at you, or kiss you, damn near impossible.''

Wordlessly, she stared at him. *Falling in love with her?* Had she heard him right?

He squeezed her fingers. ''Feel free to jump in any time you want, Ava. I could use a little help or encouragement about now.''

''Did you say you'd fallen in love with me?''

''Yes,'' he replied. ''Is that so terrible?''

It was wonderful—so wonderful, she was afraid to believe it, even though she badly wanted to accept it without reservation. ''Not terrible at all,'' she said. ''But I can't help thinking it's rather sudden. We might have known each other a long time, but we hardly know each other well.''

''Oh, I don't know about that,'' he said, sliding his arm around her waist and tugging her closer. ''It might surprise you to hear how many memories of the teenage-you were stored at the back of my mind, waiting to be released when we met again.''

''I rather doubt that. You never noticed me when I was growing up.''

''Not true.'' Laughter danced in his eyes and wove through his voice. ''I remember a girl with long, coltish legs and big, serious grey eyes and a wild mane of near-black hair. I remember her tripping over furniture, falling over her feet on the tennis court, and cursing like a trooper when she stubbed her toe on the side of the pool.''

"Exactly," she said, mortified. "Unlike Deenie, who was petite and perfect at every age and loved by everyone."

He brushed the ball of his thumb over her mouth to silence her. "I remember thinking, *Ava's going to be a knockout one day,* and I was right. When I met the grown-up version, she left me tongue-tied. She made me want to be better in every respect. To be a man worthy of a woman like her."

They were lovely words. Flattering words. They made her glow all over. But one big question still remained and until she knew the answer, she dared not give in to the happiness trying to burst free inside. "So where do we go from here, Leo?"

"That's up to you," he said. "I know what I want, and that's the chance to explore what you and I might make of a relationship based on something other than a few illicit kisses. Things like friendship and the kind of love which endures into old age. Sharing. Making plans. Learning everything there is to know about each other. Building a life together based on mutual hopes and desires."

"Those things take time."

"I know. And I'm in no hurry."

From the CD player, Frank Sinatra worked his timeless magic with "The Christmas Waltz." Leo pulled her to her feet and into his arms.

"I want to date you," he said, guiding her around the small square of floor between the sofa and the breakfast bar. "To dance cheek-to-cheek with you like this. To take you to see tear-jerker movies and lend you my handkerchief when you cry. When you walk down the street, I want people to say, 'There goes Leo Ferrante's girl.' I want them to look at me when I'm with you and say, 'He's one lucky guy.' I want to be able to get in my car and drive over to your place in fifteen minutes flat. To pick up the phone on the spur of the moment and invite you to my place to share the lousy spaghetti dinner I made."

He slowed to a stop and dipped his head to let his mouth roam over hers. "And right now, I want very badly to take you to bed."

"Oh!" She sighed, in a froth of anticipation.

He put her from him and hauled the bottle of wine out of his bag. "But I won't. Instead, I'll ply you with alcohol and leave you so befuddled, you'll agree to anything I ask, including not going back to Africa. Is there a corkscrew and a couple of glasses to be had in this place?"

"Yes," she said, reluctantly flip-flopping in her slippers to the little kitchen nook. "But if you think a glass or two of wine will make me renege on my overseas contract, you're wrong."

"I figured you'd say that," he said, watching as she set stemware and the corkscrew on a tray. "But I thought I'd give it a whirl anyway. I might as well be up front about my intentions from the start."

"Absolutely," she said. "Are you hungry?"

"Starving. I drove all afternoon to get here, and didn't stop for dinner."

"I've already sent for soup and a sandwich, but if you want to phone the main kitchen and order something for yourself, you'll find a menu on the coffee table."

"Or I could buy you dinner at the lodge. I passed by the dining room on my way over here, and it looked pretty nice. Of course," he said slyly, as he cut the foil collar on the wine bottle, "you'd probably want to change first. I'm captivated by what you're wearing, but I'm not sure I want anyone else enjoying the sight."

She scurried back behind the breakfast bar and ran her fingers up the back of her neck in a surreptitious attempt to pull loose the elastics holding her pigtails in place. "I wasn't expecting company."

"Good. I'd hate to think you were planning to entertain another man in your nightshirt."

The way he was looking at her made her elbows tingle. Oh, for heaven's sake, who was she kidding? The way he was looking at her made her tingle all over! She barely made it back to the sofa without collapsing in a soggy heap at his feet.

He poured the wine and lightly clinked the rim of his glass against hers. "To us and the future, Ava."

She saw promise in his eyes, heard it in his voice, and for the first time really began to believe that a future with him wasn't such a far-fetched idea, after all. "Do you think long-distance relationships ever really work, Leo?"

"It depends on the people involved. Nothing can come between true soul mates, not even death. Do I think you and I are soul mates?" He reached for her hand and pressed a kiss against her palm. "Most definitely."

Her toes curled. "It'd only be for a little while," she said, her voice shaking. "My contract's up in another couple of months."

"I can wait that long."

"I can't," she said, the clamour in her blood almost deafening her. "I need something more definitive to go on than mere words."

He took away her wineglass and placed it with his on the coffee table. "Will this do?" he murmured, bringing his lips to hers.

His kiss left her trembling. The strength seeped out of her, and she clung to him. "No," she managed, when he pulled away again. "It's not quite enough."

He regarded her solemnly. "I'm prepared to be patient, Ava."

"I'm not," she said.

He needed no further encouragement. So swiftly he left her breathless, he toppled her back against the cushions, buried his hands in her hair, and kissed her again. On her mouth and her jaw and her eyelids.

Down her neck to her throat. Searchingly, intimately.

With nimble fingers, he undid the buttons down the front of that chaste, unlovely nightgown. Pulled it away from her to trace his tongue over the triangle of her collar-bone.

He stripped her naked to the waist and gazed at her. In wonder. With love. He touched her breasts. Raised molten blue eyes to her face and then, with almost holy dedication, lowered his mouth and tugged gently on her nipple.

If he'd thrown a lighted match into a can of gasoline, the outcome could not have been more inflammatory. A shaft of pleasure arrowed to the pit of her womb to awaken an answering damp heat between her legs. Tiny quivers, delicate as wind chimes, vibrated within her.

Lucid thought fled, chased away by the passion spurting through her veins. In a frenzy of desire, she met his demands with her own. Stroked her hands over the hard and lovely planes of him. Raised his sweater to claw the T-shirt underneath from the waist of his blue jeans so she could explore the warm, smooth expanse of his back...of his front.

Moments passed, awash with wonder and pleasure and discovery. Somehow she was naked, and so was he, though the precise order of how that happened escaped her. Had she hurled his sweater clean across the room? Was he the one to remove her nightgown completely and send it flying over the back of the sofa? Did he lift her to lie on the sheepskin rug on the floor in front of the hearth, or did they tumble down there together?

Did it matter? Or was the only thing of any importance the sense of completion which engulfed her when, at last, with control fast slipping from his grasp, he gave way to the passion ignited that first night in the stable, and entered her? Possessed her. Locked her in deep and pulsing rhythm with him. Whispered hoarsely that she was beautiful and he could look at her forever and never grow tired of her loveliness.

He took her to places she'd never been before. To heights of ecstasy beyond anything she'd ever imagined. To depths of emotion so critically moving that she felt tears streaming down her face. And when he surrendered to the ruthless forces overpowering him, he held her secure in his arms until the tumult had passed and they'd arrived safely at a new, sublime level of closeness and understanding.

She dared then to tell him what she'd known in her heart for days. "I love you, Leo."

"That's good," he said, sounding shaken. "Because I love you, more than I knew I could love anyone. You hold my heart in your hand, Ava. Treat it gently, please. It's never experienced anything like this before."

*   *   *

"I promised your parents I'd have you home by tomorrow afternoon," he said later, when they'd made themselves respectable enough to open the door to the busboy who brought the celebratory lobster and champagne Leo had insisted on ordering. "They've invited a few people over, to ring in the new year, including my parents and the duchess. I hope you'll be able to weather her remarks when she sees us together."

"I'll manage," Ava said.

"But we can spend the morning on the slopes before we head back. Start on that dating routine I mentioned earlier."

"I'd like that."

"Of course," he said, "we ought to make an early night of it and there are no rooms to be had at the lodge. Do you mind if I sleep here, on the sofa?"

"Certainly I mind," she said. "There's a perfectly good king-size bed down the hall. It's much too big for one person."

"Sounds perfect to me. The only snag is, you might not get much sleep."

She laughed, and oh, it felt wonderful! She hadn't laughed in such a long time. "That's what I'm counting on, Leo, so don't disappoint me."

"Forward hussy!" he said, with an endearing leer. "Do you think you can contain yourself a bit longer? There are a couple of other things I'd like to take care of.''

''I'll try.''

He reached for the black canvas tote again and withdrew the package he'd left with her on Christmas Eve. ''Your mom gave this to me when I stopped by your house. Maybe now that I've made my intentions clear, you'll accept it.''

Her fingers shook as she pulled away the gold-embossed paper, then opened the white cardboard box inside and held in her hand a tiny, exquisite Victorian house encased in a crystal dome filled with liquid through which floated a hundred minute silvery snowflakes.

''To remind you of home when you're far away,'' he said, tracing the outline of her cheek with his finger. ''And to remind you that I'll be here waiting when you come back again.''

''Oh, thank you!'' she breathed. ''It's beautiful—and reminds me of that gorgeous old house we looked at.''

''Which brings me to the last item of business.'' He pulled a legal-looking document from the bag and handed it to her.

''What…?''

''It's a deed of sale. To that very same house.''

''Someone bought it?''

''I did, Ava. Because I want you to know how very serious I am about having you in my life. But

I'll put it back on the market if you don't think you could be happy there, or if you'd rather—''

''I can be happy anywhere, as long as I'm with you, Leo,'' she told him, leaning against him. ''But if you're asking me if I'll be satisfied with this particular house, I can promise you I wouldn't change it for the world. It's perfect.''

''Good. I was hoping you'd feel that way.'' He tucked the deed down the front of her velour robe. ''Merry Christmas all over again, angel, and happy New Year!''

And it would be, she knew. It would be the first of many. With him.

A SEASONAL SECRET
Diana Hamilton

CHAPTER ONE

THE short winter day was drawing to a close as Carl Forsythe cut the Jaguar's speed, slowing right down as he entered the narrow main street of Lower Bewley village.

Shadows were deepening and the ivy that clothed the stone walls of the ancient church looked black, as black as his mood, he recognised drily, his dark grey eyes brooding beneath clenched black brows.

Perhaps it had been a mistake to come back at all. The first visit to Bewley Hall since his uncle had passed away three months ago would be tough, adding to his sense of failure.

But accepting one of the many invitations from the friends who had stayed loyal to him after he and Terrina had split up hadn't seemed like a good idea either. He was no fit company for anyone, especially at Christmas time.

Three days to go before the Big Day and the normally sleepy main street was positively throbbing with expectation. Lights blazed from the bow-fronted windows of the butchers and greengrocers, their displays of turkeys and pheasants, piles of oranges and rosy apples, all decked out with festive sprigs of red-berried holly. And cottage windows were brightly lit, each with its own glittering Christmas tree. People burdened with shopping, buggies and toddlers, bumped into each other, grinning. Everyone was happy, stocking up for the coming festivities.

With a grunt of relief he edged the sleek car past the last straggle of cottages and out onto the winding country lane that led to the Hall.

Reminders of Christmas, family togetherness, he could do without.

Today his divorce had been finalised.

Failure.

Love, or even the pretence of it, had been absent for a long, long time. But when he'd made his marriage vows he'd meant them. For better or for worse. So if everything had so quickly fallen apart was it down to him? If he'd been the husband Terrina had wanted she wouldn't have looked elsewhere.

Or would she? Were his friends right when they said his now ex-wife was a promiscuous tramp? Had he as her husband been the last to know?

Throughout his uncle's long illness he'd kept the true state of his marriage from him. Kept his lip tightly buttoned on the subject when Terrina had demanded a divorce so that she could marry her French lover. 'Pierre knows how to have fun,' she'd told him. 'He knows how to have real fun. He doesn't expect me to have children and ruin my figure or spend dreary weekends in the country keeping a crabby old uncle company!'

So today he had told his executive PA that he was taking two weeks off, had locked up his apartment off Upper Thames Street and headed for his old home in Gloucestershire, where he would spend the so-called festive season sorting through his uncle's personal possessions, and his own which were still in the small suite of rooms that had been his for twenty years—since Marcus has taken him in when his parents had both died in a motorway pile-up when he'd been just seven years old.

His throat clenched as the powerful car snaked along between high, winter-bare hedgerows, the headlights making the bleached, frost-rimmed grass glitter. The next few days promised to be pretty depressing.

The Hall would be empty, unheated. The staff dismissed with generous pensions.

Another failure.

Marcus had never married and had looked to him, Carl, to bring his wife to live there, start a family, carry on the Forsythe dynasty.

The decision to auction the Hall and its contents hadn't been easy. But Carl had no intention of remarrying. Once had been enough. More than enough. So, no wife meant no children, no continuity. Pointless to keep the place on.

Smoky-grey eyes grew stormy. Guilt piled

heavily on top of failure and intensified with a stabbing ferocity as he glimpsed a solitary light in Keeper's Cottage, beyond the trees that bordered the grounds of the Hall. Obviously the new owners had moved in.

So where was Beth Hayley now? What had happened to her? His heart kicked his ribs. If he knew what had happened to her, knew that she was happy and successful, then maybe he'd finally be able to forget that night—forget how badly he'd behaved, say goodbye to dreams that were threaded through with past scenes, like snatches of a videotape constantly replayed. Her silky blonde hair, her laughing green eyes, the dress she'd been wearing, a shimmering deep green silk that had made her eyes look like emeralds. The way her taut breasts had felt beneath his touch, the ripe lushness of her lips. And the deep shame that had come afterwards…

Eight years was a long time for a recurring dream to last. Too damn long…

In the fading light the sprawling Elizabethan house looked lonely, almost as if it were an animate thing, endlessly waiting for light and warmth, the sound of human voices, laughter.

His mouth tightening, he pushed that thought aside. It wasn't like him to indulge in flights of fancy. It was time he pulled himself together and started to do what he was good at: getting the job done.

Locking the Jaguar, he took the house-key from the side pocket of his jeans-style cords and mounted the shallow flight of stone steps to the massive front door.

The main hall was almost pitch-dark, the last feeble rays of light struggling through the tall mullioned windows. Turning on the mains electricity was obviously the first priority. Swinging round to go and fetch the torch he always carried in the glove compartment of the Jag, he froze, his spine prickling.

Laughter, childish laughter, echoed from the upper reaches of the house. Disembodied whispers, a burst of giggles. The shadows of the children his uncle had wanted to see and hear? The new generation of Forsythes that would never be?

Get a grip, he growled inside his head. Failing the uncle who had meant so much to him was making him think irrationally for what was probably the first time in his life!

Young tearaways from the village, he decided grimly, taking the uncarpeted oak stairs two at a time.

The sound of his rapid footfalls had struck terror, judging by the breathy gasp, the sudden, frantic scuffling of feet.

He caught the two of them near the head of the stairs. Boys. Younger than he'd expected.

Keeping a firm but painless grip on their slight

shoulders, he demanded sternly, 'What do you think you're doing?'

A beat or two of unhappy silence and then the slimmer, slightly taller of the two said quakily, 'Exploring, sir. Mum said no one lived here any more.'

'So you broke in?'

'Oh, no, sir. We found an open window downstairs. We didn't break anything. Honestly.' It was the shorter, heavier child who spoke now, and Carl's grip relaxed slightly. The boys were well spoken and even called him 'sir'!

'Your names?'

The taller of the two answered first, 'James, sir.'

'Guy.' A sniff. A wobble in the young voice.

Both were probably on the verge of tears, Carl decided sympathetically, remembering some of the scrapes he had got into as a child and the avuncular trouble he'd landed himself in. They obviously hadn't broken in with felonious intent. Just two small boys having an adventure.

'How old are you?' he asked gently, and two quavering voices answered in unison, 'Seven, sir.'

'And where are you from?'

'Keeper's Cottage,' James supplied miserably—no doubt expecting parental wrath, Carl deduced with a flicker of wry amusement followed immediately by an icy feeling, deep inside his heart, which could be translated, when he really thought about it, as a strange sense of loss.

New owners at Keeper's Cottage, the former home of his uncle's head gardener and his wife. A dour couple who had brought up their granddaughter, Beth. None of their dourness had rubbed off on her; she had been all light and laughter, a joy to be with.

During his holidays from boarding school they'd spent a lot of time together, getting into all kinds of scrapes. Then, in his teens, he'd often brought a schoolfriend home with him and they hadn't wanted a girl tagging along. In a funny sort of way he'd missed her company, although he had seen her around the estate and had found himself red-faced and tongue-tied when they'd actually stopped to talk. Her emerging coltish beauty had made him feel uncharacteristically unsure of himself.

All that had changed on the night of the annual end of summer party Marcus had always given for the estate workers and their families. Eight years ago now, Beth had been seventeen and the loveliest thing he had ever set eyes on. He had been nineteen and should have known better.

New owners at Keeper's Cottage. He would never see her again, never find out what had become of her, and he would never be rid of the memories that had forced themselves into his dreams, where they had no right to be.

Guilt, he decided grittily, and said, 'I'll walk you back home. Go carefully down the stairs.' It was pitch-dark inside the house now, but outside the starlight in the clear, frosty heavens enabled him to see both boys more clearly. Guy was a stocky kid, built a bit like a tank, with floppy blond hair, while James, taller, was wiry, full of grace, with a mop of dark hair. Both seven. Twins, then? Though assuredly not identical.

'We'll walk back through the trees,' he told them as he fetched the torch from his car and flicked on the powerful beam of light. 'It will be quicker than taking the car round by the road, and your parents will be worried enough as it is.'

And serve them right! he thought starkly. No boy worth the name would pass up the chance to get into mischief. He blamed the parents. If he had seven-year-old sons he would make sure he knew where they were, what they were doing, at all times. Make damn sure they were home before dark! And as it was his house that had been the object of the boys' mischief he had the right to make his opinions known!

Putting that aside, he shepherded the boys along the narrow track and was assailed by a memory so sharp and clear it hurt.

Walking Beth back to the cottage before dawn on the morning after the party. Deeply ashamed of himself and knowing that saying sorry wasn't nearly enough. But he'd said it, anyway, and she'd been— been just Beth. Sweet and considerate. Kind. The way she'd put the palm of her hand gently against the side of his face, the way she'd smiled, the warmth in her voice as she'd told him, 'Don't be. Please don't be sorry,' as if the taking of her virginity hadn't been his fault but hers.

He hadn't taken this four-minute walk since then. Soon after that night he'd left for America, as arranged, to take his place at university to study Economics. He'd written to her shortly after he'd arrived in the States, asking her to keep in touch, to tell him if there had been any repercussions from that night.

He'd heard nothing. The possibility of pregnancy had all been in his mind, obviously. And as she hadn't replied he'd assumed she'd forgotten everything that had happened, put it out of her mind because it hadn't been important enough to remember.

When he'd finally returned to Bewley, three years later, his marriage to Terrina all planned and ready to take his place in his uncle's bank, old Frank Hayley had died and his widow, apparently, never mentioned her granddaughter, never mind her whereabouts. But then Ellen Hayley had always been close-lipped, dour and grudging. All he had ever been able to ascertain was the fact that Beth had returned to the village briefly to attend her grandfather's funeral.

Chiding himself for thoughts that were beginning to seem much too obsessive—Beth Hayley was the past—Carl pushed open the wicket that led into the back garden. There was a light showing at the kitchen window.

'We can find our way now, sir,' James said with a staunchness that belied his tender age, then spoiled the effect by quavering, 'Mum said we were never to go with strangers. Not ever.'

'Sound reasoning.' Carl swallowed a spurt of amusement at the way the boy had regressed from burgeoning adulthood to just a baby in a split second and pronounced, 'As I found you on my premises I simply assumed responsibility for your safe conduct home.' He allowed them to swallow that mouthful as he ushered them along the path to the kitchen door, adding with spurious cheerfulness, 'Time to face the music!'

The old solid fuel cooking stove was doing its job just perfectly, Beth thought happily as she removed a batch of cheese scones from the oven and put them on the stout wooden table next to the Christmas cake she and the boys had baked earlier.

Inheriting Keeper's Cottage had been a real surprise, considering that Gran had wanted as little as possible to do with her for the last eight years. Her original intention had been to sell up, invest the money as a nest-egg for James. But since waking this morning another idea had begun to form.

James had kick-started it when he'd asked at

breakfast, 'Why don't we live here, Mum? It's brilliant here. Guy would have to stay in horrid London, but he could come for all his holidays, couldn't he?'

St John's Wood didn't really deserve the appellation of 'horrid', far from it, but Beth knew what her son meant. There was precious little freedom there, certainly nothing like the kind of freedom a boy could experience in the countryside. And as for herself, living in someone else's home, no matter how elegant or how kind her employers were, wasn't like having the independence of living under her own roof.

Besides, she had the gut feeling that she would find herself unemployed in the not too distant future.

And living so close to Bewley Hall wouldn't be a problem, she reassured herself as she placed the last of the scones on the cooling tray. Sadly, old Marcus Forsythe had died a few weeks before Gran had succumbed to pneumonia, and she'd learned from Mrs Fraser at the greengrocer's in the village that the Hall was to be sold at auction early in the New Year.

So there was no danger of her or, more importantly, James bumping into Carl Forsythe.

Turning to the deep stone sink, she filled a kettle and put it on the hotplate. Time for tea. Way past time, she thought, her breath catching and a frown appearing between her thickly lashed green eyes.

The boys had wanted to play in the garden, making a den in the ramshackle shed right down at the bottom. 'Just for half an hour,' she'd told them. That had been three o'clock. A glance at her watch told her an hour and a half had passed since she'd watched them scamper down the path between overgrown fruit bushes and rank weeds, then turned back to her baking.

Her anxiety level hitting the roof, Beth cursed herself for being all tied up with working out how she and James could make the cottage their permanent home while time had slipped dangerously by. She snatched a torch from the dresser drawer and dragged open the kitchen door to be met by a blast of freezing air and Carl Forsythe's condemnatory, 'I believe these are yours.'

CHAPTER TWO

GUY put his tousled blond head down and scampered inside, his lower lip trembling, and Carl, the son he didn't know he had still at his side, said 'Beth?' as if he couldn't believe the evidence of his eyes.

'What—what happened?' It was as much as Beth could do to get the words out, her throat was so tight. Her panic, followed immediately by bitter self-castigation because the two boys had been out in the dark and the cold for far longer than she'd realised and coupled with seeing Carl Forsythe again after all this time had sent her into shock.

And he was just staring—glints of piercing light in those sexy, smoky-grey eyes, his mouth a tight line, a muscle contracting at the side of his hard jawline. He was mesmerising her; she couldn't look away. It was James who tentatively broke the stinging silence.

'We were exploring his house, Mum. We really thought no one lived there.' His young voice wobbled as he added, 'He said it was all right to go with a stranger 'cos we were in his house and he had to bring us back home.'

Beth's eyes misted with pride. Her son was being

so brave, confessing to his naughtiness, explaining why he had broken the strict rule of never going anywhere with someone unknown to him.

That this particular stranger happened to be his own father was something only she knew. Even so, she would make sure that she explained the rule far more stringently. Her eyes swept from her son's face to Carl's and swiftly back again. They were so alike. She bit her lip. Would Carl see the resemblance? She hoped to heaven he wouldn't!

'I'll speak to you later,' she warned as sternly as she was able, given the panicky emotions that were replacing her initial shock. 'Go to your rooms now, both of you. Get washed and then change into something clean. I've never seen either of you look so grubby.'

As James walked past her he flicked her a look of mute misery which she made herself ignore, and Guy piped up, 'There were spiders in that shed. Massive humungous ones. So we can't make a den until you get them out for us.' As if that explained and excused everything.

He was sitting on the floor, laboriously undoing the laces of the trainers he wouldn't be seen dead without. Beth flattened her mouth to stop the smallest flicker of amusement showing and reiterated firmly, 'Upstairs. Now. Both of you.' And she watched them scuttle up the wooden staircase that led directly up from the kitchen and felt just a little bit safer.

Then she forced herself to give her attention to Carl. She had tried so hard to forget him in the past, but it had proved quite impossible. How could she be expected to forget him when her darling James was so obviously his father's son?

Carl had changed, and yet he hadn't. He was still drop-dead gorgeous, yet his shoulders had widened, and he now wore his thick black hair cropped closely to his head, accentuating the savagely handsome features that were harsher than she remembered. His eyes, the colour of storm clouds, were colder and sharper than they had been before.

Belatedly remembering her manners, she said quickly, 'Thank you for seeing the boys home safely. I can only apologise for their bad behaviour and for wasting your time.'

And then, because it would look mighty suspicious if she continued to treat him as if he were a stranger to whom she was obligated but of whom she wanted to get rid as quickly as possible, she invited, 'Won't you come in?'

She hoped he'd say no.

The lecture on parental responsibility Carl had meant to deliver had disappeared like a footprint covered by a fresh fall of snow. Seeing Beth in the flesh after she'd haunted his dreams on a regular basis had stunned his brain.

Her lovely eyes were wide and troubled, her narrow shoulders tense beneath the soft jade-green sweater she was wearing, and the way she'd scooped her long blonde hair back, coiling it haphazardly on the crown of her head, emphasised the tender hollows beneath her high cheekbones and made her slender neck look achingly young and vulnerable.

How could he lecture her when all he wanted to do was fold her in his arms and comfort her, tell her not to get uptight because boys would be boys as long as the world went round? It was no big deal.

'It's been a long time, Beth,' he remarked softly, and wanted to add, Too long, but didn't. 'You were the last person I expected to see. For all anyone knew you'd disappeared off the face of the earth, so I guess I took it for granted that the cottage had been sold after your grandmother died.'

Moving past her into the warm brightness of the cosy old-fashioned kitchen, he sensed her slender body flinch and his throat clenched painfully. Was his presence so unwelcome? Because she didn't want to be reminded of that one-night stand all those years ago? In this day and age it seemed a bit far-fetched.

Unless, of course, her husband was around—the father of the twins. Knowing Beth and her open nature, she would have confessed her past relationships—if one night of out-of-this-world passion could be called a relationship, he amended drily.

She might be embarrassed at the prospect of having to introduce a past lover to her husband. That could be why she was so uptight.

He wouldn't put her in an awkward position, not for all the gold in Fort Knox, so he'd take himself off, relieve her of his unwanted company. He'd spout a few conventional platitudes first, because it would look weird if he just marched straight back out again, even though she might be hugely thankful if he did just that!

'Are you and your husband spending Christmas here?' he asked as casually as he could when she turned from securing the door. He noted with entirely masculine approval the way her jeans clipped the shapely outline of her long slender legs. 'Keeper's Cottage would make an ideal holiday retreat, and the twins will love the freedom.'

He was simply making idle conversation to make his planned immediate departure seem less precipitate. The thought of returning to that cold, empty house, leaving the warmth, the homely scent of baking, leaving her, leaving all the questions unanswered, was starkly unappealing.

But his seemingly casual question seemed to have thrown her. She looked as if he'd been speaking in Swahili. Her finely drawn brows tugged together and the green of her eyes deepened as she muttered, 'Twins?' and shook her head. 'Do they look like twins? Guy is my employers' son. I've been his nanny since he was six months old. He and James were brought up together.' She relaxed just a little, smiling slightly as she confided, 'Guy's mother is expecting a new arrival any time now. She wants a home birth, so we all thought it best if I brought the boys away and gave them a proper Christmas here. So it's just us. I don't have a husband. James's father and I never married.'

Then she dragged her lower lip between her teeth and bit it. Hard. Why couldn't she keep her big mouth shut? But the tension she'd read in his face had been wiped away, she noted uncomprehendingly. Because of what she'd said? She had no idea.

The trouble was, she had always found him so easy to talk to. Nothing had changed there. She should have had her wits about her—invented a husband—a father for her son—who was working overseas—and put him off the scent. But lying to anyone simply never occurred to her. Never had and never would.

Her eyes wide and troubled, she watched him pull a chair from beneath the old wooden table and sit down, uninvited, one arm hooked over the backrest, his long legs outstretched. He was smiling that slow, utterly disarming smile of his now, and his eyes were as warmly intimate as she'd always remembered them.

He was wearing a soft leather jacket over a dark polo sweater and sleek cord jeans he might just as well have been poured into. If he'd been a film star he'd have had women swooning in the aisles!

Her stomach squirmed and tightened in a sensation she'd almost forgotten it was possible to experience. Raw sexual attraction, she decided, deploring the fact that he could still have this effect on her.

'Tell me more,' he invited smoothly. 'As I said, it's been a long time. You and I have a lot of catching up to do.'

'I—' Aware that all her nerves were standing to attention, her breathing shallow and fast, Beth made a conscious effort to relax. Behaving like a cat on hot bricks would only make him suspicious. She pulled in a slow breath and offered, 'I was just about to make tea. Would you like a cup?'

'Love one. It's been a long day.' His eyes narrowed as he watched her turn away to take the now furiously boiling kettle from the hotplate. The girl who had woven herself into his dreams for so many years had matured into quite a woman. Five feet five inches of seductive, enticingly feminine curves. Why hadn't the father of her son married her? She was lovely to look at and had a nature to match. He couldn't think of a man on the planet who wouldn't be proud to call her his wife.

Unless her lover had been already married.

He would never have put her down as the type to get involved with some other woman's husband.

She'd been so sweet, innocent and trusting. Which was why he'd been so ashamed of himself for taking something so rare and precious and sullying it.

He frowned heavily, black brows meeting over darkening eyes. Her son was seven years old. He didn't need a degree in advanced mathematics to work out that she must have jumped out of his bed and straight into another's! Had the air of innocence and openness that had so enthralled him been nothing but a clever act?

Jealousy and a sense of bitter disappointment twisted a sharp knife deep inside him—and that was both warped and ridiculous! For heaven's sake, what had happened was well in the past. He had been married himself in the intervening years; he had no damned right to have any feelings whatsoever about what she might or might not have done with her life!

Oblivious, Beth settled a knitted cosy on the teapot and reached cups and saucers from the dresser, milk from the fridge. In the bedroom overhead she could hear the boys clumping about. From long experience she knew that getting washed and changed could take anything from twenty manic seconds to an eternity.

The latter today, she devoutly hoped. They would surely spin the chore out as long as humanly possible in view of the telling-off they were due to receive the moment they presented themselves downstairs!

Which would give Carl time to drink his tea and her time to make a more normal impression—make something approaching normal conversation. After all, they had been childhood friends. He would think it odd if she didn't make some attempt to do some of the catching up he'd talked about. Not too much, though. She needed him out of here before James reappeared and gave him time to note the almost uncanny resemblance between the two of them.

'I was sorry to hear of your uncle's death,' she said quietly as she set the tea in front of him. 'I liked him a lot. He always had a kind word for me and apparently a bottomless pocketful of toffees!' Her smile was unforced; she had genuinely happy memories of Marcus Forsythe.

'I miss him,' Carl admitted heavily, his smoky eyes darkening. 'He was one of the best.' He gave her a slight smile. 'I think the fact that we were both without parents drew us together when we were kids. But you drew the short straw. Your grandparents were pretty forbidding.'

'They did what they thought was best,' Beth said defensively, soft colour washing over her cheeks. They had been good to her after their own fashion, and she wouldn't hear a bad word against either of them. In spite of saying she'd washed her hands of her, Gran must have felt something for her. Otherwise, why would she have left this cottage to her? She could have willed it to the church she'd been such a staunch member of, or any number of charities.

Her chin lifting, Beth met Carl's eyes across the table and earnestly explained, 'I think they must have both been born with a strong Puritanical streak—it was in their nature, so they can't be blamed for the way they were. And after what had happened with their only child, my mother, they were doubly strict with me.'

As pain flickered briefly in her lovely eyes Carl instinctively reached over the table and took her hand. 'I remember how upset you were when your gran told you the truth about her,' he said softly.

Home from school for the Easter break, he had found her sobbing her heart out down by the stream, where the wild primroses grew. Gradually she'd blurted it all out. Her mother, a first-year student at a Birmingham college, had got pregnant. The first Beth's grandparents had known about it had been when their daughter had arrived at Keeper's Cottage with a newborn baby. Twenty-four hours later she had walked away and had never been back.

A card—the only one that had ever been sent—had arrived to mark Beth's first birthday, with a note enclosed for Frank and Ellen Hayley saying that their daughter had met and married an Australian and would be going to live in Darwin.

Carl had been fourteen years old to Beth's twelve and he hadn't known what to say to ease her misery, so he'd simply hugged her. And she'd clung to him until she was all cried out. Looking back, that was when his feelings for her had begun to change. Certainly during the next few years he'd felt awkward in her company, increasingly inclined to blush, get tongue-tied and sweaty.

His fingers tightened around hers now, and something sweet coiled around his heart as she responded with increased pressure of her own. 'It was a tough nut to swallow, knowing your mother hadn't wanted you, but it didn't make you bitter and twisted—I admire you for that.'

'Why should it?' Beth's face went pink. She snatched her hand away from his. What did she think she was doing? Holding hands—and loving it—with a married man! So, OK, she'd had a huge crush on Carl Forsythe for almost as long as she could remember, and he was the father of her son, but that didn't excuse or explain why she should still feel so inescapably drawn to him.

Knotting her hands together in her lap, trying to erase the sheer magic of his touch and bring herself down to earth again, she drew herself up very straight and staunchly defended what her grandparents had regarded as indefensible. 'My mother was very young and probably couldn't face the responsibility of bringing a child up on her own. My grandparents would have given her a hard time. They certainly didn't take the modern, relaxed attitude to single parenthood.'

As she had discovered for herself!

'You did. You shouldered the burden of responsibility,' Carl put in quietly. 'Did Frank and Ellen throw you out?'

'Of course not!' But their disgust and outrage at the way she'd followed in her mother's footsteps and brought shame on them had made it impossible for her to stay. 'And James has never been a burden. I wanted my baby!'

Flushed and flustered, she pushed herself to her feet and cleared away the teacups. Why did talking to him, opening her heart to him, seem so right and natural? She wished he would leave. Any minute now she might say something that would alert him to the true situation. Hadn't Gran always complained that she didn't know how to keep a still tongue in her head?

Rinsing the cups out under a furiously gushing tap, she desperately hoped he'd take the hint and leave. But his hand on her shoulder killed that hope stone-dead, and she could have cried with frustration as he reached over and turned off the tap.

He was too close, far too close. Her breath ached in her lungs. His body heat burned her. They were nearly touching. Almost against her will, but unable to stop herself, she tilted back her head to look up at him.

He had a beautiful mouth. Her eyes lingered on the wide, sensual contours. As if it had been only yesterday she could remember exactly how that mouth had felt as it had plundered hers, so sweetly and gently at first, and then with a passion that had swept her away in a floodtide of feverish longing. And love.

A shiver raced through her as she heard him whisper her name, and her long lashes flickered as she raised her eyes to meet his. There was something in the slow, smoky burn of that intent gaze that made her gasp air into her oxygen-starved lungs.

'Beth—' Lean strong fingers reached out to touch a wildly beating pulse at the side of her lush mouth. 'You don't have to put on a brave face for me. Things must have been tough for you, and I'd like to help for old times' sake. You say you're working as a nanny. I assume that means you and your boy are living under someone else's roof at your employer's beck and call night and day? It shouldn't have to be that way.'

Beth was watching the way his mouth moved, inhaling the fresh masculine scent of him, fighting the insane impulse to wind her arms around his neck and move closer, close enough to be part of him. His words merely grazed the surface of her consciousness, drowned out by the thunder-beats of her heart.

But when he asked gently, his fingers sliding

down to briefly caress her delicate jawline, the slender line of her neck, 'Beth, what happened? You didn't marry your boy's father—wouldn't the relationship have worked out?' she was jolted back to stark reality with a vengeance, like the shock of having been suddenly plunged into a pool of icy water.

What in heaven's name did she think she'd been doing? Having lustful thoughts about another woman's husband, her whole body responding to his touch, the seductive velvet stroke of his eyes...

And, just as dangerous, she heard the squeaky hinges of the boys' bedroom door, tentative footsteps on the top of the stairs.

Jerking backwards, she uttered thickly, 'I don't think that's any of your business, do you? Now, if you'll excuse me—' she walked to the door on legs that felt as if they didn't belong to her and dragged it open '—I have a lot to do.'

And she willed him to go, right now, right this minute, before the boys reached the foot of the stairs and he had the time and the leisure to really look at James and begin to wonder...

CHAPTER THREE

'THERE—that should do it.' Beth snipped off one final piece of scarlet-berried holly, added it to the unwieldy bunch she'd already collected, and slipped the secateurs back into one of the capacious side pockets of the cosy fleece she was wearing. For the boys' sake she was doing her level best to be bright and cheerful, to act as if decorating the cottage for Christmas was the only thing on her mind. But inside she was quaking. Did Carl know? Or at the very least strongly suspect that James was his son? Or was her guilty conscience making her imagine things?

'There's loads more over there,' Guy objected.

'You can't take it all,' James countered. 'The birds will be hungry if we have all the berries. Mum,' he added on that reminder, 'I'm hungry now.'

'And me.' Guy put on his pleading face, and Beth hoisted the bundle of holly more securely in her arms, forced her own fears aside and grinned down at them.

The cold wind had whipped rosy colour into their cheeks, banishing city pallor, and the fresh air had turned what had been often picky appetites into something worthy of a couple of navvies.

Which was just one more reason why the idea that she and James should make Keeper's Cottage their permanent home was becoming more firmly fixed with every hour that had passed since they'd arrived here five days ago.

The village primary school was excellent, and surely she could find a part-time job—cleaning, helping in the village stores—anything that she could fit in around school hours. What she had saved during her years with the Harper-Joneses would keep them while she hunted for something suitable.

'Lunch in an hour,' she promised, marvelling at the way they could be hungry after the piles of pancakes and bacon she'd cooked at breakfast-time. She called after them as they scampered back through the trees to the lane that led down to the village. 'Don't run, and watch out for traffic!' Though very little of that passed this way.

Following more sedately, she watched the two small figures—both dressed identically in bright red anoraks, miniature combat trousers and green wellies—and knew they would miss each other. But their separation was bound to happen, whatever she decided about the cottage. Angela Harper-Jones had dropped several hints since her pregnancy had been confirmed.

Angela and Henry Harper-Jones were both barristers and Guy had been unplanned. At the time of his birth Angela had had no intention of giving up her career, which was why she'd advertised for a full-time nanny, child no objection. The fact that Beth had had a three-month-old son had been viewed as a bonus.

'They will be company for each other,' Angela had said, making Beth view the reasonably paid, live-in position as the godsend it had been.

She hadn't had to farm her precious baby out while she went out to work, and they hadn't had to go on living off the state in a flat in a run down high-rise building the council had provided.

But now Angela was ready to be a full-time mother, and with the resident cook-housekeeper who had been with her throughout her married life she would have no need for a nanny. Beth's days in the Harper-Jones household were numbered.

Scrambling down the last few feet of muddy track to the lane, where the boys were waiting patiently— well, as patiently as seven-year-old boys could be expected to, kicking up the piles of fallen leaves that had gathered at the edge of the band of woodland— she made her mind up.

She and James would move in here when she was made jobless and homeless—he had already told her he wanted to stay for ever. It was a good place to be.

Despite her strict upbringing she had had a wonderfully happy childhood, and she wanted the same for James. The village of Lower Bewley was a close-knit community, rather like an extended family. Her precious son would have so much more freedom than was possible in London, and as for her—well, the Hall would soon be sold, so she wouldn't run the risk of running into Carl and his wife.

Frowning, she tried to empty her mind of thoughts of him. There had been far too many of them. Deeply disturbing thoughts, hinging on the way her body still responded to him, the singing of her pulses, the weakening of her bones, the aching desire to touch and be touched.

It couldn't be love, not after all this time. It simply wasn't feasible. She had long since outgrown the moonstruck state she'd inhabited all through her teens. Of course she had. Lying awake last night, she'd finally managed to convince herself that it was just an inconvenient chemical thing—hormones.

Seeing the only man she'd ever made love with had made her celibate body react alarmingly. Regrettable, but quite natural.

She wouldn't think of him, or his sleek and suitable American wife.

And she'd do her level best to forget the way he'd stood his ground last night. She'd wanted to physically push him right out of that door and bang it shut behind him. But he'd simply stood there, watching as the boys had entered the brightly lit kitchen, saying nothing, his darkening eyes narrowed on James as if he'd been committing the boy's features to memory. It had been a truly frightening situation.

Then, after what had seemed like for ever, he'd turned his attention to her, smoky eyes unveiled by the enviable sweep of thick dark lashes and fixed on hers for several heart-stopping moments, before he'd swung on his heels and walked out.

She'd felt like screaming, her nerves in shreds. Instead she'd lectured the boys on their bad behaviour, explaining that entering someone else's property without their permission was against the law of the land, not to mention the laws of polite behaviour, and had firmly withheld their usual bedtime story session.

And then spent the rest of the evening wondering if Carl suspected that James was his son.

And what he would do if he did.

Nothing, she assured herself now, shepherding the boys along the narrow lane in the teeth of an increasingly bitter wind. He wouldn't want to publicly acknowledge his son. It would mean having to confess to his wife that while he'd been getting engaged to her an eighteen-year-old, back in England, had been giving birth to his child.

He might have his suspicions, strong ones, but

she'd bet her bottom dollar that was as far as it would go.

The thought reassured her. She really didn't know what she'd been worrying about. Carl had married his pedigreed American beauty; he wouldn't want to dredge up a spectre from his past in the shape of the humble granddaughter of his uncle's gardener.

Besides, in all probability he had already left the area, heading back to spend Christmas in some highly sophisticated environment with his perfect wife. His visit to the Hall, the childhood home he had once loved but which was now apparently surplus to his adult and more blasé requirements, would have been a flying one—checking up that there was nothing personal left behind before the public auction of the house and its contents.

Their paths would never cross again.

Good, she thought staunchly, ignoring the sharp pang of loss she hadn't the remotest right to experience as a shriek of delight from James caught her attention.

'Mum—it's snowing! Look!'

Beth lifted her face. A few flakes were falling from a sky that looked heavy with the stuff. She'd been too enmeshed in the tangled web of her thoughts to notice how the clouds had rolled in.

A white Christmas would be story-book perfect, of course. The children would love it. And so would she. All she could hope for was that it would hold off awhile—allow her to drive down to the village after lunch to buy a tree—if any were left. She wouldn't want to risk the car Angela had lent her by making the journey to Bewley.

Then the warning note of an engine approaching from behind focused the whole of her attention on the two small boys. 'Car coming. Keep well into the side.' Her back to the oncoming vehicle, she heard it slowing down. Well, it would have to; the lane was very narrow and full of sharp bends. Drawing level, the car stopped, and only then did she turn to look at it.

'Carl!' She spoke his name without even thinking about it, her stomach turning a series of utterly sickening loops. So much for telling herself he would have already left the area!

Opening the driver's door of the sleek Jaguar, he unfolded all six feet two inches of lean masculinity, planting his feet wide as he instructed, 'Hop in. I'll give you a lift back.'

'There's no need,' Beth countered, feeling the heat in her face and wishing she didn't blush so easily. There was something very different about him this morning. He looked every inch the forceful, intimidating male, and his eyes were as cold as an arctic sea—completely different from the man who had walked back into her life last night.

He looked formidable.

Glancing down at the boys, she saw wide apprehension in both pairs of eyes. They had trespassed on this large and daunting man's property, and although she'd given them both a stern ticking-off they probably thought they were in for more of the same from him. Only worse, judging by his frozen expression.

'We don't have far to go.'

She stated the obvious as firmly as she knew how, only to watch him open the rear door and tell the boys, 'In you get.' Then he turned cold eyes on her. 'You have at least another half-mile to walk and the weather's turning atrocious.'

She'd rather walk a dozen miles than endure his company, Beth thought numbly, her feet dragging reluctantly as she obeyed the imperious movement of his head and joined him at the rear of the car. Lifting the boot, he took the bundle of holly and laid it beside a carton of groceries.

Her heart sank. He wouldn't be stocking up on fresh provisions if he intended to leave the Hall within the next day or two. And this new, bleakly angry mood could only mean one thing: he strongly suspected that James was his son.

Was he about to confront her with his suspicions? And how could she possibly justify what she'd done? she thought guiltily as she slid into the passenger seat and Carl checked that the boys were safely strapped in the rear.

Her stomach was tying itself in knots. She felt

nauseous as the worst-case scenario punched itself
into her brain: Carl, with his wealth, power and influence, fighting for custody, painting her as feckless
and sneaky for denying him the basic right of knowing he had a child, denying that same child all the
material and social advantages his father could give
him.

But she wouldn't think of that. She would not!

Maybe the sense of guilt she had tried to quash
over the years was making her see problems where
there weren't any? Perhaps his dark mood was down
to something else entirely? A quarrel with his wife?
Or having to face a longer stay at the Hall than he'd
anticipated? Hence this morning's drive down to the
village to collect extra provisions? And the long,
searching look he'd given James last night might
have been his way of impressing upon him his displeasure at childish naughtiness.

Reacting to his mood wouldn't set her mind at
rest, she decided as he slid in beside her and turned
the key in the ignition. The only way to discover
whether he was angry with her or with some other
situation in his life was to pretend everything was
normal—do a bit more of the catching up he had
expressed an interest in last night.

'I heard through the village grapevine that you
intend selling the Hall,' she ventured for starters,
wishing her voice hadn't emerged sounding so thin

and squeaky. Swallowing hastily, she lowered her tone. 'Marcus might be turning in his grave!'

Not a nice comment, she admitted with immediate regret as she glanced at the harsh perfection of his classical profile and saw his long mouth tighten, a muscle clench at the side of his jaw. But, against the grain of her nature, she'd wanted to hurt him because the way he'd so obviously changed made her heart ache.

The Carl Forsythe she had grown to love with an intensity that had been inversely proportionate to any hope that he might love her in return would never have contemplated disposing of the home that had been in his family for countless generations. Bewley Hall had been in his blood. He'd been so proud of the lovely house and the generations of family history wrapped up within its walls. Now he couldn't wait to get rid of it.

The tough, angular line of his jaw tightened further, and the lean fingers on the steering wheel flexed until his knuckles grew white, but he offered nothing in his own defence.

Her remark had hit home; she could see that very clearly. But the arrogant banker who could trace his ancestry back to the fifteenth century saw no need to explain himself to a nobody like her, Beth thought with deep inner misery, mourning the Carl she had practically grown up around, learned to worship.

The car's wipers were only just coping with the

amount of snow that was falling now, but in a thankfully short space of time they drew up in front of
her cottage, pulling up behind the car Angela had
lent her for the journey.

After helping the two boys out from the rear, Beth
walked stiffly to the back of the Jaguar and held out
her hands for the bundle of holly Carl had already
taken from the boot.

'Thank you for the lift.' She didn't mean it, and
the patently insincere words were difficult to frame
because her breath was so tight in her throat. She
wanted him to go away, yet she wanted to look at
him for the rest of her life. Snowflakes were dusting
the dark sheen of his hair, settling on the expanse
of black leather that sheathed his wide shoulders.
She wanted to look away, walk away, but she
couldn't.

Pulling herself together took a monumental effort
of will, but she did manage it. The holly clutched
tightly against her chest, she took an unsteady step
away. She couldn't afford to have him around James
for one moment longer; it was far too dangerous.

She could have groaned with frustration when
James himself prolonged that moment, sliding along
the snow-covered ground and thumping to a stand-
still against the side of Angela's car, piping up, 'Can
we go down for the Christmas tree now, Mum? Can
we?'

Beth's eyes clouded as she tugged her lower lip

between her teeth. She hated to disappoint her son, but taking the car on the three-mile return journey down to the village would be asking for trouble in the worsening weather conditions. And doing the journey on foot with two small boys in tow was out of the question.

Surprisingly, it was Carl who came to her rescue. More surprising still, he had obviously read the situation completely. She was sure she wasn't imagining it—the man who had been positively simmering with some dark internal anger was actually smiling down at James, his eyes soft, his honeyed voice warm and gentle as he vetoed the trip to the village.

'The roads are too slippy to drive on, and in any case I'd guess the best trees have already been sold. How about if I cut one from the estate and bring it round later this evening? I think I can find a box of lights and stuff. I'll bring those too, and maybe we can decorate the tree together in the morning.'

He looked and sounded supremely relaxed, Beth thought on a shiver of bleak anxiety. As if such a toing and froing between their two very different households was as natural as breathing.

James said nothing. He just stood there, a huge grin splitting his attractive, boyish features, until he gave a whoop of joy and turned and wrestled Guy to the ground.

And Beth just stood there too, watching the boys

roll around in the snow like a pair of young puppies, squealing and giggling. A release for the excitement that was spiraling as Christmas Day approached.

Crazily, she wished she could join them. Anything to release the dreadful tension that was building inside her.

It was a tension that was in danger of exploding all over the place when Carl, the tightness of banked-down anger back in his face, sharpening his voice, said, 'I need to talk to you, Beth. This evening. About nine. Make sure the boys are in bed. I don't want their holiday spoiled.'

And on that ominous statement he swung abruptly away, getting into the Jaguar without a backward glance and reversing down the track onto the lane that would take him to the Hall—and the wife who would be waiting for the groceries she'd sent him to collect.

He knows!

The thought sent a river of panic through her veins as she stared at the tracks his car had made in the steadily falling snow.

CHAPTER FOUR

As soon as the boys were tucked up in bed Beth put a match to the fire she had laid in the small cluttered room Gran had always referred to as 'the parlour' and had only used on rare special occasions, such as when the minister came to tea.

Crammed with an overstuffed three-piece suite of undoubted antiquity, which was starchily protected by stiff linen antimacassars, a forest of Victorian side-tables and whatnots, its walls festooned with gloomy framed prints of dour-looking Highland cattle set in landscapes of ferocious dreariness, the room had a musty, claustrophobic, unused atmosphere.

But if she kept a good fire burning and draped the brightly berried holly all over those depressing pictures then the room would be really cosy and cute, in a quirky kind of way. And the boys could open their presents here on Christmas morning and have fun.

Making plans was a way of taking her mind off what was to come. She'd made no special concessions in preparation for her dreaded confrontation with Carl. She was still wearing the same jeans and comfortable darker blue sweatshirt she'd worn all day, and instead of piling her long hair haphazardly on top of her head to keep it out of the way as she normally did she had scraped it severely back in a ponytail and secured it tightly with a no-nonsense rubber band.

No prinking and preening. Not like that other fateful night, eight years ago, when she'd pulled out all the stops and then some.

Remembering how she'd saved every penny she'd earned helping her grandfather in the gardens of the Hall out of school hours with the precise intention of buying something special for that longed-for evening opened the floodgates, releasing the memories that were as sharp as if they'd happened yesterday.

She didn't need this! She didn't want to relive that night again. But, sitting cross-legged on the hearthrug, watching the flames leap and crackle, she was powerless to hold back the memories she'd hidden away for such a long time.

Early in June, eight years ago. That was when it had really started. Her grandfather had put her to weed the long double herbaceous borders that were such a feature of the Hall's extensive grounds. Hot, back-breaking work, but necessary if she was to pay her way through college after taking her A levels.

If she closed her eyes and concentrated she could still feel the sun burning her bare arms and legs, the way her sleeveless T-shirt and old cotton shorts had stuck to her overheated body, still hear Carl's laughter as she'd almost run him down with the loaded wheelbarrow on her way to the compost heap.

Still feel the punch of sexual awareness that had made her heart tremble and her legs turn to jelly and then almost give way altogether as she'd registered the same awareness in the smouldering charcoal eyes that had held hers with an intensity that had opened up a bone-deep yearning, made her fear she was about to pass out.

There'd been something different about him. She hadn't been able to put her finger on it. For ages he'd seemed to avoid her, had seemed uncomfortable in her company whenever they'd run into each other when he'd been home from boarding school.

She'd really mourned the loss of their earlier close friendship and had sometimes woken at night with tears running down her cheeks, just aching to hear his voice, see his smile, be admitted to the magic circle of his friendship again.

But that day he'd looked delighted to be in her company. He had led her to a bench in the old courtyard, left her in the shade of the walnut tree while he'd fetched iced lemonade from the kitchens in long tall glasses, and their fingers had touched as he'd transferred one of the glasses to her.

Something had shuddered inside her and their eyes had met. Then his had dropped to her mouth and lingered and she'd known he wanted to kiss her. But he hadn't; he'd talked to her instead. And that day, precisely then, she'd fallen headlong in love with him. Looking back, she realised that she had always loved him and falling in love, as a girl on the brink of adulthood, had been a natural progression.

Swamped by an emotion that had transcended anything she had ever experienced in her seventeen years of living, she had barely heard a word of what he was telling her, her huge eyes drinking him in, the sensation of exhilaration making her head spin.

'So you'll be there?'

'Sorry?' She shook her head so hard her hair whipped across her face. She hadn't taken in what he'd been saying. He would think she'd turned into an idiot. But he smiled that gorgeous, heart-stopping smile of his and reached out to sweep her bedraggled hair away from her face. She wanted to capture his wrist, put a kiss in his palm, but didn't have the nerve.

Her eyes widened and her own mouth trembled into a radiant smile as he repeated, 'I'll be back at the end of the summer. You will come to my uncle's party this year, won't you? I'll be looking for you. If you don't turn up I'll come and get you!'

'I wouldn't miss it for worlds!' she vowed, meaning every single word with a vehement passion.

And she spent every waking minute of those waiting months going over every detail of that last meeting. The way he'd looked at her, the way she'd felt.

Holding tightly to the sudden, shattering ecstasy of falling in love for the very first time.

And planning.

At the end of every summer all the household staff, estate workers and their families received an invitation to attend the party Marcus gave for them at the Hall. And every year her grandparents politely declined. They didn't hold with such wasteful and unnecessary goings-on. They would never give her permission to attend, and while she lived under their roof she would do exactly as she was told. That had been drummed into her more times than she cared to remember.

Somehow she was going to go without them finding out.

Thankfully, they always went to bed early, so creeping out of the cottage after they'd retired for the night, wearing her old school coat over the wickedly expensive dress she'd dug deep into her savings to buy in Gloucester was the only option.

When the Hall came into view, all the downstairs windows flooded with light, she almost lost her nerve. She had wasted all her precious savings on frivolous underwear, the green silk dress that was far more daring than anything she'd ever imagined herself wearing, matching silk-covered high heels and a confusing mass of make-up that had demanded hours of secret experimentation before she had been able to achieve the right effect.

All of which would have to be continually hidden away—because if Gran ever discovered this evidence of what she would call flightiness there would be hell to pay!

And for what?

Just because Carl had asked her if she would be going to his uncle's annual party. Probably because he felt sorry for her, knew she was denied the sort of fun most girls took for granted by over-strict grandparents. And for the sake of old friendship he'd joked about it. 'If you don't turn up I'll come and get you!' Not really meaning it. It was one of those things people said.

Hovering on the edge of the drive, feeling foolish, she suddenly realised what the change in him she'd seen back in June was. It was the patina of sophistication that came naturally to a young adult male with wealth, centuries of breeding behind him, looks to die for and a deeply entrenched certainty about who he was and where he was going.

Carl Forsythe had the world at his feet and he knew it. She might have gone and fallen in love with him, but he would never feel more than moderate friendship for his old playmate—the humble granddaughter of one of his uncle's employees.

A feeling of hopeless misery wrapped itself around her heart as the bright embers of her hopes and dreams crumbled to ashes. Then her sense of self-worth emerged from where it had been hiding, prodding her forward, towards the main door which was flung hospitably wide.

She would go to the party. The money she had spent wouldn't be completely wasted. Besides, she liked the way she looked. And there was little fear of her grandparents discovering her perceived sins.

Grandad never gossiped with his fellow estate workers and Gran never conversed with anyone who wasn't a member of the chapel. A terse nod of acknowledgement was as much as most people got. In any case, she didn't know what she was feeling so strung up about. Carl probably wouldn't be there. He would have better things to do than hob-nob with a crowd of country bumpkins!

But he was there. Entering the huge, raftered inner hall after handing her old coat to the maid who was in charge of the cloakroom she saw him almost immediately. Head and shoulders above the rest, his crisp white dress shirt contrasting sharply with his dark dinner jacket, his strikingly handsome features tanned from a foreign sun, he made her heart stand still.

After a brief murmur of apology to the group he was with he walked towards her, his smile flattering in its sincerity, the sultry gleam of his eyes lingering on her face before dropping to skim her silk-clad body, making her flesh burn as though he was actually touching her…

*   *   *

It was still snowing, Carl noted as he collected the handsome five-foot-tall tree he'd cut earlier and left in the barn. It swirled, a pattern of wildly dancing flakes, in the beam of the powerful torch he carried. And it meant, he decided grimly, that Beth Hayley wouldn't have been able to take the sneaky way out again and drive off, disappearing with his son.

Anger beat at his brain with the harsh insistence of a machine gun. If James wasn't his son he was the Queen of Sheba—he'd stake his life on it!

The dates were right, exactly right, and the boy had his colouring, not his mother's. He had spent an hour tracking down old photograph albums, searching for what he needed. Proof. He'd found it in the last shot that had been taken of him with his parents, only weeks before they'd been in the accident that had claimed both their lives.

The seven-year-old boy grinning at the camera could have been the twin of Beth's son.

His son. He was damn well convinced of it.

His mouth hardened in a line of grim determination as he set out for the cottage. If he was right— and she'd have to come up with some cast-iron reasons why he wasn't—then he'd move heaven and earth to claim rights over his child. How dare she keep his son's existence from him?

He wouldn't have believed the open, sunny-natured, almost painfully innocent girl he had tended to put on a pedestal capable of such duplicity.

Innocent! The word intruded, hammered at his mind. His steps halted as he closed his eyes on the knife-thrust of guilt, letting the snow-laden wind push against him.

That night. That fateful night he'd never been able to get out of his head. The images, the feelings of shame coming back to taunt him when he'd least expected it.

He hadn't meant to seduce her, take away her innocence—he'd swear by everything he held dear that he hadn't. Suggesting—no, demanding that she attend the annual party hadn't been done with any dark ulterior motive. Simply a desire to see her have some fun for once in her sheltered life.

Her upbringing had been severely restricted. Seeing her friends outside school hours strictly forbidden. In case, he guessed, they'd led her astray. Her childhood friendship with him had only been tolerated because her dour grandfather had worked for his uncle.

So he'd believed his insistence that she join them had been motivated by compassion, conveniently forgetting that he'd been sexually attracted to her for some time but had been too young to know what to do about it.

He should have recognised the warning signals when he'd found himself watching for her arrival. He'd put his edginess down to jet-lag. He'd been back at the Hall a mere matter of hours since returning from Mexico, where he'd spent the last three months doing volunteer work for a charity which helped homeless children.

When he'd seen her arrive his heart had lurched, an anguished protectiveness taking him over. She'd looked so lovely standing there, the green dress skimming and flattering those lush curves, and so achingly vulnerable, too.

Her beautiful green eyes had been darkened by an apprehension he had never seen her display before, as if she had no right to be there, and her soft mouth had opened, her hands twisting together in front of her, as her eyes had been drawn to the party decorations that dominated the hall. She'd looked as if she had never seen anything like them in her life.

And the poor kid probably hadn't.

Only she hadn't been a child any longer.

Her heartbreakingly lovely face had lit up when she'd seen him, her huge eyes glowing like emeralds. He'd walked towards her, his heart thumping with pleasure, and they'd been playing a waltz—his uncle on the fiddle, Mrs Griggs the stout old housekeeper pounding the piano, and young Tom the stable boy on the flute.

Taking her in his arms, he had swept her into the dance. Holding her close had been heaven. He'd felt utterly, gloriously complete. They had moved together slowly, her full breasts brushing against him, thighs clinging. His hand had slid further down her back, holding her closer, and when the trio of players had launched enthusiastically into something modern and lively the older couples had left the floor to the youngsters who, he'd noted through eyes that felt decidedly unfocused, were dancing apart.

Compromising, he had rested both hands on her hips, keeping her swaying body against his, unable to relinquish this tormentingly intimate proximity. And Beth, with a tiny sigh, had looped her arms around his neck and pressed closer, so that he had known she must feel the engorged evidence of his desire. Through a dizzying red mist, he had known that she welcomed it. The way she'd tilted the feminine arch of her pelvis against him, parting her thighs just a little to accommodate him, had made his heart pound with suffocating ferocity.

The cessation of the music and his uncle's announcement that supper was waiting in the dining room had come just in time to stop him completely losing it.

Even so, it had taken quite a time to get his body back under control. Loosening his grasp, he had inched them apart a little, just as she'd dropped her arms back to her sides.

His throat had tightened with an emotion he hadn't been able to name as he'd seen her soft mouth tremble. There had been a rosy wash of colour on her cheeks and her eyes had been slumbrous, hazed, the look she'd flicked up at him through thick sweeping lashes oddly shy, uncertain.

'Would you like to eat?' His voice was thick because his breathing was still haywire.

'Not hungry.'

A tiny bead of perspiration nestled in the tantalising cleft between her breasts. He wanted to put his mouth there, take that tiny drop with his tongue. Battling with the almost overwhelming urge, he shuddered convulsively. Both of them were overheated, on a different planet. They needed time out to recover from what had happened.

He pulled himself together. He had to stop behaving like a lust-crazed fool. He'd be leaving for North America in three days' time, and by the time he came back, after his stint at university there, she would almost certainly have flown the uncomfortably rigid family nest and be making her own life. Their paths mightn't cross again for years. If ever.

'Stay right where you are,' he instructed thickly. 'I'll find us something cold to drink.'

People had already begun to emerge from the dining room with heaped plates of fork food when he came back with a bottle of chilled wine and two glasses. 'Let's find somewhere cooler to sit.'

And quieter. He could explain about the degree course in Economics he was due to take, before joining his uncle in the family-owned bank, and find out what she meant to do after leaving school.

Take a friendly interest, nothing more. Show her that their earlier close friendship still counted for something, but dismiss what had happened on the dance floor as a simple aberration by not referring to it at all.

Leaving the heat, the sound of people enjoying themselves behind, he led her up the wide staircase to the first-floor landing, where a squashy two-seater sofa was placed between an ancient suit of armour belonging to one of his distant ancestors and a low table that carried a bowl of flowers.

His fingers weren't quite steady as he poured out two glasses of the sparkling white wine. The lighting was more subdued here, but he could see the rosy flush that grazed her cheekbones, the slight trembling of her lush pink mouth. She looked adorable, her silvery blonde hair tumbling around her shoulders. The green silk of her dress left her arms and shoulders bare, and the straps that looped around the back of her neck were so delicately fragile they looked as if they would snap if he were to touch them.

Swallowing hard, he carefully placed the bottle and his glass on the polished surface of the low table and turned back to her, her glass in his hand. She bent forward hesitantly to take it and the dip of her neckline revealed the edge of her lacy bra, curving so lovingly against the creamy perfection of her breast.

Whether it was the unsteadiness of his hand or the trembling of her fingers he didn't know, but drops of the liquid spilled on the fine silky fabric that shaped the lush globes of her breasts.

His throat too thick to get an apology out, his heart galloping, he felt in his pocket for a handkerchief. He hadn't got one and, leaning forward, he used his fingers to brush away the offending droplets. Lightly at first, quickly. Until the fingers of both hands took on a will of their own and curved around the breasts that were peaking, spilling into his palms.

She was breathing rapidly, her lips parting, and his blood ran hotly through his veins as his hands shaped her, his fingers playing with the engorged nipples, his head spinning as this thing between them became a wild conflagration.

With a catch in his throat he brought his head down and kissed her, and he heard her low moan of pleasure as she responded with a generosity that made his heart quiver with emotion. Almost without knowing what he was doing, knowing only that this was the most perfect thing that had ever happened to him, something he had been unknowingly waiting for all his life, he swept her up into his arms and carried her to his suite of rooms.

He had never forgotten that night, or the beauty of it, he thought now, his mind jerked back to the present by a vicious gust of icy wind. But how could he reconcile the Beth who had blossomed so generously and sweetly for him on that long-ago night with the woman who had unconcernedly refused to respond to his letter, who had heartlessly deprived him of his own son? he thought with grim cynicism as he strode through the snow towards the lights of the cottage.

Were people never what they seemed to be? Was Beth, like his ex-wife, all sweetness and light on the surface and twisted and devious underneath?

Time to find out, for sure.

Propping the tree up against the side of the porch, he put his thumb on the doorbell. Beth Hayley had a whole load of questions to answer...

CHAPTER FIVE

IN WELCOME contrast to the bitterly cold night air Beth's kitchen was warm, redolent of seasonal baking, mouthwateringly spicy and sweet. Terrina had boasted that she didn't know how to boil an egg. Their sterile, elegant London apartment had been filled with the scent of her sultry perfume and Christmas had come in hampers from Harrods.

But he certainly hadn't come here to mull over his ex-wife's deficiencies in the home-making department, he decided grimly as Beth wordlessly took his ancient, snow-dampened sheepskin coat and hung it on a peg on the back of the kitchen door.

Her features had lost the softly rounded quality of her teenage years, were more finely drawn—even more lovely, he thought, an ache settling in the region of his heart. But she was very pale and her full lips were compressed, unsmiling.

He had kissed those lips. Held her and kissed her until they were both delirious.

Snapping that totally irrelevant thought aside with dark impatience, Carl demanded tersely, 'Are James and Guy in bed?'

Unguardedly, Beth lifted her eyes to the beamed ceiling, and Carl recalled hearing those muffled scuffles and thumps after she'd sent them up to get changed the evening before. Remembered eventually hearing the sounds of their feet on the stairs, the way she'd tried to get him out of the cottage.

Because she hadn't wanted him to get a good clear look at James.

And this morning she'd been on edge, spiky.

She knew he knew.

No wonder she looked pale. The eyes that had thus far refused to meet his own were dark-ringed and haunted.

Guilty conscience. He'd stake his life on it.

The thought that his son was sleeping overhead, unaware of his very existence, made his gut wrench with anger, pushing any compassion he might have felt for her clear out of sight. Controlling it took all his concentration, so he merely followed leadenly when she murmured, 'Through here,' and led him into a time warp.

A smile—unbidden, out of place in view of the fraught circumstances, and most certainly unwanted—curved his lips. The room looked as if it hadn't changed in a hundred years. Pure late Victoriana. Terrina would have wrinkled her aristocratic nose and pulled her mouth down in distaste, while Beth fitted unquestioningly into the old-fashioned surroundings, as she would fit in wherever she happened to find herself.

Catching himself up sharply, he hardened his

mouth. He didn't know why he kept comparing her with the cold, grasping creature he had been misguided enough to marry. Despite appearances, and his misplaced long and fond memories of her, Beth was as sneaky and devious as his ex.

Closing the door behind him, he turned to face her. She was standing on the hearthrug, her back to the fire. She looked, he noted grimly, as if she was getting ready to face her own execution.

And she'd be right about that!

He paced forward, moving closer because he needed to be able to read her expression and find the truth.

Since the scales had fallen from his eyes a few short weeks after his marriage he'd become expert at knowing when a woman was telling lies, bending the truth to suit her own selfish ends.

He questioned, slowly and deliberately, so there would be no possible mistake about what he was implying, 'How promiscuous are you?'

For a split second Beth's blood ran cold, then bubbled hotly through her veins. The bone-clenching trepidation that had grown steadily worse while she'd waited for him was swept away in a flash flood of rage.

'How dare you ask such a thing?' Her eyes clashed with his. If she'd had a brick handy she would have thrown it at his head!

Yet Carl looked so coolly controlled, as if he

hadn't just asked her the most outrageous question he could think of. And to push the impression home he followed on flatly, 'I got James's birth-date out of him while I was fastening his seat belt this morning. If I'm not his father you must have gone from my bed straight into another's. That would make you promiscuous.'

Beth felt the ground shake beneath her feet. She'd been sure he had strong suspicions, but she hadn't known he'd questioned James about his actual birth-date. That would have made his suspicions a rock-solid certainty. She felt sick. Her hands flew to her mouth, her fingers trembling against her overheated skin.

'Well?' he prodded remorselessly. 'Did your initiation into sex give you a taste for it? So much so that you hawked yourself around to get more of the same?'

His anger was cold, pent-up, dangerous. But hers sprang to answering, blistering life.

Taking two fraught steps towards him, she knotted her hands into fists, to stop herself from actually hitting the loathsome swine. Yet.

But he took the wind from her sails, completely deflating her, as he tacked on softly, 'Or is James my son?'

Beth's heart juddered, all her strength seeming to ebb away. Head and shoulders above her, his powerful body clothed in thigh-moulding jeans and a black roll-necked sweater, he looked terrifyingly intimidating, his hair clinging in damp tendrils to his beautifully shaped skull, his devastatingly handsome features hardened with cruel determination.

What to say? Brand herself as promiscuous or admit the truth? Run the real risk of him trying to take her son from her?

'Been struck dumb, have we?' His velvety voice held a sardonic bite as he took her chin between his thumb and forefinger, forcing her to look at him, to meet his cold, dark eyes. 'Not to worry. A simple DNA test should do the talking for you.'

Beth's throat convulsed. She was living in her worst nightmare. But she would fight to the death to stop him doing anything to upset her son.

James had recently started asking about his father. Guy had a daddy, why didn't he? She'd told him as much of the truth as she felt his tender years fitted him to handle. Explained that his father was a wonderful man and that she'd loved him very much. But that their lives and backgrounds had been too different to allow them to live together, that it was best if she was both mummy and daddy. It was an explanation he had accepted without any further questions.

So no way was she going to allow Carl to upset and confuse him, demand rights in his life, demand to have him with him for weekends or parts of his school holidays. His wife would certainly resent his very existence, and possibly show it.

She would not allow that to happen.

Jerking her head away from his punitive grasp, she told him fiercely, 'James is mine. I carried him, gave birth to him, cared for him and loved him for every minute of his life. He is everything to me. He is nothing to you—how could he be? Your only input was one night of lust you immediately forgot about!'

Momentarily pain flooded his eyes, the stab of it tightening his mouth, tugging at his breath, and Beth wished she hadn't voiced that last statement. She had wanted to hurt him and had succeeded, but it made her feel ashamed of herself.

She hadn't been a victim. She had wanted him to make love to her—wanted him with a desperation she could still so clearly remember. And he had written to her from America, asking her to keep in touch. She could have told him she was pregnant, but for reasons that had seemed good at the time she hadn't.

She took a step towards him, wishing she could take the wounding words back, her teeth biting into her full lower lip. But Carl, obviously furiously recovered, stated lethally, 'I take it that's your confirmation? James is my son. I have rights. He has rights. He is the new Forsythe generation. He is all Marcus ever wanted.'

Beth wanted to cry but wouldn't let herself. Her voice wobbling, she threw at him, 'Don't drag your uncle into it! You weren't thinking of his wishes when you decided to sell the Hall—he would have hated that!'

She was beginning to wail. She clamped her mouth shut. If he had said James was all he, Carl, had ever wanted then she might have softened, tried to work out a way of him getting to know his son without upsetting the little boy. But he hadn't, and it really, really hurt.

'There wasn't going to be a new generation of Forsythes,' he answered tensely. 'So there seemed no point in keeping the place on. The situation has now changed. I have the heir I never expected to have. The auction will be cancelled.'

Beth sank onto the nearest chair. Her legs were giving way beneath her. She put her hands over her mouth, her fingers flattening her lips.

She could see it now. Obviously his wife couldn't have children and, knowing how he took pride in his lineage, that would have been a dreadful blow. But now he had his heir he would move heaven and earth to claim him, to bring him up as a Forsythe, taking no account whatsoever of her or James's feelings. Then another thought took hold and threatened to shatter her precarious control. If his wife was barren, as he seemed to be implying, then she would resent James even more!

She couldn't let that happen! But how on earth could she stop it?

There was only one way. She took it. Lowering her hands, tears now streaming unashamedly down her pinched face, she pointed out, 'Your wife might not agree with you. I suggest you leave now, go back to the Hall and discuss it with her before you start trying to throw your weight around. And—' she gulped back a throatful of tears '—I have a say in my child's future, too.'

'What say, what rights, did you allow me eight years ago, when you knew you had conceived my child?' he demanded witheringly. 'None. If some quirk of fate hadn't brought us together, now, I would have gone to my grave never knowing I had a son! So don't try to plead your case with me. You don't have one!'

He swung round on his heels and stalked out of the room, and Beth wrapped her arms around her body and tried to pull herself together.

At least he'd done as she'd suggested—gone back to his wife to discuss the matter. Hopefully, she'd talk him out of what Beth was sure was in his mind—having his illegitimate son live with them. That his wife wouldn't be able to talk him out of anything, or would raise no objections, didn't bear thinking about.

Carl Forsythe was a powerful man in the banking world, and centuries of believing that what he wanted was his as of right had been bred into him. How could she hope to fight that?

Despite the roaring fire she was shivering convulsively, cold right through to the centre of her bones, and she leapt out of her skin when Carl walked back through the door. She had been so sure he'd left the cottage.

'Drink this.' He put a mug in her shaking hands. 'Hot, strong tea. You need it; you're in shock.'

For a moment her bewildered eyes met his. The last thing she'd expected from him was this brusque, rough-edged compassion.

Quelling a shiver, she gripped the mug in both hands to hold it steady. The ache at the back of her throat spread down to her chest. She couldn't blame him for being angry, and she should have remembered that even as a young boy he'd had a caring, compassionate heart.

A sudden memory flashed through her troubled mind, of Carl, probably nine years old at that time, finding a tiny baby frog on the gravel driveway in the full glare of the sun, the careful way he'd picked it up and carried it to the long damp grass which bordered the pool in one of his uncle's meadows, his grin of pleasure as the little creature had hopped away to safety.

So was it so surprising that he should put his anger aside momentarily and have a care for the mother of his child?

Straddle-legged, his back to the fire, he hooked his thumbs in the pockets of his jeans and told her flatly, 'I have no wife to consider. Terrina left me for her current lover, and we're now divorced.'

Every scrap of colour drained from Beth's face. When she'd heard of his engagement, his marriage, she'd been gutted, hair-tearingly jealous. She'd loved him so and had wanted him for herself, even though, deep down inside her, she'd known it could never happen.

But she was older now, and very much wiser. Except for their son's existence the past was dead and buried. Any residual fondness he might have felt for her had been wiped from his heart by what he had learned.

And he was free, which put her at an even greater disadvantage. No wife's feelings to consider meant he was free to do exactly as he wanted. He'd lost a wife but gained a son. He would do everything within his considerable power to keep him.

'I'm sorry.'

She muttered the expected polite response, wondering if he knew exactly how sorry she was, and why, and inwardly quaked at the harsh bitterness in his voice when he shrugged those impressive shoulders of his and stated, 'Don't be.'

Beth shivered. He seemed to fill the room with his presence, his controlled anger making the air sizzle with tension, and even before he spoke again she knew he would want answers. To her own horror, her defence now seemed unbelievably shaky.

'Why didn't you tell me you were pregnant?' he sliced rawly. 'What did I ever do to make you keep my son's existence from me?'

Guilt swamped her. He sounded so driven. It tore her in two. She had thought at the time that she was doing the right thing, and during her years as a single parent she'd found composure, remained convinced that the decision made so long ago had been the best for all concerned.

And now he would tear her defences into shreds.

She lifted reluctant eyes to his, her heart thudding heavily, then heaved a sigh of cowardly relief as she heard James pattering down the stairs, his voice wobbly as he called for his mummy.

'Darling!' She was out of her chair and opening the door immediately, strength flowing back into her weakened limbs, her only thought now to comfort her child.

Standing on the bottom tread of the staircase in his red and white striped pyjamas, his quivering mouth turned down piteously, the grey eyes beneath a rumpled lock of dark hair flooded with tears, the boisterous seven-year-old had returned to unashamed babyhood.

Her heart swelling with love, Beth hunkered down and held out her arms, murmuring, as he launched himself into her loving embrace, 'Bad dream, darling?' She dropped a kiss on the side of his soft little neck as he nodded wordlessly and took a noisy gulp of air into his heaving chest, burrowing his head into her sweatshirt.

He rarely suffered from nightmares, and she guessed tonight's had been caused by the excitement of the approach of Christmas and the naughtiness of the previous evening. Cuddling him closely, she could feel his slight body shivering. The upstairs rooms were decidedly chilly, and the sooner she got him safely tucked up under his cosy duvet the better.

But first, 'How about a drink of warm milk, poppet?' Feeling his vigorous nod, she got back to her feet and dropped a swift kiss on the top of his head. 'Coming right up.'

She turned and saw Carl's eyes fixed upon them. Dark, brooding eyes, and a line of pain around his mouth, a line of colour along his slanting cheekbones. Her heart turned over. She knew how he was feeling. Seeing his own son in distress, unable to do anything about it.

Whether it was guilt or compassion, she didn't know, but she heard herself calmly suggesting, 'Jamie, why don't you go through and sit by the fire with Mr Forsythe while I heat that milk?'

She held her breath. Would James do that? Or would he remember the ticking-off he'd had for trespassing and hang his head, cling to her, refuse to do any such thing in case the formidable stranger started telling him off all over again?

But James simply nodded and took Carl's outstretched hand, and as they walked back into the sitting room Beth heard, 'Call me Carl. I brought you a Christmas tree. I said I would, remember? I'll come by tomorrow and we'll put it up together.'

And then the door closed and Beth released the breath she hadn't known she was holding. She would have felt utterly, drainingly dreadful if James had refused to have anything to do with his father. Though why she should care about Carl's feelings when she knew his intentions regarding the future of his son—a future which would see her relegated firmly to the sidelines, a weekend visitor at best, if he had his way—she had no clear idea. And the thought of him coming here tomorrow to help decorate the cottage for Christmas appalled her.

There was too much between them. The past with its lovely bittersweet memories, the future with its threatened dangers, and the spiky tension of the present. She didn't know how she would handle having him around.

She had to get a grip, she told herself fiercely as she poured creamy milk into a pan, slid it onto the hotplate of the Rayburn and reached down a mug.

Her emotions had been going haywire ever since she'd opened the door and found him standing there with the shame-faced little boys. Found the old at-

traction still alive and kicking and become the unwilling recipient of memories she'd thought she had
buried, battling with the fear that he might suspect
James was his son, her feelings of horror and help-
lessness when those fears had been verified.

She just had to start thinking positively, she lectured herself firmly. What court in the land would
take a child from its mother and hand him to his
father? And if he went ahead and hired the best lawyers in the universe she would fight him.

Never mind if all she had to offer was unstinting
maternal love when Carl could offer every advantage known to man that influence, wealth and position could bring. She would still fight him!

Her chin high, she carried the mug of warm milk
into the sitting room, only to have her feeble heart
melt inside her. They looked so right together, the
resemblance truly remarkable.

Carl was sitting on the chair she had used, near
to the crackling fire, with James curled up on his
lap, his dark head resting against the big man's
shoulder. They looked so relaxed, so peaceful.
James's tears had dried and his cheeks were flushed
with pink, and Carl's eyes were warm, his smile
gentle as he helped the little boy sit upright to take
the milk, his strong arms anchoring the warm little
body.

'Carl was telling me a story about Mole and Ratty
and the riverbank,' James announced sleepily. 'His

daddy used to read it to him when he was little.' He took a long swallow of milk and came up with a creamy moustache. 'I wish I had a daddy.'

Beth's stomach churned over. James had just unwittingly given Carl even more ammunition. She didn't dare look at him, not even when he put the empty mug down on one of the many little tables and got fluidly to his feet, his son in his arms.

'I'll carry you up and tuck you in,' he was saying in a low, conspiratorial whisper. 'We'll be very quiet, like mice, so we don't wake Guy. And I'll see you in the morning. Say goodnight to Mummy.'

A milky kiss brought tears that stung the backs of her eyes, her skin prickling with goosebumps. She could recognise bonding when she saw it!

And recognise unfairness, too. She had deprived Carl of the first seven years of his son's life, deprived her child of a father.

Pacing the floor, feeling sick, she waited for Carl to reappear. They had to sort something out. He was angry with her, and she could understand that. She would have been spitting tacks, throwing things, had their positions been reversed.

But when he cooled down they should be able to work something out—gently break the news that Carl was James's father, agree on visiting rights. Weekends, certainly, and if, as he'd stated, he would be keeping the Hall on, then maybe James could spend time with him there. It was only a matter of a couple of hundred yards away...

Then her mind went blank as she heard Carl coming down the stairs, his feet quiet on the old oak boards. Her mouth had gone dry and she couldn't stop her fingers twisting together, over and over, as if she were trying to pull the joints out of place.

His face, when she could see it clearly, was unsmiling now. The warmth, the softness that had been there for his son utterly wiped away.

'He went out like a light,' he informed her coolly as he reached for his coat. Shrugging into it, he turned to face her. 'I'll see you first thing in the morning.' He turned the fleecy collar up and took his torch from the kitchen table. 'As I see it, there's only one thing to do in this situation. Marry. As soon as it can be arranged.'

Marry him! Something inside her rose on a rushing tide of tantalising hope. It was all she'd dreamed of at one stage in her life. But the surge of hope died, dropped like a stone.

Her mouth stiff, she parried, 'Don't tell me you've fallen in love with me!' She heard the note of sarcasm in her voice and applauded it. It was the only thing that stopped her from bursting into hysterical tears.

'Of course not.' His voice was flat. 'I want my son. And he wants a father—you heard him. He needs two parents. Full-time. To achieve that we have to live together, marry. I lost both my parents when I was a few months older than he is now. Marcus did his best to replace them, but there was a big hole in my life for a very long time.'

He turned for the door, swung it open, and the bitter wind blew a flurry of snowflakes at his feet. 'You can refuse, of course, but I warn you the consequences won't be pleasant for any of us.' One final look speared contempt into her wide, shell-shocked eyes. 'Don't fight me on this, Beth. You won't win.'

CHAPTER SIX

BETH was woken by muffled thumps and shrill giggles from the room next to hers. The boys were already awake, full of beans and ready to start the day.

Christmas Eve.

She groaned. She didn't want to be awake yet. It was still pitch-dark. And last night she hadn't been able to fall asleep for hours. She felt exhausted.

Marry him!

The reminder of what he'd said just before he'd left the cottage last night, the reason she had paced the floor for absolutely ages and been unable to sleep when she'd finally gone to bed, attacked her brain, brought her fully, stingingly and regretfully awake.

She hadn't wanted to have to think about it. Not again. Not yet. She'd gone over and over it last night and it had got her precisely nowhere.

Her stomach tying itself in increasingly tight knots, she wriggled over and reached for the bedside light. A glance at her watch told her it was barely six o'clock. It wouldn't be light for another two hours!

Pulling a warm woollen robe over her serviceable cotton pyjamas, just as an ominous crash was followed by a breathless silence and then a crescendo of giggles, she heaved an irritated sigh. Obviously her hopes that she could persuade them to go back to sleep were dead in the water. Her opinion consolidated when she opened their door and flicked on the light.

Mayhem. Pillows and feathers everywhere.

James, sitting on the floor beside the upturned night-table, offered spurious innocence, making his eyes seem even bigger than they normally were. 'I fell out of bed, Mum.'

'So I see.' She spoke repressively, but she hadn't the heart to read the riot act. The two small faces were alight with excitement. After all, it was Christmas Eve. Consigning at least another hour of much needed sleep to the dustbin of dashed hopes, she said, 'Get dressed. And tidy this room up before you come down for breakfast. And if you behave yourselves—and only if you do,' she stressed, 'I'll help you make a snowman when it gets light.'

'Wow!'

Guy bounced off the bed and James, grinning from ear to ear, announced, 'Carl can help as well. He's coming to put up the tree. He said so. Where is it, Mum? Is it a big one?'

'Big enough.' She'd seen it propped up in the porch when Carl had let himself out last night. She wished he hadn't promised James that he'd come and set it up. She didn't want to have to face him again until she'd got her mind sorted out.

Besides, they had nothing to dress it with. Christmas trees and glittery baubles hadn't featured in her grandparents' scheme of things. She'd fully intended to buy some decorations yesterday, when picking up a tree from the village, but the sudden heavy snowfall had put a stop to that.

But that had to be the least of her worries. Leaving the boys' room, she closed the door and leant back wearily against it.

What Carl had suggested was out of the question. How could she marry a man who'd vehemently stated that he didn't love her, who actively and openly despised her?

He had wanted her physically once, briefly, and now he obviously thought she was the pits. That she had loved him, adored him, could safely be relegated to the past. Of course it could.

What she had experienced when they'd been talking after he'd brought the boys back from breaking into his house had been simple animal lust. He had matured into a wickedly attractive male. A woman would have to be blind not to fall victim to his vibrant masculinity.

Marriage would be a form of torture. There had to be another way. But her brain seemed incapable of functioning sensibly.

Using all her will-power, she propelled herself

into the bathroom, shutting her ears to the noises coming from the bedroom where James and Guy were clumping around, hopefully tidying up the mess they'd made.

She needed more time to get her head around Carl's cold insistence on marriage, to work out a compromise that would be acceptable to both of them. She needed a breathing space—but she clearly wasn't going to get one.

Back in her own room again, she pulled on the first things that came to hand. A pair of warm fawn cord trousers, an old navy blue jumper that had stretched in the wash and a pair of suede ankle boots that had seen better days. Dragging a brush through her long hair, she met her eyes in the mirror and groaned at what she saw there. Utter bewilderment.

The brush dropped from her fingers, clattered on the dressing table.

She had never known who her father was, only that he had been a student at the college where her mother had been studying at the time. As a child she had hopelessly daydreamed that both her parents would come and claim her, make her part of a close-knit, loving family. It had never happened, of course.

Had she any right to deny her own son the security of the love and care of both parents? True, he had a mother who loved him, but he needed a father too.

Full-time, as Carl had stated.

Could she handle it? She simply didn't know. Her heart twisting alarmingly, her forehead creased with confusion, she padded downstairs to make a start on breakfast. It was going to be a long, long day.

She already felt like a piece of chewed string and the day had barely started!

Carl found what he'd been looking for at the far end of the attics. The box of Christmas decorations.

In less enlightened times this series of small rooms leading off a narrow corridor had provided sleeping quarters for the servants. But things had changed for the better. Mrs Griggs, his uncle's housekeeper, and her husband Cyril—a cheerful, willing helper around the house and grounds—had occupied a light and comfortable suite of rooms above the kitchen quarters. A phone call early this morning had established the fact that they were only too happy to return.

They would take up their positions immediately after Christmas, hire the extra staff needed and make sure that everything was running like well-oiled clockwork when he took up permanent residence.

With his son.

His heart swelled inside him until he thought it might burst, and he felt strangely light-headed as he lifted the box and walked the length of the corridor to the door at the head of the attic stairs.

He was making decisions. He didn't have to think about it because it came naturally. And he didn't have to think about the possibility of Beth refusing his offer of marriage. He would make damn sure that the consequences of her refusal would make her blood run cold.

A few days ago remarriage had been out of the question. But now it was the only option if his son were to have a permanent place in his life, the privileges he himself had enjoyed, the security of two loving parents, his heritage and all that entailed.

The Hall was big enough for him and Beth to lead virtually separate lives—only sharing mealtimes when James was around, joining forces when the three of them needed to do things together: celebrating James's birthday, school sports days, that sort of thing.

He clattered down the narrow staircase. No one had ever said that such an arrangement would be easy, but if he could live with that, for their son's sake, then so could she. That would be the first thing he would make sure she fully understood. No arguments!

As he passed the small sofa on the first-floor landing his mouth tightened as an unidentifiable pain clamped around his heart. She had been so sweet, so responsive and loving on that long-ago fateful night. Had she, even then, been concealing a devious nature, a disregard for anyone's feelings and needs except her own?

He would never forgive her for denying him his rights as a father.

Outside, the air was crisp and cold. An overnight frost had hardened the thick layer of snow, just as her duplicity had hardened the carapace around his heart where she was concerned.

Once, he had been besotted with her, and if circumstances hadn't removed him he knew he would have pursued her with all the tempestuous ardour of puppy-love. He'd written, asking her to keep in touch, and after weeks and months of waiting for her non-existent reply he'd done what any sane guy would have done—got on with his studies, enjoyed his social life, and forgotten her.

Except in his dreams.

But those erotic, tormenting dreams were a thing of the past. He was no longer a besotted, callow youth, inexperienced in the ways and wiles of women.

Beth was switching off her mobile phone as Carl walked, unannounced, into the kitchen of Keeper's Cottage. She had an arm round Guy's shoulders and her face was pink.

Guilty conscience? Had she been phoning her solicitor? Her current man-friend? Trying to find a way out of the situation she found herself in? Her obvious embarrassment, and the absence of James, certainly pointed that way. If she was thinking along those lines she'd have to damn well think again!

Beth felt her face run with hot colour. She hadn't expected him this early. It was barely eight-thirty. And he looked so dangerously attractive her heart stood still. Gorgeous simply wasn't the word for it. Perfect, very male features, a lean and sexy physique—but cold, killing eyes. He looked as if he hated her.

It was Guy who broke the tension. Beth heard his bright young voice as if it came from a great distance. 'My mummy says the new baby is coming soon, and my daddy says Father Christmas knows where I am. He won't leave my presents at home by mistake.' He squirmed out of Beth's hold and dived over the kitchen floor for his wellingtons. 'My dad says he doesn't mind if the baby gets born a girl or a boy. But I want a boy to play with, 'cos James says he wants to live here for ever and ever.'

'We phone Angela and Henry every day, so Guy can speak to them.' Beth's explanation was shakily delivered, and the hand that placed the mobile on the table was far from steady.

Carl felt the tension ebb from his shoulders. But whether it was because that phone call had been innocent and not what he had suspected, or whether it was because his son apparently seemed keen to stay in the area—relieving him of the worry that he might not want to be uprooted—he couldn't say. A mixture of both, he decided, and he put the bulky cardboard box down on the table just as James came clattering down the stairs.

He was wearing a long woolly scarf round his neck and carrying another, which he bunched into a ball and threw at Guy. His face lit up when he noticed Carl. 'Mum said she'd help us make a snowman. You can help, too.'

'I'd like that, Jamie.' Carl's voice was slightly husky, warm. The cold, killing look had disappeared. His smile would have melted an iceberg.

Beth shivered. She hugged her arms around her body. What had she done to this man? She'd deprived him of the first formative years of his son's life and turned what had been a fondness for her into implacable hatred.

How could she marry him, knowing that?

How could she live with Carl until their son was of age, making his own way in the world, loving him and knowing that he despised her?

Biting her lower lip until she tasted blood, she made a swift and vehement mental correction. Of course she didn't still love him! It had been the best part of a decade ago, for pity's sake. Love didn't last that long without anything to feed on!

He was helping the boys into their coats, asking them if they'd like to see over his house and look for a hat for the snowman. He was sure they could find something—there were several old trilbys that had belonged to his uncle in the garden room. Marcus wouldn't mind, Carl was explaining, he'd be glad they were making use of something he didn't need now.

As Beth listened to the gentle baritone she felt swamped by lonely bitterness. Of course Marcus wouldn't mind his great-nephew using his cast-offs. The bloodline was all-important to the Forsythes. She felt surplus to requirements. The outsider.

She had never felt that way in those long-gone happy days when she and Carl had been practically growing up together. But everything had changed. And that was the loneliest feeling in the world.

'Ready?' Carl turned to her, one dark brow gliding upwards. The boys were fidgeting, anxious to get outside. 'You'll need your coat; it's bitterly cold out there.'

He sounded polite, friendly even, Beth thought hollowly. He wouldn't want James to pick up bad vibes. But she wasn't going to jump when he told her to.

'Now you're here to supervise I'll leave you to it,' she came back with a manufactured saccharine-sweetness, an airiness that belied the heaviness of her heart. 'I've got loads to do inside.'

Their eyes clashed for long fraught moments, then his face froze over. Two strides took him to the door. He flung it open and the boys, needing no encouragement, raced out into the pale winter sunshine.

'Sulking, Beth?' he enquired in soft, level tones that sent shivers down her back. 'Grow up, why don't you? You brought this on yourself and it's time you took responsibility for your sins of omission. And by the way—' there was a sharp edge to his tone now '—I'll give the boys lunch at the Hall. It's time James got familiar with the place he'll be calling home. I suggest you use the next few hours to decide when we tell our son who I am and break the news of our forthcoming marriage.' He walked through the door, turned back to her and stated coolly, 'It's going to happen. Just get used to it.'

It was growing dark when they returned. Beth heard the boyish voices ringing out on the frosty air well before Carl pushed open the kitchen door.

Frantically, she pinched her wan cheeks to coax some colour into them. She didn't want him to see her looking as if she were knocking on death's door. She had more pride than that!

She'd changed into fresh blue denim jeans and a pale aqua silk-knit sweater, brushing her hair until her scalp stung and leaving the soft blonde mass loose around her shoulders. No way would she let him know she'd spent the intervening hours in a state of blind panic at the way he was taking over, keeping James away from her for the greater part of the day without so much as a by-your-leave. Excluding her.

That she could have gone with him if she hadn't stubbornly decided to make a point was something she hadn't contemplated as she'd thrown herself into a mindless whirlwind of cleaning and polishing, baking and ironing, doing anything to stop herself from feeling like a spare wheel, stop herself from thinking.

Now, as the boys rushed past Carl into the warm kitchen, babbling excitedly, their cheeks rosy, their eyes over-bright, she wished she'd been with them and been a part of their fun day.

'The snowman's humungous!' Guy gabbled, kicking off his wellingtons so wildly they flew into a far corner. 'His name's Bert and he fell over, but we builded him up again and gave him a hat and an umbrella.'

'And pelted him with snowballs until he disintegrated again,' Carl put in with a wry smile. 'However, Bert Mark Three is still standing, guarding the approach to the Hall—Guy, be a good chap and pick your boots up and find your slippers—'

'And Carl's house is brilliant, Mum,' James, sitting on the floor and removing his boots more circumspectly, cut in. 'You should see it—millions of rooms and he's lived there since it was built!'

'Which would make me getting on for five hundred years old,' Carl said with a grin that made

Beth's heart turn over. She dragged her eyes away from him, her face hidden as she busied herself helping the two boys out of their coats, hanging them up on the back of the door.

Carl in this kinder mood sent a lonely sigh around her heart, where it curled up and stayed right where it was, leaving her feeling bereft because none of this warm gentleness was for her benefit.

How could it be?

'I fed them beans and sausages for lunch,' Carl imparted as James and Guy scampered up to the bathroom to wash their hands, as instructed.

Beth, pulling herself together, but not quite to the point where she could actually turn to look at him and see all that hurtful hating back in his eyes, collected the discarded boots and scarves and told him, 'Thank you. I've made a seafood pie for supper. Will you join us? Or would you rather skip that and come back later? We need to talk.'

She felt calmer then. However unpalatable the facts were, they had to be faced. The fact that she was now willing to do so, and was no longer in denial, had restored some of the sense of self-worth that had been leaching away ever since he'd told her he knew James was his son.

'I'd like that.' Carl knew his voice had come out with an intimate slow huskiness, and felt his eyes soften, grow heavy, as he watched her move around the kitchen. Even putting the diminutive wellington boots in a tidy row at the side of the stove, folding the scarves and placing them in one of the dresser drawers, her movements were sheer grace.

The soft denim fabric moulded the elegant length of her legs, clipping the rounded feminine curve of her hips, just as the sweater she was wearing followed the proud curve of her beautiful breasts. The way she moved had always fascinated him.

And he'd missed her today, he admitted. Wanted her to be with them.

Running out of things to occupy her, she turned and faced him. Her silky blonde hair was tumbling around her face, curving around her slender neck. A faint wash of colour was creeping across the delicate arch of her cheekbones and something deep in the emerald depths of her huge eyes made his stomach clench with a desire that should have died years ago.

The sensation made him want to hit something. His mouth twisted bitterly. He had forgotten what love was, but his body remembered hers.

Lust. That was what it was all about. And lust he could handle simply by ignoring it. He surely hadn't wanted her with them today for any other reason than getting James used to seeing them as a threesome. Sure, he'd like to join her for supper, but only because it would give him the chance to continue the bonding process with his son.

She owed him that much, and a damn sight more! To hammer that point home, for his own sake as much as for hers, he informed her coolly, 'It's important that Jamie and I spend as much time as possible together before we break our news. And yes, we do need to discuss the timing. Also—' he shrugged out of his coat and hung it with the others '—I promised them we'd decorate the tree.'

The hope that his attitude towards her was softening had been a very faint glow in the darkness of his overt dislike of her, and his coolly delivered words had brutally extinguished it.

No big deal, she told herself staunchly. She would be a fool to hope for anything other than implacable dislike from him.

The thought of that dislike stretching through the years to come, until, when their son was grown, Carl could safely get rid of her, made her feel nauseous. But he wasn't going to see that.

Making herself smile—a thin one, but a smile just the same—she said, 'Then perhaps you could make a start while I see to supper? The boys will come down any time now. I put the tree in a bucket and wedged it firm with split logs. The box of decorations is through in the parlour, too. And while you're in there make up the fire, if it needs it.'

Then, feeling her control begin to slip away, she knelt to bring the seafood pie from the fridge. When she stood up again the parlour door was closing behind him and her eyes filled with tears.

CHAPTER SEVEN

CARL had made coffee while Beth had been settling the boys for the night. The aroma, usually so enticing, turned her stomach.

'Through there.' He lifted the tray and walked into the parlour and Beth had no option but to follow. Crunch-time, she thought, her face paling as her heartbeats threatened to choke her.

The cheerful blaze of the fire drew her. She sank into the chair nearest the hearth to relieve her wobbly legs of the necessity of keeping her upright. Outside, the wind was howling around the little cottage. It sounded like a wild animal. They were in for another snowstorm; she was sure of it.

She felt trapped. By the weather, but mostly, she admitted, by Carl. She shuddered.

'I've decided to set a date for the wedding towards the end of January,' Carl announced unilaterally, his back to her as he poured the coffee. 'It will give time for the banns to be called.' He turned, a mug in each hand, his features expressionless. 'A register office ceremony might be more appropriate, under the circumstances, but traditionally Forsythes have always married in the village church.'

'And we mustn't go against tradition, must we?'

Beth was amazed by the strength of her sudden anger, but grateful too. At least the surge of hot, savage emotion injected life back into her wilting spirits. 'This is all about your precious family tradition, isn't it? Did you divorce your wife because the poor woman couldn't produce a Forsythe heir? If you hadn't been the last in the line of your wretched dynasty you wouldn't have given a damn about my son, would you?' she accused heatedly.

Her breasts heaving, she shook her head and crossed her arms over her midriff, refusing to take the coffee he calmly held out to her.

Carl's impressive shoulders lifted in a slight shrug as he put the mug down on the nearest low table within her reach. His voice was as calm as his actions when he countered her blistering accusations.

'Terrina refused to have children—a fact she had neglected to share with me before our marriage. She preferred to take lovers. Her primary aim in life was to look beautiful, spend money, attract men. She had her second husband lined up when she demanded a divorce. I give him six months at best. She has a low boredom threshold.'

He took a mouthful of coffee and, cradling the mug in his hands, told her forcefully, 'Remarriage was not on my agenda. I decided to sell the Hall because the old house cries out for a family. If I'd been so obsessed with what you choose to call the Forsythe dynasty, I'd have mothballed the place until I could find some fecund young thing willing to marry me and give me an heir. You should think things out before you make judgements.' His face tightened, closing up implacably. 'Now everything's changed. I have a son. Flesh of my flesh. Satisfied?'

Beth caught her lower lip between her teeth. She wished he'd sit down. Looming over her, he made her feel small. She already felt two inches high and shrinking after hearing what he'd had to say.

How any sane woman could even look at another man when she had Carl's love, his wedding band on her finger, she couldn't begin to imagine. He must have been truly, deeply hurt.

But that didn't alter her own unenviable situation. She said, as calmly as her rioting nerve-ends would let her, 'And if I don't agree to be legally tied to a man who loathes me? I could decide to have nothing to do with your crazy ideas!'

His mouth flattened, but there was a thread of danger in his voice as he imparted, 'Then you will regret such a decision for the rest of your life. Be very sure of that.'

He sank into the chair opposite hers while he waited for his words to sink in. He watched the whole gamut of emotions cross her features, like clouds racing over the landscape—saw the pain, the uncertainty in her deep green eyes, and wanted to hold her, kiss the pain away, assure her that he would care for her, always care for her.

Clenching his hands, he reminded himself that she deserved everything he was dishing out, that in her own way she was no better than Terrina. But for some damn fool reason he heard himself qualifying, 'I don't loathe you. I admit I don't want a real marriage—the Hall's big enough for us to rattle around in without having to have much to do with each other—but I don't loathe you. When you opened the door when I brought the boys home that first night, it was like meeting a warm ray of sunshine on a bitter winter's day. That was before—'

He broke off, leaving her to draw her own conclusions. She knew what he meant. Miserable guilt was written all over her pale and lovely face. 'Why didn't you respond to my letter?' he pressed quietly. 'Why didn't you tell me you were expecting my child? I didn't just walk out on you—you knew I was due to leave for the States; I told you.'

Or had he told her? His eyes darkened beneath clenching brows. He knew he'd meant to tell her, had taken her to that secluded place for that reason. He had already known that something pretty monumental was coming to life between them and he'd been trying, for both their sakes, to cool things down.

He'd been nineteen years old, and pretty inarticulate as far as his emotions were concerned, but he'd known he had to make her understand that they had to be adult enough to wait until they'd both finished their education before they took their relationship any further.

But maybe he hadn't actually got around to it. He couldn't clearly remember. His brain had been in a fog ever since he'd started to dance with her. Then the wine had been spilled and events had overtaken them.

She might have seen his disappearance from the scene as desertion...

The slight contemptuous curl of her mouth as she answered his questions confirmed exactly that.

'It was days before I found out why you weren't around. I must have been the last person to know you'd flown to the States directly after that party.'

Even now she could recall exactly how shattered she'd felt at her own naivety. She'd truly believed that he'd made love to her because he loved her. When the truth was he'd simply used her, not even bothering to explain that he was due to leave the country. No wonder he hadn't suggested when they would see each other again.

He'd left the country without a word, leaving her in total ignorance, waiting for him to get in touch, tell her he loved her and wanted to be with her for ever. Fool!

'And then that letter came.' She verbalised her angry thoughts, her rage fuelled by the memory of how eagerly she'd ripped open the airmail letter, how she'd disintegrated after reading the hastily scrawled lines.

Her eyes held emerald scorn. 'Mostly about how well you were settling in at the home of your uncle's banking associate, his charming wife and their daughter Terrina. How welcome they made you feel. And then the really stiff and impersonal bit!' she lashed out. 'You would like me to keep in touch. And contact you if there were any repercussions.' She pushed her hair out of her eyes with impatient fingers, then knotted her hands together in her lap, her voice dry as she recalled, 'It took me until I realised I was pregnant to understand what you'd meant by "repercussions".'

And then she'd been afraid. So afraid.

Her grandparents would have to be told; they'd probably disown her...

'Why didn't you tell me?' He closed his eyes briefly; his face looked drawn.

'After that letter? Get real, Carl! There wasn't one word of affection, the slightest indication of caring. The dreaded "repercussions" had eventuated. You wouldn't have wanted to know—why would you have wanted something like that to mess up your perfect, privileged life? You would have probably sent money for an abortion. I couldn't face your doing that. I wanted my baby. I didn't want to have you spell out that our baby was the last thing you wanted. Do you know something?' she queried witheringly. 'I thought it best for all of us for you to be in happy ignorance!'

There was a beat of heavy silence, then Carl said wearily, 'I'm sorry if I gave you the wrong impression. When I wrote that letter I was desperately ashamed.'

Ashamed? A vein throbbed at her temples. Her jaw clenched. Her voice shook as she came back at him. 'Of course you were ashamed. The young lord of the manor, heir to a banking empire, having sex with the gardener's granddaughter! Bad form, what?' she taunted, sarcasm dripping from her shaky voice.

Never in her life had she seen anyone move so quickly. Her eyes winged wide open as he left his seat and hunkered down in front of her, taking her hands, loosening her frantic grip, taking each of them into his own. 'That is not what I meant. Then or now. Did I ever give you any reason to believe I didn't think of us as equals? I was ashamed because I'd taken something precious. You were so young and I'd taken your virginity. I'd had no control over my own desire; I'd taken no precautions. I was ashamed of myself, not of you,' he stressed. 'For pity's sake, Beth, I was besotted with you, put you on a pedestal—'

Then, just as quickly, he moved away, standing up, dropping her hands, pacing back. As if he'd suddenly remembered that, far from being besotted with her, he didn't even like her now, not one little bit.

The passion, the vehemence behind what he'd just said rocked her. Had he really felt like that about her? Might everything have been so different? Her eyes swam with sudden tears. The glittery baubles on the Christmas tree shimmered and seemed to lose all substance.

He was standing with his back to her, staring out of the window into the wintry darkness, as if the cluttered room stifled him and he wanted out. Out of the mess they had made of their lives. She could see the tension in the hard, high line of his shoulders, in the taut muscles of his back and long, lean thighs.

Beth blinked, scrubbed the wetness from her cheeks with the back of her hand and forced herself upright, taking a couple of paces towards him, talking to the back of his head. 'I know you'll never forgive me for not telling you about James. But, in my defence, the first time I held our son in my arms I knew I was going to have to. You deserved to know that between us we'd made such a perfect baby. That first time I held him I felt very close to you. It was almost as if you were in that hospital room with me.'

'Really?' His voice was flat. 'Then what stopped you?'

He didn't turn. She could see the reflection of his

grim features in the darkened window. She'd been right; he would never forgive her.

But now, while they still had to agree how and when to tell James that Carl was his father, was probably the only chance she'd ever get to put her side of the story. Already he would be regretting having confessed how he had once felt about her, wishing he could take the words back because his youthful emotions had no relevance now.

Her voice unconsciously low and soothing, she told him, 'As I said, my grandparents didn't ask me to leave. But they made their disapproval so obvious it was the only thing I could do. I found work, a room to live in, and a couple of months before James was born I was given a one-bedroom council flat in a high-rise building that was more than half empty and mostly boarded up because nobody who had any choice wanted to live there—'

'And you took my child to a place like that?' He swung round, and she was sure the hands that were pushed into the pockets of his jeans were bunched into fists. There was a savage glint in the eyes that raked her face.

'What other option did I have?' she demanded rawly. She had hated that flat—the eerie, evil-smelling staircases, the lifts that had almost never worked, the wrecked cars in the street outside, the dubious-looking characters who'd inhabited the flats that were occupied. Did he think she'd lived there because she'd wanted to? He knew nothing—nothing about the real world!

'You could have contacted me. You said you were going to, so what stopped you?' he asked icily. 'Stubborn pride or a need to punish me?'

Beth gasped as a tide of anger hit her. Resentment and agonising pain flooded through her as she remembered how she'd felt at that time. She wanted to kill him for always putting her in the wrong! 'You know nothing!' she snapped through gritted teeth. 'Two days before James was born Gran phoned to say Grandad had died. I was admitted to the maternity ward soon after—and the nurses were willing to look after James while I went to his funeral. My baby was three days old then. I'd meant to phone your uncle, to ask for your current address, but as I was going to the funeral I decided to ask him in person.'

Her cheeks burned furiously, her eyes brilliant with rare temper. 'I never got round to it. After the service one of your uncle's outdoor staff told me—in passing, as it were—that you'd just got engaged to some American beauty who could trace her ancestors back to the *Mayflower* and beyond, and your uncle was over the moon about it!'

Unaware that tears of rage and remembered pain were falling in a torrent, she slapped the open palm of her hand against the side of her head. 'So what was I supposed to do? You tell me! Announce that

I'd just given birth to your bastard? That would have ruined your engagement, disappointed Marcus— even turned him against his blue-eyed boy!' She was almost sobbing now, her breath catching, her lungs heaving. 'So I held my tongue—for your sake. Not for mine. Not because I was devious or twisted enough to believe I was somehow punishing you.'

She gulped in a long, shuddering breath, oblivious to the sheer anguish in Carl's eyes. 'We managed, James and I. The job with Angela and Henry was a godsend. I must have been with them for around three years when I read an account of your marriage in Henry's morning paper. A high society affair— and in the photograph you both looked so happy. I knew I'd been right to keep silent.'

He took a step towards her, but she backed away, her body quivering with tension. 'I loved you, Carl, even then. I wanted you to be happy.' Her voice broke. 'Only that!'

'Beth—' His face was drained of colour and he looked bone-weary; only the dark glittering eyes spoke of emotions too raw to articulate. 'I—' Whatever he'd been about to say, he obviously thought better of it. His lips tightened into a long straight line and his voice was flat when he told her, 'I've misjudged you badly. For the first time in my life I've let emotion override logic. You haven't a mean bone in your body. I should have remembered that before dishing out accusations and orders. I take them all back. Unreservedly.'

'Where are you going?' Beth voiced the question even though she already knew the answer as she watched him walk to the door.

Her stomach lurched. Everything he'd said, his insistence that they marry for the sake of their son, had been ruled out of order by his final taut statement. She should have been feeling a rush of happy relief instead of being emotionally gutted.

'Home.' He took his coat from the hook on the back of the kitchen door. 'I've inflicted too much on you for one evening.'

'What about James?' Her voice was high and wild. She pressed her fingertips to her temples. Was she going mad? He was walking away from them, no doubt thinking he was doing the honourable thing in view of how he'd admitted he'd misjudged her. She'd been praying for just such a scenario ever since he'd guessed that James was his son. So why was she feeling so churned up and desperate because what she'd wished for with all her heart was coming true?

'We'll arrange for access through our solicitors.' He sounded so controlled and sensible she wanted to strangle him. 'There'll be a generous financial settlement. You'll never have to work again, unless you want to, and my demands regarding the time I spend with my son will be reasonable.'

He had the door open. The freezing wind gusted in. Beth watched him walk out, her mouth dry, a sick feeling in her stomach, saw him turn, heard him say, 'I'll leave it to you to judge when and how to tell him he has a father who loves him.' And then she closed the door, nearly wrenching her arms from their sockets in the violent process, shutting him out before he could witness her tearful and utter disintegration.

CHAPTER EIGHT

THERE had been another heavy snowfall during the night. It bowed down the branches of the trees and glittered in the thin winter sunlight.

Beth winced at the noise coming from the parlour. James and Guy were enjoying Christmas morning with a vengeance and it was time to put the chicken in the oven, the pudding on to steam. She passed her fingers over her aching forehead. She hadn't slept last night, but she'd dressed in a figure-hugging cream-coloured cropped sweater and a calf-length swirly scarlet skirt. A heavier hand with her make-up than normal, and her hair falling softly around her face, went some way towards hiding the havoc of lack of sleep.

For the boys' sake she had to pretend she was loving every minute of the day. It wasn't their fault she felt half-dead and more than half-crazy.

She had to be half-crazy to be feeling this way. After she'd met up with Carl again she'd spent all her time wishing he'd disappear, and had been scared witless when he'd insisted on marriage. Yet as soon as that demand had been taken back she'd felt as if half of her life had been sliced away with a very sharp knife.

But she still had James. James was all she had ever wanted.

Not true, she acknowledged as she slid the roasting tin into the oven. She had wanted Carl as well. As a lover, a best friend, her husband, the father of her child.

She still did.

She banged the over door shut, her face flushed. But she couldn't have him. Didn't she know that? She hated herself for thinking like a fool. He had always been out of her league; deep down she'd always known that. If she hadn't she would have contacted him the moment she'd discovered she was pregnant.

Besides, she reminded herself with conscious cruelty, it was just as well he had withdrawn his threat to marry her. Quite rightly, the thought of it had terrified her. Living with the man she still loved—and a plague on her for being such a fool— having him treat her like an only-just-tolerated stranger, would have been torture. She was being a drama queen, pretending to herself that she had lost something wonderfully precious.

It was time to start getting her life back to the way it had been before he had walked in and unsettled it.

Listening to the noise level from the parlour, she wondered whether she could safely leave the boys playing with their new toys for another ten minutes while she prepared the vegetables. She decided to risk it.

As she took potatoes from the vegetable rack the phone rang. She picked the instrument up off the table, stamping firmly on the fluttery hope that it might be Carl. He didn't have her mobile number; the caller couldn't be him.

It wasn't. It was Henry.

'Angela had a little boy just over an hour ago—both of them are fine, but I'm exhausted! We shouldn't have let the housekeeper go to her sister for the holiday; the house is an utter shambles and I spent the whole night making pots of tea for the midwives—'

The outside door opened and Carl walked in. Beth lost the thread of what her employer was saying. Carl's hands were pushed into the pockets of his sheepskin, the upturned collar framing a face that was white with fatigue, the skin stretched tightly over the fabulous bone structure, the eyes deep-set, unsmiling.

Beth's stomach performed a series of somersaults. She hadn't expected him to show his face until everything had been arranged through his solicitor. She felt warm colour steal across her cheeks, her lips curve into an unstoppable smile. She knew she shouldn't read anything into his unexpected arrival, but couldn't help herself hoping...

Holding the phone against her upper chest, she

asked softly, 'Carl, would you fetch Guy, please? His father has news for him,' and watched a brief smile touch his gorgeous mouth, a gleam of understanding flicker in his eyes, before he strode past her into the parlour, where the noise was reaching ear-splitting levels.

A pulse was beating madly in her throat as she gave her fractured attention back to Henry, offering sincere congratulations and the information that Guy was having a great time and would talk to him in a moment.

The little boy scampered in, his face flushed with warmth from the fire and happy excitement. Beth gave him the phone, her heart lurching as Carl re-entered the room. Jamie was holding his father's hand.

'I dropped by to wish these two merry Christmas,' he said quietly. 'I'm not stopping.'

Stay! Beth's eyes pleaded, and she could have hugged Jamie when he vocalised the word she hadn't had the courage to force past her lips.

'Stay! Please! I want you to.' Huge eyes shining, the little boy tugged at his father's hand. 'You can play with my train set and have some Christmas dinner! And Guy's got a new football and a Man United away strip. You could be goalie!'

Her mouth running dry, Beth met Carl's eyes. What she read there made her bones go weak. He needed his son and Jamie needed a father. Mums were okay, as far as they went, for kissing sore places better, giving hugs and cuddles, making food. But mums knew zilch about football teams and hadn't got a clue about rolling stock and signals. A boy needed his dad.

'Stay.' She added her own entreaty, making it easier for him by tilting her head towards Guy, who was now capering wildly around the room.

'I got a brother!' he was shouting, over and over, until she felt dizzy.

'I really could do with some help.'

Some of the tension eased out of his hard, handsome face as he conceded, 'So I see,' and his smile was wide and magical as he captured Guy's flying figure with one strong hand and suggested, 'Why don't we go and see how Bert's weathered the snowstorm? If he's okay we could make him a wife for company. A man gets lonely when he's on his own.'

Was she meant to read something into that? Beth wondered hectically, her hand going to her breast, where her heart was pounding violently. She hardly registered Guy's shriek of, 'And make them a baby. A boy baby. If I'd had a soppy sister I'd have given her away!'

As the two boys raced to collect their coats and boots in a competitive jostle Carl said, 'I'll keep them out of your hair for a couple of hours. The fresh air and exercise might calm them down. What time would you like them back for lunch?'

She held his eyes. 'We'll eat at two. You included,' she ordered firmly.

'I didn't intend—'

'I know you didn't.' She cut through the stiff beginning of what she was sure would amount to a stiltedly polite refusal to accept her order. He was used to dishing them out, not taking them. As an inducement he couldn't back away from, she added, 'James would be really disappointed if you didn't share Christmas lunch with us.'

She saw the way his broad chest expanded on a sudden intake of breath, heard the huskiness of his voice as he countered, 'How about you? Would you be disappointed?'

Dragging in a breath just as deep and as ragged as his had been, she answered, 'Very,' and heard the lightening of his tone as he collected the boys and led them outside.

Everything was ready on the stroke of two: the table spread with Gran's best cloth, scarlet crackers by each place-setting, the plump golden-brown chicken surrounded by crisp roast potatoes on a serving dish, vegetables and cranberry sauce, lighted candles and sprigs of holly, glasses of fruit juice for the boys.

And Beth's stomach was being attacked by a plague of butterflies. While she'd been on her own she'd made up her mind to tell Carl how she felt. Exactly how she felt. She had nothing to lose but her pride—and pride didn't count for a row of beans when love was at stake.

She'd managed to convince herself that he did feel something for her. Hadn't he sincerely denied it when she'd accused him of loathing her? Admitted to having been glad to see her again—a warm ray of sunshine on a bitter winter's day? And he'd said he'd been besotted with her all those years ago.

His insistence on marriage—a clinical, in-name-only relationship—had been dropped when he'd realised she had only kept quiet about James for his sake.

If she still felt the same after all these years then maybe he did, too. All she had to do was find out.

But she was tongue-tied, almost paralysed with the fear that she had got her wires crossed.

The boys were upstairs, washing before lunch, and Carl was opening the champagne Henry had given her to wet the new baby's head. This was her opportunity to say something, let him know how she felt. But the words wouldn't come.

The cork popped with a minor explosion and Carl turned to fill the two glasses she'd put ready. He handed her one and their fingers met.

His brilliant eyes shimmered over her flushed face and his voice was low, almost strangely hesitant, for a man who, she was sure, had never suffered a moment's hesitancy in his charmed and privileged life.

'Did you mean it when you said you were in love with me all those years ago?'

Emboldened by the intensity in his dark and beautiful eyes, she answered breathily, 'I was in love with you. I can't remember a time when I wasn't.'

She saw him wince as if he were in pain, and then there was no opportunity to hear what he might have replied because the boys came thundering down the stairs—and no one could have a meaningful and intimate conversation when crowded out by a pair of chattering, hungry, still over-excited seven-year-old boys.

But it was a happy crowd around the table; she had to admit that. Maybe the champagne helped— and the unspoken messages she was receiving from Carl's eyes certainly did. If she was reading them correctly, she amended.

'Why don't you boys go through by the fire and rest up while Beth and I clear the dishes?' Carl suggested after the last scrap of pudding had disappeared, the last cracker had been pulled and the last stale joke read out to gales of childish laughter.

'You could each choose one of your new books to read.' Beth put in her pennyworth, her heart beginning its now familiar skittering again. Did Carl want to continue that earlier interrupted conversation? She had her internal query confirmed when she started to pile up the dishes.

'Leave it.' He caught her hand and a jolt of

wicked sensation burned its way right through her. He stood up, facing her, and she wanted to drift her fingers over the lines of his sexy mouth so badly it hurt. There was a moan in her throat and he must have heard it, because every line of his face softened and his voice was a caress that threatened to send her spiralling out of control.

'Do you still love me, Beth? Tell me the truth. There have been far too many misunderstandings already.' He took her other hand and her knees wobbled. She nodded, too choked up to speak. Was he going to laugh at her, or, far worse, tell her he was sorry for her?

His eyes darkened emotionally and then he pulled her into his arms, holding her head against his heavily beating heart for one long delirious moment before he cradled her face between his hands and kissed her.

The wild passion of his mouth as it plundered hers, the fevered touch of his hands on her body, her own abandoned responses to every move he made were just as she'd always remembered them— but better. Far, far better. A million wildfire sensations shot like molten fire through her blood and she could have cried aloud in frustrated need when he eventually held her away, his voice rough-edged as he told her, 'We could have company at any moment, my darling.'

He brought his hands up from the curve of her

hips, lightly grazing the narrow span of her waist and then up to brush against the pout of her breasts, making her cry out with the need that was a pulsating fire deep inside her. Silencing her protest with the soft brush of his lips, he murmured against her mouth, 'I have always loved you. Always.'

It took her a little time to recover, to shake her head and remind him, 'You married someone else, remember? Don't tell me what you think I want to hear.'

Carl cupped her cheekbones, his voice rueful. 'I'm telling the truth, Beth. It was something I hadn't fully realised until I saw you again a few days ago. In all those wasted years apart you were often in my thoughts and always in my dreams. Listen, and believe me. When you didn't respond to my letter—and, boy, did I watch the post every day for months on end—I decided that I obviously meant nothing to you, that what we'd shared had meant nothing. I had to stop myself becoming a total wreck, so I worked hard, played hard—and Terrina was there, literally throwing herself at me, vowing she was crazy about me.

'One thing led to another, and that led to an engagement. I wasn't in love with her—I firmly believe the real thing only happens once in a lifetime—but I was fond of her. Marcus, on the one visit he made to the States while I was studying there, thought she was eminently suitable wife material. And she was beautiful. But I didn't love her. I couldn't feel the passion I'd felt for you. I was still in love with you, but I refused to let myself even think about it.'

Beth slid her hands up to his shoulders. Of course she believed him. It had been the same for her. He'd never been far from her thoughts, never vacated that special, secret place in her heart.

'You'll marry me?' His heart beat heavily against hers as she moved closer, her shining eyes alight with love. 'A real, true and lasting marriage? Not merely for our son's sake but for us?'

The parlour door creaked open and James announced, 'Guy's gone to sleep.' He sounded disgusted.

Beth whispered, 'Of course I will—just try to stop me!' and turned to their son.

She took Carl by the hand as the three of them tiptoed back into the parlour, careful not to wake Guy, who was curled up on the sofa, exhausted by the excitement of the day.

The daylight was fading rapidly. Beth closed the curtains and the baubles on the tree glowed in the firelight. When she turned James was snuggled up on Carl's knee and Carl was saying to him softly, 'I didn't expect to meet up with you, so I didn't have a gift for you this morning. But come the New Year we'll find something special, I promise.'

'Excuse me for contradicting...' Beth knelt with

a swirl of scarlet skirts in front of the two dearly loved males in her life. 'But Carl does have a gift for you, Jamie. Carl is your daddy. And very soon now we're going to get married and spend the rest of our lives together.'

There was a heartbeat of silence while Jamie's face went red with sheer happiness, then he wrapped his arms around his father's neck, and when he emerged from the stranglehold he said, 'That's the very best present ever. In the whole wide world!'

Carl caught Beth's hand and brought it to his mouth, and their eyes said to each other, It's been a perfect day.

If you enjoyed what you just read,
then we've got an offer you can't resist!

Take 2 bestselling novels FREE!
Plus get a FREE surprise gift!

*Four bestselling authors bring you the magic,
wonder and love of the holiday season...*

The Christmas Collection

AN ANGEL IN TIME
by *New York Times* bestselling author Stella Cameron

'TIS THE SEASON
by *New York Times* bestselling author Vicki Lewis Thompson

DADDY'S ANGEL
by *USA TODAY* bestselling author Annette Broadrick

AN OFFICER AND A GENTLEMAN
by *USA TODAY* bestselling author Rachel Lee

Look for these classic stories in October 2004.

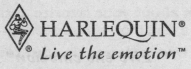

HARLEQUIN®
Live the emotion™

www.eHarlequin.com

RCCC1

eHARLEQUIN.com

The Ultimate Destination for Women's Fiction

Your favorite authors are just a click away
at www.eHarlequin.com!

- Take a sneak peek at the covers and
  read summaries of **Upcoming Books**

- Choose from over 600
  author **profiles!**

- Chat with your favorite authors
  on our **message boards.**

- Are you an author in the making?
  Get advice from published authors
  in **The Inside Scoop!**

**Learn about your favorite authors
in a fun, interactive setting—
visit www.eHarlequin.com today!**

A night she would never forget...

Logan's Legacy

Because birthright has its privileges and family ties run deep.

THE BACHELOR

by national bestselling author

MARIE FERRARELLA

With a full-time job and a son to care for, event planner Jenny Hall didn't have time for men. So when her friends pooled their money at a bachelor auction to buy her a date with Eric Logan, she was shocked—especially when she found herself falling into bed with the billionaire playboy!

Coming in October 2004.

Where love comes alive™

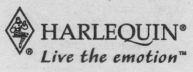